Christmas Royale

By

Dena Garson

Christmas Royale
Copyright © 2019 Dena Garson
Edited by Heather Long

Cover art by Desiree DeOrto (Dark Queen Designs)

ISBN: 978-1-945075-17-9 (print)

DEDICATION

For my boys -
I love you even when you don't clean your rooms.

ACKNOWLEDGEMENTS

I've said it before, I'm sure I'll say it again: Lauren Smith is an angel for patiently answering my questions about historical England and the appropriate use of titles. Thank you!!

I also need to tell Dawn Kaaihue thank you for her gentle nudges to finish this book (so she could read it - LOL).

 1

AN airship drifted across the moonless night sky almost as silently as its neighboring clouds. Below, a pair of night watchmen exchanged jokes as they patrolled. Their voices echoed off the cobblestone street in the narrow alleyway.

James Bennett—Vernon Wright when he wasn't on assignment for the Royal Intelligence Office—waited until the men had passed before slipping through an open window of Genoa's largest banking institution. Inside, he found exactly what he expected. Several storage cabinets lined the one windowless wall. A relatively plain desk had been centered in the eastern half of the room, facing the door. Other than the painting of one of the city's fountains that hung on the wall behind the desk, the entire room lacked ornamentation.

Vernon aimed a narrow band of light into the drawer he searched. File after file of banking records, loans, and investments revealed nothing but error-free documents. Everything meticulously organized.

That alone screamed impossibility for a bank this size.

Footsteps echoed on the wood floor outside the office warning him of the need to hide. He flicked the shutter on the slender light device he held to cast the room once again into darkness. Then he slid the drawer shut and ducked behind the door. His dark suit and hat as well as his brown hair and neatly trimmed beard helped him blend into the shadows.

A key rattled in the lock then the door opened part way. A security guard glanced about the room then closed and relocked the door and moved farther down the hall.

Vernon waited for the footsteps to recede before coming out of his hiding place. He checked the room for hidden storage compartments and recently used documents then tidied the area so that no would know it had been searched. Once he was satisfied he had obtained all the information he could on Signor Romano's day-to-day transactions, he tucked his notebook away and pulled on his sticky gloves. He'd left his shoes with the sticky pads on the floor near the wall to minimize the noise he made. The ingenuity of the devices that allowed him to momentarily cling to any surface never failed to make him feel like a kid with a favorite toy.

With the gloves and shoe pads in place, he departed the way he had entered – through one of the windows near the ceiling.

Once he escaped the office, he accessed the roof and scurried along the shadowed edges to the side of the building with the fire escape ladder. He'd only just removed the gloves and shoe pads when a man yelled, "You there! What are you doing up here?"

Vernon tipped his hat then dashed for the end of the roof in the opposite direction.

"Stop! You can't—"

Vernon couldn't hear anything else the man may have said over the sound of his own heartbeat and the wind rushing in his ears as he leapt off the building. The gust of cold air in his face as he began his descent very nearly made his breath catch, but he ignored it.

He extended his arms out from his sides and waited for the leather wings hidden inside his jacket to spring out. As soon as the air cradled him from below, he smiled. The sticky pads were fun but they were nothing in comparison to his false wings. Since it was the middle of the night, he refrained from yelling out in glee as he glided almost effortlessly through the next two alleys.

The landing was always a bit tricky but he'd recently figured out how to coordinate both the retraction of the wings and getting his feet under him. He was proud he no longer had to take a tumble to come to a stop. That never made for a dignified landing.

Once both feet were on the ground, he continued his

forward momentum and hurried out of the alley and further down the block. By the time he reached the next block he had slowed his pace to a leisurely stroll. To alter his appearance, he tucked his hat into one of his pockets, pulled up the collar on his coat, and extended the length of the baton he pulled from his pocket used it as a walking stick.

He smiled in satisfaction. At a glance, anyone who passed would think he was nothing more than a young man on the way home from a late night at one of Genoa's many clubs.

2

"I'M going to the gala and that is final."

Phoebe Elizabeth Ashdown silently counted to ten as her sister, Sophia, stormed out of the sitting room in a huff.

"It is the biggest event of the season, my dear." Aunt Gladys set her teacup on the table. "Surely you don't expect her to pass up the opportunity?"

Phoebe crossed her arms. "I do if the opportunity could end badly."

"You must be exaggerating. Sophia is a lovely, spirited young woman. It's quite natural for her to want to experience the world."

"I do know that." Phoebe paced back and forth behind the floral patterned settee. The heavy skirts of her dress rustled with every agitated step. "I just don't understand how or why she was invited in the first place. After all, we have only been in Genoa for a little more than a week."

"Do you think it could have been the young man she introduced us to at the art museum?"

"Agapito Romano?" Phoebe asked.

Phoebe's aunt nodded making her greyish-blonde curls bounce. "He did say he was from Genoa."

"I don't know who else would have sent it," Phoebe admitted.

Her aunt waved dismissively. "Well, there you have it."

"But don't you see?" Phoebe grasped the back of the settee. "That's one of the reasons I'm worried."

Her aunt patted Phoebe's hands. "Perhaps you worry too much."

Phoebe pressed her lips together. Worrying wasn't

something she made a habit of. Her instincts screamed there was more to Agapito Romano, Sophia's current focus of infatuation, than just polished manners and a pretty face. Her skin crawled every time he came near her or her sister. There had to be a reason for it.

Sophia, however, was completely taken with him. And all it had taken was one waltz. Since that night, she hadn't stopped talking about him.

When their aunt had mentioned she had always wanted to go to Italy, her sister had immediately pushed for a trip. Apparently it had been a good thing that their mother insisted she travel with Sophia. As much as she loved their aunt, she was incapable of keeping a close enough watch on the bundle of energy and emotion Phoebe called sister.

She groaned just thinking of everything that could go wrong at a crowded ball in a foreign country where they knew very few people.

Aunt Gladys' friends Signor and Signora Bianchi had been very accommodating hosts during their stay. But they, too, were older. She doubted they would be able to keep up with either of them throughout the evening. And since Gladys tended to be a bit flighty, the bulk of the responsibility of chaperoning Sophia would fall on her shoulders.

That was fine. It wasn't as if she had any expectation of socializing with friends at the event. After all, the only people they knew in Genoa were her aunt's friends.

All in all, she had enjoyed their trip but she was ready to return to England. It was only a few weeks until Christmas and she missed her family. If it hadn't been for Sophia's insistence that they stay until after this gala, they would have been most of the way home by now.

"You know we will have no peace until Sophia gets her way," Aunt Gladys pointed out.

"Yes. I know." Phoebe sighed and dropped onto the sofa closest to her aunt. She pulled her spectacles off and rubbed the bridge of her nose. Resigned to her fate she sighed. "I'll say nothing more about it if you promise to not let her buy the frilliest gown she finds at the dress makers."

"I doubt she will have much to choose from at this late date," Signora Bianchi reminded them.

"It is a shame we didn't have time to visit that dressmaker I love so much in Paris. What was his name, Charlotte?" Gladys asked her friend.

"Hmmm. Let me think." Signora Bianchi tapped her own cheek thoughtfully. "Wise." She frowned. "No, Worth." Her expression brightened. "Worth was his name."

"Yes. That's him," Aunt Gladys reached for another biscuit. "Lovely man. Beautiful gowns."

"It might be considered bold for a young lady her age but I think Phoebe would look lovely in emerald green," Signora Bianchi suggested.

"You know, I was just thinking the same thing," Aunt Gladys said, almost conspiratorially.

The two matrons rattled on about the gowns they both had purchased on their last visit to Paris together while Phoebe drifted into her own thoughts.

Around this same time last year, Phoebe had been making plans to attend the Lockwood Ball with her friends. It turned out to be a huge success for one of them. Her friend Charlotte was now engaged to the Viscount of Huntingdon. Even though it had yet to be settled, Phoebe's other close friend, Lillian, had also made a promising connection that same evening with the Earl of Derby.

Which left Phoebe largely on the shelf.

Even though she was ecstatic for her friends to find good matches—matches that included love—it wouldn't be long before she would be standing alone on the side of dance floor. Once they were running their own households, her friends simply wouldn't have as much time to spare for her.

She wasn't bitter. She was realistic. After more than four seasons, the odds of her making a good match had narrowed considerably. And while she had always dreamed of a suitable match and starting her own family, she could be content to be the eccentric aunt and ladies' companion to her friends.

At least she hoped she would be content.

For now, though, she needed to ensure that Sophia didn't do anything foolish to ruin her chances at a good match. Sophia might be beautiful, but that would only go so far if their family were to face another scandal.

She just needed to make it through one ball and then quelling Sophia's flights of fancy could once again be their mother's responsibility. How hard could that be?

 3

VERNON Wright poured a healthy splash of amber liquid into each of the two crystal glasses and waited for his current partner to arrive. The heavy footsteps on the creaking wood floor above him told him that he wouldn't have to wait long.

Sure enough, before he could finish digging through the maps they had collected during their month long investigation, Lawrence Moretti staggered through the door.

"You're late."

"Not by much." The red-haired Scotsman grinned.

Vernon assessed his partner's state. Clothes wrinkled. Cravat askew. Hair mussed. The faint smell of cigars and at least two brands of tobacco he couldn't recognize as well as brandy and ale clung to Moretti's person. "And you've been drinking."

"Admittedly." Moretti flipped his chair around and straddled it.

"Did they fall for it?"

Moretti scoffed. "Of course." He pulled a document from his jacket pocket and tossed it onto the table.

"Good." Vernon approached the table that served as their workspace. "Let's see what we've got." He unfolded the document and used his palms to flatten the creases.

Moretti turned the crank on the lamp closest to him making the false-flame brighten the room further. Both men bent over the paper and studied the information.

"You're sure this is the Casa de Romano?" Vernon asked.

"My source swears it is."

"Did you look at it?"

"Only long enough to verify it was the correct map."

Vernon looked up from the document. "And you think it's accurate?"

"Based on what I know of the property, yes, it is."

Vernon nodded. "Tell me what you expect to happen the night of the gala."

Moretti downed the contents of his glass and then pointed to a place on the map. "This is the ballroom. Most of the event will be held here." He slid his finger to one of the connecting rooms. "There will be refreshments set up here. Musicians here." He moved farther across the page. "This room will likely be used for entertainment."

"Entertainment such as?"

"He always hosts card games."

That information piqued Vernon's interest enough to make him look up. "What kind of stakes?"

"Nothing you can't handle. The one you need to worry about will be here." Moretti slid his finger across the page to a smaller drawing in corner. "Romano's private study. High stakes. Excusive entry. Romano senior will be here."

"So this one," Vernon pointed to the large room, "Is merely for entertainment of his guests?"

"Yes."

"Understood."

"But to get to the exclusive room you have to prove yourself worthy there." Moretti gestured to the first picture.

"Not a problem."

"Probably not for you."

Vernon didn't try to deny it. He had a knack for cards and making his own luck, as they said. He just needed to make sure he produced plenty of it come Saturday. "And where will you be while I'm working my way up the proverbial ladder?"

"Mingling amongst the common folk."

"Hardly."

"Well I assume you don't need me hovering over your shoulder so I will likely make my way through the crowds and ensure nothing goes awry while you're hob-knobbing and canoodling with Romano under the table."

Vernon sorted. "Canoodling?" He shook his head.

"What else would you call it?"

"Working for Queen and country."

"Hmmmm." Moretti pointed at Vernon with his glass. "What did you learn today?"

"In truth not much. His bank records are virtually spotless and so are his investments."

Moretti frowned. "How often does that happen?"

"Only when someone is taking drastic measures to hide something." Vernon sighed. "It's a bit of a shame, really. I admire a man who keeps tidy records."

"So you don't think it's because he's well organized."

"No." Vernon scoffed. "Even the best banker or clerk makes mistakes from time to time. Neatness and criminal activity are two different concepts."

"But still bedfellows."

Vernon saluted Moretti with his own glass. "True." He gestured to the diagram. "So tell me where I can find Romano's office or where ever he is most likely to keep important documents."

"It should be here." Moretti circled an area on the map with his finger. "Whenever he conducts business at home, this is where he brings them." He pointed to one room on the diagram. "But that room has been searched and nothing was found."

"What about hidden safes?"

"Not that we've found."

"Does it lead to any other rooms around it?"

"Yes." Moretti pointed to the small marks on the map. "Here and here."

"Do we know what is in those rooms?"

"Not thoroughly. Only from glimpses."

"Cleaning staff won't say?"

"They're not allowed in. Only his personal valet is permitted."

"Interesting." Vernon's brows rose in surprise. "What about possible exits?"

"There are two windows and a small balcony overlooking the gardens on this room. Just one window on this one and no other exits."

"Last detail, how do we get in?"

"We walk in."

Vernon cocked a brow. "Just show up and expect to be allowed admittance to not only a social event but also the big game? A game that locals talk about for months ahead of the event."

"These..." Moretti pulled two more documents from his pocket and dropped them in the center of the table. "Will get us into the event."

Vernon scanned the embellished card. "Invitations."

Moretti dipped his head. "They are indeed."

"How did you—" Vernon shook his head. "Never mind, don't tell me.

Moretti chuckled.

"You could have told me that from the start."

"That would far too easy for you, my English friend."

Vernon snorted. "I suppose we should pop in to see a tailor."

"You might, but I'm set."

Vernon shook his head. "Please tell me you brought something other than your plaid as formal wear."

"What's wrong with wearing my colors?"

"Nothing, if you want to stand out."

"As if your pale skin doesn't stand out."

"No more than yours."

"Bah," Moretti scoffed.

"What do you know of guards and their patrol?" Vernon asked.

"Not a lot. The dogs are rather effective but we believe they will be secured during the event."

"What about hired security? Romano keeps a staff of men to guard himself and his family, doesn't he?"

"Yes. He put a call out last month to increase his numbers, but I haven't been able to confirm how many." Moretti tapped his finger on the table. "Do we know who was included on the guest list?"

"All of the wealthy families, of course. Anyone he personally conducts business with, and, of course, friends of the family."

"Hard to believe that hornswoggler has friends."

Vernon refilled his glass, this time with water. "I suspect most of them are either friends with Romano's wife or seeking some sort of connection to him. Although why they bother baffles me. That man does no one favors when it comes to business."

Moretti grunted.

"Who will we have for back up?" Vernon asked.

"That largely depends on how far you want to push Romano."

"As far as we can without tipping our hand."

"I have five men lined up to be on the grounds as hired staff. Two as guards, the others as servers." Moretti pushed his now empty glass aside. "My local contacts will be there as guests but we can't count on them to bail us out if we get in a bind. They will be there mostly to observe and warn us if they notice anything peculiar."

"So we're mostly on our own."

"Isn't that how we usually operate?"

Vernon shrugged. "Yes."

Moretti leaned back in his chair and crossed his arms over his chest. "Personally, I'd like to take that bastard out but Glastone keeps shooting that idea down."

"He's a stickler for the rules."

"Shame that."

Vernon went to the sideboard and splashed more brandy into his glass then flopped into his chair. "Do you think we'll ever get a mission that allows us to do more than gather information for someone else to act on?"

"Wanting to get into the action, are ye?"

"I certainly wouldn't mind a little more action." Vernon swirled the amber liquid in his glass. "But mostly, I'd like to finish a mission knowing that what I had done actually made a difference."

"Aye." Moretti turned pensive. "That would be a nice for a change, wouldn't it?"

"Indeed."

 4

PHOEBE pulled her wrap tighter around her shoulders and
followed Aunt Gladys into the carriage. Signor Bianchi
climbed inside and settled in next to his wife, Lady Charlotte.

"Are you girls excited about this evening?" Lady Charlotte
asked.

"Oh, yes," Sophia exclaimed as she clasped her hands
together. "I can't wait to see all of the dresses and hear the
music."

"Signor Romano always has the very best musicians for his
events," Lady Charlotte told them.

"I'm going to dance every dance," Sophia declared.

Aunt Gladys patted Sophia's knee. "And you should my
dear."

"Just don't forget there are rules here too, Sophia. Just
because we aren't in London doesn't mean that people do not
talk."

"I know, Phoebe." Sophia waved her hand toward Phoebe.
"Stop worrying. I promise I won't do anything to embarrass
you or our generous hosts." She smiled at Signor Bianchi and
Lady Charlotte.

To change the subject, Phoebe faced Lady Charlotte's
husband. "This is a lovely carriage, Signor Bianchi. Papa has
been thinking of retiring his favorite horses in favor of a steam-
powered carriage. They're all the rage in London."

"I will say that we have enjoyed it immensely. There are
fewer horses for my stable master to care for. This one doesn't
require food or shelter. Nor do we have to worry about injuries
to our mounts whilst out on a run."

"That is a good thing," Phoebe remarked. "But I'm curious,

how does yours operate? What propels it forward?"

Signor Bianchi chuckled. "The mechanics would likely bore you, my dear. But suffice to say, we add fuel in the back to heat the boiler and Renzo controls the motion and speed up front."

"But doesn't that leave Renzo vulnerable up front?"

"Well, I suppose it does to a small degree, but he has become quite adept at handling this machine. I have every confidence that he knows what he's doing and that he would do everything in his power to limit any risks to us and himself."

"Well it's certainly warmer in here than expected," Phoebe pointed out.

"The boiler and the mechanics are located right under us. The steam warms the interior nicely." Signor Bianchi patted the seat they sat on.

"That's why I told you that you didn't need your heavy cloak." Her aunt fluffed the pouf of material that jutted out from her shoulder. "Besides, your new wrap is far more festive."

"I'm surprised you bought anything at the dressmakers, Phoebe." Sophia shook her head in disbelief. "You never spend money on frivolous things."

"I wanted something made locally to remind me of our trip and I knew it would provide a little extra warmth," Phoebe explained. "So it serves more than one purpose."

"Well it looks lovely on you. Goes well with your coloring, doesn't it, Charlotte?" Aunt Gladys said.

"It does indeed." Lady Charlotte tapped Phoebe on the knee with her fan. "You'll likely turn more than one head this evening."

"I suppose you have no interest in meeting any of the local gentlemen though, do you?" Sophia asked with a roll of her eyes.

"Not particularly." She smiled at Lady Charlotte and her aunt. "While I'd be happy to dance with any gentleman who presents himself well, it is not my intention to win the attention of anyone in attendance tonight."

"I don't see why not," Aunt Gladys said with surprise.

"You're a lovely young woman. There are likely to be a dozen gentlemen who might catch your eye."

"And they would all be lucky to have you," Signor Bianchi added.

"Well, thank you, but I simply don't have the same interest in marriage that Sophia does," Phoebe admitted.

"Oh, pish, my dear. No one said that just because you dance with someone, you have to marry them."

"My heavens, no," Lady Charlotte agreed.

"Even I don't believe that should be a rule," Sophia said from the other side of their aunt. "None of the gentlemen worth having would dare enter a ballroom if it were."

Charlotte and Aunt Gladys murmured their agreement.

When the carriage made the final turn onto the drive leading to Plaza de Romano, Sophia and Aunt Gladys cooed in approval. Oversized wreaths had been hung on the brick pillars marking the entrance. The drive was lined with gas lanterns. Festive bows connected garlands of greenery to each lantern. Whoever chose the decorations must have exceptionally good taste.

Because of the number of guests attending, it took a bit of time for their carriage to reach the brightly lit courtyard. A number of footmen scurried between carriages, rushing to aid those who needed assistance.

Finally, their party made it from the carriage and into the ballroom. Festive greenery had been hung wherever possible. Ladies wrapped in layers of silk and gentlemen wearing dark suits milled about chatting with friends and neighbors alike. Two white marble staircases circled down onto the dance floor. Windows filled the opposite wall and reflected the lights flickering from the chandeliers. The brightly lit interior spilled out onto a terrace beyond the wall of glass then drifted out into what appeared to be a veranda.

Phoebe wished for a moment that she could forget about her promise to her mother to keep an eye on Sophia. She might very well have been able to view the gala as a magical evening.

The gowns were a delightful blend of colors and fabric.

London fashion had become rather predictable. At least to the extent that she always knew who would be buying from which dressmaker and perhaps even what color they would wear.

Here in Genoa she was delighted to find an entirely new sea of colors.

"Sophia, why don't we—" Phoebe turned to ask her sister a question only to find her darting through the throng of guests without so much as a backward glance.

"And off she goes," Aunt Gladys said happily.

"Why can't she be sensible?" Phoebe muttered under her breath and quickly followed.

Phoebe took care to slip in and out of the crowd without jostling anyone or getting stepped on while watching where her sister went. Sophia's blonde hair was easily identifiable which made her task somewhat easier.

When she finally caught up to Sophia, Phoebe had to swallow the lecture their mother had given them more than once about the dangers of navigating a ballroom alone. It would only be a waste of breath. "Sophia, would you please show a modicum of restraint?"

Sophia let out an exasperated sigh. "Phoebe, why can't you simply go and enjoy the ball and leave me be?"

"Because you are my sister and I don't believe you understand the predicament you could be putting yourself into. So, no. Mother is not here therefore it falls to me to ensure that you do not make any fatal missteps and ruin your reputation along with your chance at a good match."

"Agapito Romano is a good match."

Phoebe shook her head. "Not for you."

Sophia's neck and ears turned pink. A sure sign that she was angry. "You don't know that."

"I know enough, Sophia. If you would only listen—" Phoebe reached for Sophia's wrist but she jerked it away.

"How could you know? No one has ever even offered for you."

Phoebe flinched. She often wondered if gentlemen avoided courting her because of her spectacles. Although, her closest friends said it likely had more to do with the number of fortune hunters she had set back on their heels. Her own mother tried to convince her that if she could pretend to be a fluffy-headed debutante until she landed her husband she could be as outspoken as she wanted after the vows were read.

"I'm not like you, Phoebe. I want to enjoy my time in the ballroom and know that I did everything I could in order to find my Prince."

"I know but you need to do it sensibly," she pleaded.

"You mean like you?"

"No. I mean—"

"Your way does not seem to be working."

"I don't have a way, Sophia. I'm just trying to keep you from doing something you will regret later just because you didn't take a moment to think about your actions."

"I have. Why can't you trust that?" Sophia spun on her heel and charged back into the crowd.

Phoebe sighed but let her get away. It was pointless to say anything more. Sophia was determined to not listen to any words of caution. That meant all she would be able to do was keep an eye on her from a distance. Despite her frustration, Phoebe made her way across the now-crowded room to find a spot where she could observe the dancing.

Her aunt and Lady Charlotte soon joined her. Lady Charlotte introduced them to an older couple who were passing by. Then another couple paused to speak to Lady Charlotte making their small group slowly grow. Phoebe ensured she remained in a position to see most of the room, while keeping track of the conversation with Lady Charlotte's acquaintances.

Sure enough, not long after the first dance began, Phoebe spotted Sophia talking with a group of gentlemen. Agapito Romano was included in that group. Surprisingly it was one of the other young men who escorted Sophia onto the floor for a lively country dance.

In a way she envied her sister's carefree attitude. If their sister Lily had not experienced such a scandalous season,

Phoebe would likely be as daring. Fortunately, Lily managed to make a good match and was now happily married. However, ton gossip about someone else's indiscretions very nearly ruined Lily's reputation along with their family name. Since then, Phoebe had taken great care to never put herself or her family in a similar position.

But sometimes she wished she could be free of society's constraints and prying eyes. Life would be so much more enjoyable if everyone could dress as they please and dance with whomever they wish.

Phoebe half-listened to the conversation around her while she continued to track Sophia's whereabouts. As her gaze swept across the dance floor, a familiar face caught her attention. She took a step back in order to get a better look. Sure enough, she managed to locate the man she thought she had seen.

Inwardly she cringed. Of all the people she might run into, why did it have to be Mr. Vernon Wright? Although, as Lord Bartley's youngest son, and a confirmed rake, it was likely that he had been chased out of London after yet another scandal.

His hair was a touch longer that the last time she had seen him, but he was just a devilishly handsome as before. Much to her dismay. For her first three seasons, she and Vernon crossed paths at every major ball and even a few smaller events. As friends of friends, he was always charming, they had even shared a dance or two, but after his cruel treatment of one of her closest friends, she had made it a habit to avoid him.

Now that she thought about it, it had been some time since she'd last seen him. As she struggled to recall exactly how long it had been, Mr. Wright's gaze locked onto hers. Instead of the charming young man she was accustomed to seeing, she found something distinctly harder and far more serious in his countenance.

It set the butterflies loose in her belly.

For a moment she thought there had been a flicker of pleasant surprise in his eyes. But then a small group of people crossed between the two of them and their connection broke.

She raised up on her toes to look for him but Mr. Wright had disappeared. Not that she really wanted to see him again. No matter how handsome he might be.

 5

VERNON excused himself from the group he had been talking with. Surely, that had not been Phoebe Ashdown he had spotted across the room. He ducked behind a crowd of people to avoid being seen by her again. He couldn't risk blowing his cover.

At first he wasn't sure that she had even recognized him, but her expression gave everything away. He just prayed that none of Signor Romano's men noticed.

He tracked Lawrence Moretti down and signaled that he needed to talk with him. As agreed prior to the event, they both made their way to the gaming area.

As soon as they deemed it safe Vernon whispered to him, "I have a situation."

Moretti counted his chips and slid them across the velvet-clad table. "How critical?"

Likewise, Vernon added his own chips to the pile. "A family connection."

Moretti's expression didn't change but the hand that had been fingering a random chip paused. "And?"

"She could be a wild card."

"Do you need assistance?"

"Not yet." The dealer swept the bets that had failed from the table. "I will let you know if I do."

Without a glance back, Vernon got up from the table and went in search of Phoebe. It was only fair that he notify his partner of any changes to their situation. But it didn't mean he needed to halt their plans. After all, he might very well be able to deal with Phoebe on his own.

Inwardly, he cringed. Although, it was far more likely that

he would receive a frosty reception. He had pretended a greater interest in one of Phoebe's friends than he should have in order to gain to complete his first assignment from the Royal Intelligence Office. While he had never pressed his advantage with the girl, and had been careful to never give the impression that a proposal of marriage would be forthcoming, he later learned that she had been hurt by his sudden disinterest. Not to mention his being caught in an awkward situation with a young widow.

Vernon's sister had warned him that he had blown his chance of making a match not only with the girl but also her friends. That included Phoebe. At the time, he had dismissed it as the price to be paid to fulfill his mission. Queen and country, and all of that.

But it seemed fate had a wicked since of humor.

It was far too risky to simply ignore Phoebe's presence. In his experience, the best way to deal with an unknown threat was with a direct charge.

His height allowed him to peer over the top of the crowd. He spotted Phoebe at the edge of the dance floor. Her posture radiated tension and her eyes remained glued to one couple in particular. Following her line of vision, he found Agapito Romano, Signor Romano's youngest son.

He frowned. Surely Phoebe wasn't interested in Agapito. He was as crooked as his father, if not more. What connection could she possibly have with him?

A second glance at the waltzing couple provided the missing clue. Agapito was dancing with a young lady who looked enough like Phoebe that she had to be related. Most likely one of her sisters. Based on the girl's dreamy expression, she was smitten with Agapito.

Vernon's stomach clenched.

When the song ended Phoebe tried to follow her sister and Agapito from the dance floor to the veranda but was quickly crowded out by other guests. Vernon seized the opportunity and moved in from behind.

Phoebe stiffened in surprise when he brushed against her

side. "Vernon."

His name—his real name—on her lips soothed a raw place in his soul that he had long ignored. In a harsher tone than he meant he whispered, "Please don't use my name. I'll explain when we get outside."

She gave him a frosty glance. "I don't know why you think I should do you any favors." She raised up on her toes and tried to peer over the crowd.

"I assume that is your sister you are following, is it not?"

Once again she jerked her gaze at him in surprise. "Yes. How did you know?"

"The two of you share several of same features." From his vantage point Vernon could see Agapito taking liberties and whispering into the girl's ear. "Does she know who her dance partner is?"

Phoebe grimaced. "She thinks she does. I am not convinced."

"You have good instincts."

He took Phoebe by the arm to steer her to the right side of the crowd but she jerked it away. "What are you doing here?"

He regained his grip on her arm and whispered, "Again, I'll explain in a moment."

He wasn't certain, but he thought Phoebe mumbled something rather un-lady like under her breath. With a chuckle, he used his stature to protect and guide her through the crushing crowd. When they finally reached the terrace he pulled Phoebe to the shadowy area off to one side so her sister or Agapito wouldn't spot them.

He laid Phoebe's hand on his forearm then covered it with his free hand so she couldn't pull it away.

"I don't know why you think I want anything to do with you, Mr.—"

"Yes, I know." He cut her off before she said his name. "You're quite put out with me." He led her toward the stone path that Romano had taken. "I'll give you the opportunity to list all of my faults later."

The harrumphing sound she made succeeded in drawing a

chuckle from him.

They followed the couple at a distance until they reached the fountain in the center of the garden. Vernon pulled Phoebe deeper into the shadows so they could watch without drawing anyone's notice.

"You promised to explain your earlier demand," she reminded him.

"As far as anyone in Genoa knows, my name is James Bennett." He held her gaze allowing her to see how serious he was. "And it needs to remain that way."

"Why?"

A simple question with many dangerous implications. "I cannot tell you that." She opened her mouth to say something but he cut her off. "On this too I must beg your indulgence. There are far too many lives at stake over this one simple detail." Based on her questioning expression, he could tell she was undecided about whether to believe him. "I could arrange to have you immediately transported back to England but I would rather not do that. It's messy and tends to irritate people."

Her eyes widened in alarm.

"All the years I have known you, we have shared mutual acquaintances but never knew each other well. I should like to think we could have been friends." He looked at her, as if seeing her for the first time. "Perhaps if circumstances had been different we could have been good friends."

"Perhaps." Despite the darkness around them, she looked directly in his eye. "If you were not a rake and a bounder, we might have been."

The need to kiss her slammed into him like a fist, jarring him back to reality.

"I, for one, take exception to my friends being ill-used," she said with a lift of her chin.

"Which friend might that be?" Vernon asked, even though he knew full well whom she meant.

Her eyes narrowed in warning. "Emma, of course." He couldn't tell if the flame glittering in her eye was a reflection on her spectacles from a nearby torch or the ire he had stoked inside of her.

"Ah. Yes. Emma." He nodded. "I heard after I had left for Paris that she had assumed she and I might someday marry." He raised one brow. "Despite the fact that I had stated quite the opposite from the start."

"I'm expected to believe that you told her plainly that you were not interested in marriage?"

He shrugged. "Believe it or not, that is the truth."

"And what did she have to say when you told her marriage didn't interest you?"

"Something about every man thinking that until they meet someone."

Phoebe cringed. "Until they meet their match."

"Yes. That sounds right."

She looked away. After a moment she told him, "Emma always believes the best of people. That is what made me so angry about what you did."

"If it's any consolation, I didn't mean to hurt her."

"Then why did you pretend to be a suitor for so long?"

He grimaced. "Quite frankly, to pacify my mother."

"Surely getting caught in Lord Grantham's study with Crenshaw's widow didn't make your mother happy." Phoebe's delicate brow arched in disapproval.

"No, it did not." He frowned at the memory. His mother had been quite cross with him. However, if he had been caught with the documents he had just taken from Lord Grantham's vault, she would have been far angrier.

"My father said that Lord Grantham was charged with conspiracy the day after that ball."

Vernon pasted an innocent expression on his face. "Is that so?"

"And as I understood it, you were never seen associating with Mrs. Crenshaw again, either."

"That is correct."

"And now you're here in another country, using a false name, asking me to support your deception."

He glanced to where her sister and Agapito huddled on the edge of the fountain. "You have always struck me as a person who sees more and reasons things together faster than most. I would never ask you to do this if it weren't vitally important. Will you grant me this one favor and remain silent about who I really am? Most especially who my family is."

Her gaze bore into him. Finally, she dipped her head in acknowledgement. "Very well."

The knot that had settled in his gut loosened ever so slightly.

She held up one finger. "I have one condition."

He hated to speculate what conditions she would place on her silence. Even worse, he hated to think how far he would go to guarantee it. "What might that be?"

"Tell me everything you know about Agapito Romano."

Vernon's gaze hardened when he looked back at the pair sitting next to the fountain. "I cannot tell you everything I know about him as it pertains to the reason I am here. But nothing I know about him is good. I would caution you to do everything in your power to separate your sister from him."

Phoebe took a step toward her sister but Vernon held her back. "You do not want to cause a scene. Especially not here. She is safe enough for now."

"But—"

"There are many people here. As long as she remains in public view, you will only succeed in embarrassing yourself and your sister. And if you push too hard, you will catch Agapito's father's attention. That, I assure you, is not something you want to do."

"So what should I do?"

"Exactly what you have been doing. Stay close. Watch her carefully. Never let her be alone with him. And if at all possible, never let him or his men catch either of you alone."

A shiver ran through her. "Very well."

Agapito offered Phoebe's sister his arm. It galled Vernon how polite and polished some people could behave while evil intent ran through their veins like ice water. It only proved how little you really knew people. He prayed that his trust in Phoebe was not misplaced.

"They're going back inside," she said.

"Then so, too, shall we." He offered Phoebe his arm. This time she readily accepted it. As before, they strolled at a leisurely pace while keeping to the shadows. When they reached the doors of the veranda Vernon paused so he could check which direction Phoebe's sister had been led. He spotted them at the edge of the dance floor.

Across the room, lingering near one of the columns, he found Moretti flirting with one of the guests. With the slightest nod of his head he let Moretti know all was well. Then he pasted a charming smile on his face and looked down at Phoebe.

"If your card is not too full, would you care to dance with an old friend?"

She glanced after her sister then dipped her head. "I would be delighted."

 6

WITH practiced ease Vernon maneuvered them into the flow of dancers where they could easily keep an eye on Sophia. Never before had a man's touch made Phoebe's heart skip a beat. It unsettled her knowing Vernon was the cause.

Or rather, James. That was what he called himself, wasn't it? James Bennett. She needed to remember that so she didn't slip up.

Her curious nature had roared to life when she learned of his alternate identity. There had to be a story behind it. Perhaps someday he might tell her.

"Are we old friends now?" she asked.

He gazed down at her even as he spun her through a complicated turn. "What if I told you that I should very much like to be?"

Despite believing the worst of him for so long, she sensed a kernel of truth in his statement. "Perhaps we could be."

He smiled. "Then that settles it. We shall be the oldest of friends. You do realize that by accepting this position, you are agreeing to write to me every year so that I can keep track of how you fare, don't you?"

She couldn't stop herself from smiling. "So often?"

"Absolutely. We shall need some way to prove our friendship." He quickly clarified, "No more than we see each other."

"I believe I could manage a few pages for you each year." She gazed up at him. "You shall be my Christmas pen pal."

He glanced about the room with just a touch of wonder. "It is that time of the year, isn't it?" He chuckled. "I didn't realize that was what the ribbons and greenery were for."

"Have you been so busy that you haven't taken notice of the celebrations going on around you?"

"It would appear so." He shrugged. "My business associates have made no mention of the holiday so it hadn't occurred."

She frowned. "How long have you been away from home?"

"Between university and my travels abroad, I've been away a rather long time."

Phoebe's heart ached for him. Determined to return to their happier topic, she told him, "Well, I for one have enjoyed my visit to Genoa. I do believe that I should like to see it during the warmer months."

"It is lovely to visit when the gardens are in full bloom."

"I'm sure it is. The buildings and homes are lovely. And the views of the port are breathtaking."

"I agree." He tipped his head.

They spent the rest of the dance exchanging polite but simple conversation appropriate for two people still getting to know one another. At the end, Phoebe found herself directly behind Sophia.

"Phoebe. I dare say I'm pleasantly surprised to see you dancing." Sophia glanced meaningfully at Vernon.

"I'm afraid I insisted," Vernon interjected with a smile.

"Sophia, this is the—" With a subtle squeeze of her fingertips, Vernon reminded her not to use his title. "This is a former acquaintance of mine, Mr. James Bennett." To Vernon she said, "Mr. Bennett, this is my sister, Sophia."

"I am pleased to meet you, Miss. Ashdown." Vernon smiled and squeezed Sophia's fingers.

"And this is Signor Agapito Romano," Phoebe gestured at Sophia's dance partner.

"*Buonasera*, Signor Bennett," Agapito said as the men shook hands. "Did I hear it correctly that the two of you knew each other before tonight?"

"Yes, actually, you did hear that correctly," Vernon told him.

"We met a few years ago at one of the Anderson girls' coming out balls," Phoebe added, for Sophia's benefit. The

Anderson balls were always such a crush that even Sophia could never question whether or not it was true.

"We have been crossing paths a few times each year ever since." Vernon smiled down at Phoebe making her heart flutter in an odd way.

"Well it sounds to me that the two of you were destined for each other." Sophia gave Agapito a dreamy smile. "Don't you agree?"

"So it would seem." Agapito regarded Vernon with open curiosity while Sophia rambled on about how wonderful the music had been and how much she enjoyed seeing the festive decorations.

"Sophia, I think I see Aunt Gladys gesturing for us," Phoebe said.

"So soon?" Sophia almost whined.

"It is well past midnight." Phoebe barely restrained herself from stepping on her sister's foot to drive her point home.

"Ladies, I would be happy to escort you to your Aunt's side," Agapito said politely.

"That won't be necessary, Signor Romano," Phoebe protested. "I'm sure you have other guests to attend to without us taking up so much of your time."

"Alas, this is very true." Agapito's expression was one of forced resignation.

"But what about the dance you promised me?" Sophia asked with a slight pout.

"Sophia," Phoebe put her hand on her sister's arm and said in a gentle but firm tone. "We shouldn't monopolize Signor Romano any more than we already have."

"But—"

"Signor Romano, I noticed earlier that you had a room for games of chance. I have enjoyed learning the various card games played here in Genoa," Vernon inserted, effectively cutting off Sophia's plea.

"You are a card player, Mr Bennett?" Agapito asked.

"Only when I find a table that strikes my interest," Vernon impressed Phoebe by how easily he diverted Agapito's interest away from Sophia.

"My father has a room set aside for special guests," Agapito told him. "Perhaps you and I can find something to catch your attention there."

"In hopes that I'll leave a few of my hard earned coins on the table?" Vernon joked.

Agapito laughed. "Naturally."

Vernon dipped his head at Sophia. "Miss Ashdown, I am happy to have made your acquaintance." He then took Phoebe's hand and placed a lingering kiss on her knuckles. "Miss Ashdown, I am quite glad to have run into you again."

Tingles rippled across Phoebe's hand and arm. "And I you, Mr. Bennett."

"Perhaps we'll run into each other again before we each return home."

She smiled. "Perhaps we will."

"Ladies, I am pleased you were able to come to our gala this evening," Agapito was all polish and charm. "I do hope you enjoy the rest of your evening."

"Thank you for inviting us, Signor Romano." Phoebe looped her arm through her sister's and steered her away. "Good night, gentlemen."

Phoebe didn't breathe a sigh of relief until they climbed into the Bianchi's carriage and were rolling away. Perhaps now Sophia would be safely out of Agapito's reach and they would be able to enjoy the rest of their journey.

That wasn't too much to ask for, was it?

 7

IN under an hour of playing, Vernon had earned an invitation to join the elder Signor Romano's game in the upper west wing. Those games were played with far more intensity and finesse. Admittedly, the older men in attendance gave Vernon the first real challenge he had in some time.

The final hand came down to a single flip of a card.

Tension hung in the air like the smoke from the fine cigars they had smoked throughout the evening. None of the players who had dropped out of play spoke a word. Everyone's eyes were on the last two players, Vernon and Signor Romano.

When Vernon was dealt the final card, one of the two he needed to win, a hush echoed around the room as everyone waited for Signor Romano's reaction. Had they been playing under a different roof using someone else's dealer, Vernon suspected his win would have likely been called into question. As it was, Signor Romano had no choice but to grudgingly offer his congratulations.

Signor Romano gestured to the pile of chips and bank notes in the center of the table. "Well played."

Vernon held Signor Romano's gaze but made no move to collect his winnings. "My compliments to you and your associates. This has been the most challenging game I've played in some time."

Signor Romano's only acknowledgement was a slight nod of his head. "Perhaps a fresh round of drinks. Ilaria!"

One of the young serving girls hurried to the bar and returned with a bottle and four glasses.

As they shared a post-game drink with two of the men they played with, Vernon asked Signor Romano, "I don't suppose I could impose upon you to convert my winnings into a more transportable form of currency, could I?"

"Something in your Queen's coin, I suppose?" The chill in Signor Romano voice made the two men they shared drinks with pause. Their gazes bounced from one man to the other.

Vernon raised a brow as if Signor Romano's displeasure didn't concern him in the least. "Certainly not. I had rather hoped you might have something that could easily be deposited at your bank." He shrugged. "In the event that I need to finalize any of my business deals in an expedited fashion."

Signor Romano's expression didn't change as he considered Vernon. "You say your funds are handled by us?"

"But of course." Vernon raised his glass in salute. "Only the finest institution would do."

"Perhaps I can accommodate you after all." Signor Romano's smile made Vernon wonder if he was about to be led down a dark alley. "Right this way."

Vernon set his glass on the table then snagged three of the larger notes from his winnings and slipped them into his pocket before turning to follow.

Two of the brawny men guarding the door fell in step behind them as Signor Romano led the way. He stopped just outside the office Vernon had been hoping to gain access to. One of the guards used a key he fished from his pocket to unlock the heavy door. He scanned the interior before stepping aside to allow them entrance.

Despite the lack of obvious heat source, the air inside the room was more comfortable than Vernon expected. The desk and locked cabinets gave the appearance of a functional ledger room but the pieces were finely crafted. The sparse yet tidy appearance coupled with the security measures spoke volumes about the man who owned it. Clearly he trusted no one.

Using the ring of keys hidden secured to his vest, Signor Romano unlocked one of the cabinets and removed a ledger. He gestured to one of the guest chairs. "Please. Sit." Then Signor Romano took the chair on the other side of the desk.

As Signor Romano scribbled in his ledger, Vernon took in as much of the room as he could without drawing any more attention of the guards than he already had.

Unless there was a hidden entrance behind one of the bookshelves, the door they entered through was the only access point. He had hoped to find a window but the likelihood was small. He strongly suspected the door had been made from thick wood and unless he was very much mistaken, reinforced with metal.

Despite the overall neat and orderly appearance of the room, one of the cabinets behind Signor Romano did not line up with the others.

"I believe you will find this—" Signor Romano signed his name with a flourish at the bottom of the page. "Will allow you an expedited transfer of funds from one my personal accounts to your own." He handed the page to Vernon.

Vernon scanned what Romano had written. "Excellent." He folded the paper and tucked it into the pocket inside his jacket then held out his hand to Signor Romano.

While he waited to shake hands with the Signor, his gaze drifted to the floor in front of the awkwardly angled bookshelf. The arced scratches on the wood indicated something had been moved across the floor. Given how many lines there were, it must have been moved more than once. "Thank you for tonight's entertainment, Signor. It was a real pleasure."

Signor Romano shook with Vernon. "If you're still in town, perhaps you will allow us an opportunity to win back our losses."

"I would look forward to it." Vernon turned and nodded to the two guards. "Good evening."

One of the guards followed him out of the office and gaming room all the way to the stairway they had used to access the upper landing. He didn't have to look back to know he was being watched.

To maintain the image of jubilant partygoer, Vernon rejoined the crowd that was still milling about the ballroom. He stopped to speak to some of the gentlemen he had met in the clubs. Slowly, he made his way around the room to the terrace.

From what he had seen of Romano's office, a lot of effort had been made to secure a few ledgers and a liquor cabinet. His instincts screamed that the shipping logs they wanted were very likely be hidden in that office. He was also curious what else might be kept behind that off-center cabinet.

On the terrace Vernon found a dark corner where he could monitor the activity in the game room. Given the number of guests coming and going, there would be no way to sneak into Romano's office during the party. He would be better off attempting it after the party was over.

Unless he could devise a reason for Romano and his friends to leave. But he doubted anything short of a fire would drag them from their sport. Then again, one of the men said something about joining their wives for the final waltz.

Vernon consulted his pocket watch. The ball should be winding down within the hour. That might be his best opportunity.

He returned to the ballroom. The servers didn't appear to be nearly as rushed. The food table had been cleared. He snagged a glass from a passing server and took a sip. Sure enough, the wine had been watered down. All signs that the host would be bringing the evening to a close shortly.

Vernon engaged an older gentleman in trivial conversation until the band played the first notes of the waltz. Once he confirmed that Romano and his friends had indeed joined their wives for the last dances, Vernon slipped out of the ballroom by way of the terrace. From there he moved around the darkened edges until he reached the spot that he thought would be best for accessing the upper floor.

Using his dart gun, he launched an arrow tipped wire into the size of the building. His gloves protected his hands and helped him grip the thin rope as he shimmied up the side of the building. The window he left unlatched earlier in the evening allowed him to access the game room quietly and efficiently. As he hoped, everyone had indeed abandoned their cards in favor of the ball and their wives' good favor.

Vernon silently made his way to Romano's office and set to work on the lock. Memories of his early lessons of entering secured spaces flitted through his mind. As a beginner, he came close to being caught more than once. Where he had lacked skill with the pick, his instincts and lightness of foot had served him. Tonight, he felt certain he would need all of his skills to make it in and out of the Romano's office unseen.

The lock yielded to his manipulations in record time and allowed him to slip inside. He hurried to the cabinet he felt certain hid a secret doorway or anti-chamber. His fingers slid over wood sides seeking any kind of latch or lever. Satisfaction rolled through him when he found what he was looking for.

He started to pull the cabinet open then glanced at the scratches on the floor. Vernon pressed his shoulder against the side while he slid it open to minimize the sound of wood scraping on wood. Behind the false cabinet he found shelves full of ledgers and lock boxes.

As temping as it was to liberate some of Romano's funds, he left the cash boxes alone and concentrated his efforts on finding the shipping log he needed. He flipped through five unmarked journals until he found what he needed.

Once again, he was tempted to take the book but they only needed a few names from the logs for their investigation. A page or two were far more likely to be missed than an entire ledger.

He scanned the most recent entries, memorizing the names he could, then carefully cut one page from each shipping log that was least likely to be missed. He folded the sheets and slipped them inside the hidden compartment of the cigar case he carried.

Then he returned everything to the places he had found them and gently closed the cabinet. He used the silk scarf from his pocket to wipe the places he had touched. Romano stuck him as someone who would notice minute details like smudges on polished wood. No need raising the alarm before absolutely necessary.

Once he was assured that everything had been returned to its original state, he went to the door to check his escape route. A faint scratching at the door gave him pause. His pulse quickened when the handle turned just as he reached for it. Vernon ducked behind the door and pressed himself flat against the wall and waited to see who it was.

A man, also dressed in formal black, crept into the room and closed the door behind him. Given the stealthy way he moved and the anxiousness about him, Vernon felt certain he was not one of Romano's men.

Seizing the opportunity to lay a false trail, Vernon crept up behind the man and hit him on the back of the neck, knocking him out. The man was just small enough for Vernon to catch with ease. He propped the man in one of the chairs while he peeked out the office door.

The room appeared to still be empty.

Vernon grabbed his new friend around the chest and wrapped the man's arm over his own shoulder. He left the man in a chair in the corner of the game room then hurried out onto the balcony. Using the shadows for cover, he watched for the guards to make their pass below.

As he waited, he pulled a device that looked like a snuffbox from his pocket. He lifted the top, rotated a couple of pieces then secured it to the balcony railing. Next he snapped the lower half of the pen into two, creating two devices. These allow him to grip the thin wire and escape onto the grounds below in seconds.

With a grin of satisfaction he recoiled the wire, returning it to its snuffbox disguise, removed his gloves and slipped them into his pocket. He checked his surroundings to ensure no one saw his descent then quietly made his way around the shrubbery.

He dusted a stray leaf from his jacket sleeve then eased out of the shadows onto the walkway near the patio. He approached one of the matrons who had likely stepped out for a breath of fresh air and engaged her in conversation. She would be the perfect cover if anyone took notice of his return.

After escorting her back into the party he gracefully excused himself under the pretense of needing a drink.

As he waited for his drink, one of the women he remembered from the game room approached. Most of her dark hair had been coiled up on top of her head but one enticing lock fluttered along the left side of her face.

"Signor Bennett, is it not?"

"Indeed." He turned to face the woman. "I don't believe I've yet had the pleasure, Signora..." Vernon let his question hang in the air, hoping she would provide her name. He detected an odd lilt in her accent. While close, he suspected the local dialect was not native to her.

Her rouge-stained lips lifted in an inviting smile. "Gianna Moretti." She stepped closer while her brown eyes fluttered downward, pausing briefly where most young men concealed a pocket within their coat. "You played brilliantly this evening."

Vernon held his ground despite her uninvited closeness. He wasn't in the least bit attracted, but he was curious of her intent. "Thank you. I do so love a challenge."

"As do I." She tried to look coy as she toyed with the lapel of his jacket. "I must admit that I am surprised you didn't take your winnings and move on to more exciting entertainment by now."

He smiled as he guided her hand away from his jacket opening. "Believe it or not, tonight's events have kept me well entertained."

"Perhaps I can ensure the rest of your evening is just as eventful." She batted her eyes at him "Would you think me rather forward if I were to skip the hints and tell you outright that I'd very much like to dance with you?"

"I wouldn't think you forward at all." Actually, in the ton, her behavior would have been considered quite untoward. However, they were not in London. And he suspected she was after something other than a titled or rich husband. "Unfortunately, the dances are done for the evening, are they not?"

"I know a place we can go where the band plays until the sun comes up, if you're interested."

Vernon's gut cautioned there was more to the woman than a simple flirtation.

"Perhaps if you join me for a stroll in the garden, I can convince you." She pressed closer, brushing her breast against his arm invitingly. "I understand the gardens are quite fine under the night sky."

"I believe a stroll would be just the thing." He placed her hand in the crook of his arm and led her to the terrace. Since the evening was very nearly over, he led her down the darker pathway, hoping to speed up whatever she had planned.

No sooner hand they stepped around the row of hedges than two men leapt out of the shadows. The woman staggered backward but didn't call out an alarm.

With the smallest of effort Vernon snapped the neck of one of the attackers then stripped the knife from the other and used it to incapacitate him.

"Oh, my." Her hand clutched at her chest. "You're so brave," she cooed as she rushed to his side. "Were you hurt, Signor Bennett?"

He tried to brush her hands aside as he listened for more attackers. "No, I'm unharmed."

She ran her hands over his chest. "Do let me take a look to make sure."

"I—" A flash of movement from the corner of his eye momentarily distracted him allowing her an opportunity to pull his gun from his pocket.

She pressed it against his ribs. "Where is the shipping log?"

Damn. His gut had been right again. And just when things were getting interesting too. "What are you doing? What log?"

"Do not play dumb with us. We know you obtained the book from Signor Romano's office earlier. My men were watching."

He tried to wrap his arms around her again but she pushed his hand away. "Ah, *cher*. We were having such a lovely time." He pursued her deeper into the shadows.

"That's close enough," she cautioned. "Give me the book."

The click of the trigger warned him the gun was ready to fire. He lifted his hands in surrender.

She took one step to the side. "The log. Now."

The snap of a twig from the other side of the bushes distracted her just long enough for Vernon to move in. He knocked her hand that held the gun aside then wrenched the weapon away from her. As he struggled to subdue her without releasing or firing the pistol, a man stepped out of the shadows.

The ember of the cigar the man smoked illuminated just enough of his face so that Vernon could tell it was Moretti.

"Do you have what you came for?" Moretti asked.

"Of course." Vernon tipped his head toward the woman in his arms. "And then some."

"Do you need help with the lady or is this how you get your jollies?" Moretti's question rang with amusement.

"I believe I have the situation under control, but it would be ever so much easier if you would kindly do your magic trick. If it's not too much bother, that is."

The woman struggled against Vernon's hold and tried to back away when Moretti reached for her but she only succeeded in stepping on Vernon's boot. His body blocked any retreat she could have hoped for.

"Shhhh. This won't hurt." Moretti put his fingers on both sides of the woman's neck until her body went limp.

Vernon caught her weight and slowly lowered her to the ground. He looked at her unconscious form then at his partner. "I need to learn how to do that."

Moretti chuckled. "Ancient secret, my friend."

Vernon grunted. "I assume you took care of her backup?"

"Of course."

"Good." He gestured at woman. "I suppose we should move her somewhere that one of the party guests won't raise the alarm before we can leave."

"There is an out of the way place just a little farther back."

Vernon scooped the woman up into his arms. "Lead on."

After securing the woman's hands and feet and stashing her

out of sight, Vernon and Moretti made their way back to the villa they had leased. They left their coats in the foyer then headed to what served as their sitting room.

Alessio, their hired manservant, came in while they were helping themselves to a drink. "*Buonasera*. Did you have a pleasant outing?"

"Yes." The men exchanged glances. "I would say it was successful."

"Ah, but Signor, does not a successful evening include spending the night in a beautiful woman's arms?"

Moretti pointed with his glass. "You are right." He looked at Vernon. "So despite both of our winnings at the card tables, it seems our night cannot be labeled a success, my friend."

"Sadly, I must agree," Vernon said.

"Perhaps if you had made a little more effort to woo the woman you were dancing with when I found you then your night would have ended better." Moretti grinned unrepentantly.

"I shall keep that under advisement next time," Vernon said drolly.

 8

PHOEBE slept later than usual and yet she still arrived at the breakfast table first. Lady Charlotte and Aunt Gladys arrived shortly after she had finished her bowl of oats and berries. Surprisingly, Sophia made her appearance not long after.

As expected, the conversation revolved around the gala and the people who had attended. When the three had voiced their opinions on all of the dresses and bonnets they had seen they turned their attention to who arrived or danced with whom. Despite the fact that only Lady Charlotte knew any of them, there was much speculation on which pairings might last until the spring.

Phoebe tuned out most of what was said while she pursued the newssheets. An occasional affirmation that she had indeed seen whatever the ladies were talking about sufficed for her participation. It took far more control to stifle her disparaging remarks whenever Sophia rattled on about how handsome the young Signor Romano was in his formal attire and how lucky she was to have caught his attention. She did, however, allow herself the occasional eyeroll when Sophia wasn't looking.

Sometime during the discussion of silk ribbons, Phoebe's thoughts strayed to Vernon.

Despite her best efforts the memory of their dances transformed into one long, seductive dream. In it, the two of them danced from cloud to cloud. Even though she thought they hovered high in the sky, she felt safe and secure in his arms. So much that she never once feared slipping or falling.

By the light of day, she chided herself for such a fanciful notion. And, in truth, she was ashamed to admit to any attraction to him because of his treatment of her friend.

They might be peers, but his mother had been one of the matrons to openly shun her family when the scandal involving her sister had broken. While the incident with Emma may have been as much Emma's fault as it was his, his behavior with Mrs. Crenshaw was still scandalous.

From her perspective, there could never be a connection between them beyond passing friendship. Neither of their parents would allow it. So why was she even entertaining the possibility?

The far more interesting topic was why he needed to keep his identity a secret. Was he playing a prank on his friends? Or perhaps her?

It was possible that he left London to escape yet another scandal. But she hadn't heard of any involved Vernon's family before she left. And she felt certain her mother would have been more than happy to share that news.

Maybe he came to Italy to hide from his parents. She chuckled. That seemed the most likely answer. While she didn't know Vernon's father at all, she had the distinct impression that he had a rocky relationship with all of his children. And, not surprising, with his wife as well.

Yet she couldn't shake the thought that he had another reason for being in Genoa. A far more dangerous reason.

She'd heard whispers the Prince Regent had been recruiting some of the younger sons of the peerage. And after stumbling upon a conversation between her father and two of his friends at a dance just three months past, she believed the whispers. Her father and his colleagues confirmed they each knew of instances where the Prince Regent had indeed put some of the young men of the ton to use for the sake of the crown. One of her father's friends remarked how his youngest, after being approached by the Prince's men, left on some sort of assignment. They were uncertain of his destination or when he would return. The other man related a similar incident with another friend's son. The men speculated the recruiting efforts had to be related to something they called the Royal Intelligence Office.

When she later quizzed her brother about the Royal Intelligence Office, he became unusually silent on the subject. Normally Mathew answered all of her questions. However, in this one instance, he became more tight-lipped than a clam. That only served to fan the flames of her curiosity.

There were dozens of reasons Vernon might visit Genoa. Like many young men with the means to do so, he could also be taking advantage of his bachelor status to travel abroad. However, her mind wouldn't let go of the idea that he was here for reasons other than leisure.

A serious minded man had replaced the carefree young man she had met years ago.

If he was indeed here for reasons other than his own—reasons provided by perhaps even the Queen herself—could she have put him in compromising situation by acknowledging their former acquaintance?

Her heart skipped a beat in her chest. What if she put him in danger? What if she put herself, and by extension, her family in danger?

She blinked away the myriad of horrible possibilities.

Her gut told her that she had nothing to fear from him. And if she were completely honest, she was more intrigued than fearful of this new Vernon. She sighed. But the likelihood of seeing him again was slim. After all, her aunt had made arrangements for them to leave first thing on the morrow.

Perhaps they might run into each other at a ball after they both returned to London. It was possible.

"Since you only have one more day, we should visit the port," Lady Charlotte suggested.

Phoebe shook off her woolgathering. "Is the seaside market near the port?" Phoebe asked.

"Why yes, it is. I must admit I am surprised you would know of it."

"I—I must have heard it mentioned somewhere." Phoebe's cheeks grew warm.

"Perhaps from Mr. Bennett?" Sophia asked with a knowing smile.

"Mr. Bennett?" Lady Charlotte asked.

"Is that the young man you were dancing with last night?" Aunt Gladys asked. "I admit that I'm surprised you were willing to dance with a young man you had not been introduced to."

"Apparently they already knew each other," Sophia added smugly.

Phoebe resisted the impulse to kick sister under the table. "Yes. Mr. uh…Mr. Bennett and I share several mutual friends. We were introduced a few years ago."

"Is that so?" Aunt Gladys expression brightened with interest.

Before Aunt Gladys could ask what Phoebe feared would be a long list of questions, Lady Charlotte's maid hurried into the room. "Excuse me, Signora."

"Yes, Trisola, what is it?" Lady Charlotte smiled indulgently at the girl.

"Rocco just returned from the market. He said that Signor Romano and his son, Luciano, are dead."

Sophia and Aunt Gladys gasped in surprise.

Lady Charlotte's hand paused in mid-air where she was about to spread jam on a slice of toast. "Dead?"

Trisola nodded vigorously, making the cap she wore on top of her mass of curls bobble. "People are saying they were killed sometime last night either during the gala or shortly after." Trisola motioned with her hand to make the sign of the cross across her chest.

Aunt Gladys' teacup rattled against the saucer when she dropped it. "Killed?"

"Oh, my poor Agapito." Sophia clasped her hands to her chest. "He must be so distraught."

"Does Signor Bianchi know?" Lady Charlotte asked as she set the knife she had been holding aside then wiped her hands on her napkin.

Trisola gestured to the open doorway. "Rocco was just on the way to tell him."

Lady Charlotte nodded. "Thank you for telling us, dear.

And do let me know if you hear anything more."

"Yes, of course, Signora." Trisola curtsied then hurried out of the room.

"How dreadful," Aunt Gladys exclaimed.

"It is." Lady Charlotte's gaze strayed to the window while her nail tapped the side of her cup. "And there will likely be a number of shifts in family alliances before dinner."

"Do you suppose they were really killed, Charlotte?" Aunt Gladys asked.

Lady Charlotte refocused her gaze on Gladys. "I think it is extremely likely."

Sophia gasped.

"Romano had far more enemies than he did friends. To be honest, I'm surprised he wasn't killed long before now."

Aunt Gladys leaned forward in her chair. "I didn't realize he was so hated. He seemed perfectly cordial last night."

Lady Charlotte's brows rose. "Of course he was. His wife always made sure he played the role of generous host. But anyone who did business with him knew exactly how cut-throat he could be."

"Oh, I see," Aunt Gladys said.

"I suppose I should send my condolences to Signora Romano," Lady Charlotte muttered.

"Do you think it would be too forward of me to drop by their home and see how Agapito is doing?" Sophia asked. "I'm certain he must be devastated over losing both his father and his brother."

Phoebe was relieved when both Gladys and Charlotte looked at Sophia as if he had just asked to walk naked into the town square.

"That simply will not do, my dear," Aunt Gladys said firmly. "From what you have told me of your association with the younger Romano, it would most certainly be considered forward of you. You would wreck any chance you might have at making a good connection with him."

Sophia slumped in her chair with a pout. "But it may be my last chance to see him again before we leave."

Phoebe shook her head and reached for the pot of tea to keep herself from rolling her eyes, yet again, at her younger sibling. How could any girl be so unconcerned with making a fool of herself over a man?

"That is an unfortunate possibility," Aunt Gladys told her.

"I am afraid that I must also add that any chance of making a connection with him you might have had just vanished," Lady Charlotte told them.

Sophia sat up in her chair. "But why?" she practically wailed.

"As Romano's heir, he will have no choice but to make a strategic alliance. A local, alliance." Lady Charlotte stressed the word local.

"But—" Sophia's gaze bounced from Aunt Gladys to Lady Charlotte and back again.

"I'm sorry my dear." Lady Charlotte patted Sophia's hand. "But I do think it best that you know that now, before you become any more attached."

"But he wants me." A small tear formed in the corner of Sophia's eye. "I know he does."

"Did he tell you that?" Aunt Gladys asked.

"Well… no." Sophia hesitated as she dabbed her cheek with her napkin. "Not in so many words."

Phoebe couldn't remain quiet any longer. "It only takes four words. At the most."

Sophia frowned at her. "What only takes four words?"

"For a man to clearly tell you his intentions."

Sophia's frown deepened when Phoebe raised her hand, with one finger pointed to the ceiling. "Will." She raised another finger as she uttered each of the remaining words. "You. Marry. Me." She wiggled all four digits. "Four. That's all it takes to ensure that all parties are on the same page." She dropped her hand and looked into her sister's eyes. "Was that simple question asked of you?"

"Just because you're older than me does not mean you know everything." Sophia threw her napkin on the table and stormed from the room.

Aunt Gladys and Lady Charlotte's startled gazes returned to

Phoebe. Gladys looked reproachful while Lady Charlotte's held sympathy.

"I know you probably think I'm being cruel, but Agapito isn't nearly as attached to her as she is to him. You do realize that, don't you?" Phoebe asked of the two matrons.

"Perhaps that is so, but what harm would it do to allow her to hope?" Aunt Gladys asked

"Potentially a great deal if she throws herself at the man." Was she the only one who could see the disaster in Sophia's future if someone didn't rein her in?

Her aunt waved her hand in a dismissive gesture. "Sophia is spirited and outgoing but she can also be perfectly sensible. I don't think she would go that far."

"You give her far more credit than I." Phoebe folded her napkin and set it next to her plate. "But I probably should apologize and see how she is." She pushed her chair back. "Excuse me. I'll just check on Sophia then change for our trip into town to see the port."

"An excellent notion, my dear." Lady Charlotte consulted her pocket watch. "We should probably make ourselves presentable as well, Gladys."

"Yes, of course." Gladys took one last sip from her cup then rose from her chair.

"We'll assemble in the front parlor, as before," Lady Charlotte suggested. Then to Phoebe, she asked, "Would you let Sophia know we'd like to leave within the hour?"

"I will." With a nod she headed to the wing where hers and Sophia's rooms lay. Her thoughts were a jumbled mess. The primary thought she couldn't shake was whether or not Vernon had been involved in Signor Romano's death.

She had no reason to believe that he was a killer. But he had been at the party. And the last person she saw him with was Romano's son. And Vernon did imply that he had confidential information about the younger Romano.

Coincidence?

Possibly.

Her gut told her Vernon wasn't dangerous. Then again,

what did she really know about him? She knew who his parents and some of his friends were. She'd also seen how he behaved at balls and parties. Just because he knew how to act in public didn't mean he was a gentleman through and through.

That was what her father always told her brothers, anyway.

She wasn't sure how long she had been standing in front of Sophia's door, lost in her thoughts, before she shook them off. She needed to stop dwelling on Vernon and focus on the issue at hand.

Perhaps if she made a little effort toward making Sophia happy she would be able to salvage their last day in Genoa. Even though her sister annoyed her more often than not, she did love her and wanted to keep peace between them.

With a sigh she knocked then let herself in.

 9

VERNON hovered in the doorway of the storehouse watching the people milling about the port. He had spoken with the man he needed to make contact with but the information he had gotten didn't further their investigation. Now, he just needed to wait until Moretti finished his search.

Between the two of them they had gathered all the information they could about the captains, crew, shipments, shipping dates/times that had been listed on the log pages he had obtained. Two of the ships were sitting in the dry docks, out of commission. One they learned had been confiscated by a foreign entity. And yet another had last been spotted on the outskirts of Germany. Rumor had it that ship's captain had returned home with no plan to return.

People moved in and out of the oversized buildings carrying baskets of produce and other goods. He loved this part of his work. Watching people going about their day trying to figure out what each of their lives might be like.

The widowed woman who lived with her daughter and helped care for her grandchildren. The trio of women who didn't look enough alike to be sisters, but were close enough to make him believe they lived together. Or in the same shared accommodations.

As he pondered the possibilities a group of ladies caught his attention. Or at least one lady in particular.

Phoebe.

She and the sister he had been introduced to strolled along the edge of the pier at a leisurely pace. There were two older women with them and one younger. Based on the younger woman's dress, and her demeanor, she was likely a maid.

It had been a surprise to stumble across Phoebe at Romano's ball. Even more surprising had been how pleased he had been to see her despite his worry that she might give away his true identity. He would need to work on his explanation for his deception before he spoke to her again, but hopefully that wouldn't be until he returned to England.

Now that Romano was dead, he hoped their investigation would be wrapped up quickly so he could return home. He loved his work. And the danger and adventure certainly satisfied his wilder nature. But seeing Phoebe reminded of the few things he missed about home.

If he and Moretti gathered the information on the ships they were looking for, perhaps they could return to London before Christmas.

There was a chance that Romano's slave enterprise might crumble without him at the head. A slight chance, but still a chance. It was far more likely another snake would simply slither into Romano's place. That always seemed to be the way of it.

Vernon couldn't help himself tracking Phoebe's movements. It appeared she and her family were taking in the sights. Occasionally, one of the ladies would point to a ship and the others would nod in agreement.

He considered approaching them but he had always subscribed to the theory that it was best to stick as close to the truth as possible without telling a lie. His appearance at the docks would raise more questions than he wanted to answer. At least by anyone of the ton. Specifically, any ladies of the ton.

Just then, Phoebe and her companions made a turn and headed in his direction. Vernon considered ducking into one of the nearby shops until they passed but decided that would draw more attention. Instead he tugged his cap lower and slipped into the shadow of a nearby stack of crates.

The ladies passed by without so much as a glance in his direction.

When he felt they were far enough head he stepped around the corner to see what direction they had taken. Based on their current route, they were most likely headed to the market.

Just as he turned to resume his survey of incoming ships, he spotted two of Romano's men. Unless he was mistaken, they were the men Romano sent when dirty deeds had to be done. The pair's movements hinted they were not out for a casual stroll. The man in the lead gestured to his partner, who trailed a little father back.

They seemed to be following someone.

Now that Signor Romano was dead, one would think the men would be at the Romano estate, watching over the grieving widow. Who or what might they be looking for?

Vernon tracked the men's line of sight. His blood ran cold when the first man followed Phoebe through an open doorway into the market.

Bloody hell.

Foolishly, he had believed Phoebe and her sister would be safe from Romano. Apparently that had only been wishful thinking.

He took a deep breath. He would have to abandon his task in favor of seeing to the girls' protection. There was really no choice. His conscious would allow nothing less.

With a flick of his coat collar to hide more of his face, Vernon fell in line behind the men following the girls. He slipped a pen shaped device from his pocket and held it close to his hip. Using his thumb, he pumped the pen's tip multiple times to charge it.

When he drew close enough to pass, he pressed the end of the pen against the man's side. The device discharged with a barely audible crackling sound. Romano's man convulsed then crumpled to the ground. Vernon continued moving forward as if nothing had happened.

Behind him he heard a woman calling out. "Signor, are you all right? I think he's having a fit of some kind, Francesca."

Vernon moved as close as he dared to the next man, then ducked behind a barrel to avoid being seen. When Phoebe and her group turned the corner, Vernon ran to the end of the alley and peeked around the edge.

The girls had stopped to look at something a vendor held out to them. Phoebe smiled at the woman and shook her head, no. She tugged at her sister's arm and they continued on their way.

A second man slipped out of the shadows and follow the ladies. Once again Vernon also fell in behind them. Near the end of the row, his opponent paused next to a wooden crate. The man kept one eye on Phoebe's group while he took an apple from the nearby vendor. The merchant started to say something to the man, but was silenced by a single menacing look.

The man took bites from the stolen apple as if he had all the time in the world. It only made Vernon's ire grow.

When the girls looked as if they were about to move on, Vernon moved in. He dropped what looked like a pebble at the man's feet as he strolled past. The satisfying thud of a body hitting the ground echoed from that area and confirmed that the gas contained in the pebble had indeed worked.

Now that both assailants had been incapacitated he just needed to find a way to get the ladies away from the port without alarming them.

10

MORE than once since they entered the market, Phoebe felt a prickling on the back of her neck, as if someone were watching her. At one time she thought she spotted a man following them, but since he disappeared, she was likely imagining things.

Yet she couldn't shake the feeling. Even Sophia's excited rambling couldn't distract her from it. It appeared she was the only one who felt that way however.

"Aunt Gladys, do you think we would have time to return to that little shop that had the pretty hats and ribbons?" Sophia asked.

Aunt Gladys laughed. "Which pretty hats do you mean? I believe we have looked at dozens of them this week alone."

"The shop that had the blue hat with the long bird feathers in the window that we all admired," Sophia told them.

"I know just the one you mean." Lady Charlotte gestured to Aunt Gladys. "The one in town. Just down the street from the tea shop."

"Oh, yes," Aunt Gladys nodded. "I remember. Lovely place. What did you need from there, my dear?"

Sophia shrugged. "I thought I might get a few ribbons for Elspeth. So she doesn't feel so bad that she couldn't come with us."

"What a thoughtful girl you are." Aunt Gladys patted Sophia's hand.

Phoebe considered Sophia. She rarely thought of anyone but herself. The fact that she even mentioned their maid, Elspeth, came as a surprise. What was she up to?

"Good afternoon, ladies."

Phoebe barely contained her gasp of surprise. "Mr. Bennett." She had been thinking about Vernon and suddenly he appeared. She smiled. "What—How are you?"

"I am well, thank you." His gaze drifted to her sister and the others, reminding her they were not alone. "I am glad to see that you took my advice."

Aunt Gladys stepped forward. "Phoebe, are you going to introduce your friend?"

"Of course. Aunt Gladys, this is Mr. James Bennett." To Vernon she added, "Mr. Bennett, this is my aunt, Lady Gilbray and Lady Charlotte. And I assume you remember my sister, Sophia?"

He gave them all a gracious smile, one that made her insides flutter. "Ladies. I do hope you are enjoying this fine weather."

"We have," Aunt Gladys said.

"So much nicer than we expected for this late in the year," Lady Charlotte added.

"Phoebe tells us that you too are from London proper, Mr. Bennett?" her aunt prompted.

"I am," Vernon told them with a dip of his head.

"What a lovely coincidence that both Phoebe and Sophia happened across someone they knew," Aunt Gladys beamed.

Vernon and Phoebe exchanged glances. "Quite the coincidence."

"And what brings you to Genoa, Mr. Bennett?" Lady Charlotte asked. "I wager that a handsome young man like yourself isn't here to take in the sights."

"Actually, today I am," he told them.

Aunt Gladys gestured to Lady Charlotte. "Charlotte was just delighting us with some of the local history. Would you care to join us as we tour the docks?"

"I'm sure Mr. Bennett has far more important things to do today." As much as Phoebe would have liked the opportunity to visit with Vernon, the idea of him being exposed to her sister's fluctuating moods, much less her shopping habits, filled her with dread.

"Actually, I was able to complete my business and I find

myself at loose ends today. I'd be delighted to hear some of the history of the area." Vernon's smile seemed to work on experienced matrons as well as innocent misses. Her aunt and Lady Charlotte both cooed with delight when he offered them his arm.

At first, Phoebe's pulse stuttered at the thought of spending time in his company. But she soon forgot her original nervousness and found herself enjoying their exploration of Genoa. Lady Charlotte's stories enhanced the visual delights. But it was Vernon's knowledge of ships that truly held her attention. He was also able to answer most of their questions about the shipping companies and what merchandise each of them specialized in. Despite his charm and the humorous antidotes, Phoebe couldn't help but think he was distracted by something. More than once she caught him looking behind them, as if expecting someone to sneak up on them.

"Mr. Bennett, would you care to join us for tea?" Lady Charlotte asked, drawing his attention back to their group.

He smiled. "I don't wish to intrude on your day any further."

"You would not be intruding," Phoebe's aunt quickly assured him.

Vernon glanced at Phoebe as if wanting confirmation. "Aunt Gladys would never lie about something as important as tea."

"Well, in that case." He offered Aunt Gladys his arm. "I would be delighted to join you."

Phoebe smiled to herself. Yes, he was indeed a charmer.

When they reached the main entrance to the docks, Vernon hailed a hackney. The driver pulled the carriage near their group then Vernon handed each of them up. He climbed in after them and sat next to Phoebe.

With six of them in the carriage they were forced to sit tightly pressed against each other. Phoebe's knee brushed against Vernon's every time the driver turned a corner or made any abrupt motions. By the time they arrived at the villa, she could barely form a complete sentence in her own head much less audibly.

When had a man ever affected her so?

Never. Not once.

In her previous experiences, most men were just there, taking up space. But Vernon somehow pinged her consciousness on a level that she had never experienced before. She was a little unsure how to process it much less how to react to it.

When the carriage stopped in front of the Bianchi villa Vernon disembarked then handed each of them down from the carriage. Despite the gloves she wore, even the touch of his hand on hers made the butterflies in her belly flutter.

In the foyer Lady Charlotte handed her bonnet to one of the maids who had come to assist them. "Paolo please have Corina bring a tea tray to the library."

"Of course, Signora."

They each handed their jackets and scarves to the footman who had appeared then proceeded into the library. Phoebe waited until Lady Charlotte and her aunt had taken their seats then took one that would put some much-needed space between her and Vernon.

Luckily, Sophia took the available space at the opposite end of the sofa that Vernon hovered near. Somehow they managed to make it through refreshments without Sophia embarrassing herself. Before Phoebe knew it, she was walking through the front garden with Vernon so they could say their farewells.

"I am glad to have crossed paths with you again, Phoebe," Vernon told her.

She felt her cheeks grow warm. "Actually, I am as well."

"I do hope your trip home is pleasant. Your aunt indicated you leave tomorrow?"

"That's correct."

"Good."

Something in his tone made her pause. She stopped and faced him. "Are you so anxious for us to depart then?"

"No, not at all. Why would you think that?"

"Because the way you answered just now. I dare say it

sounded as if you were relieved."

"I am just relieved to see you and your sister leaving before…" Again, he forced a smile. "Well, before anything happened."

She considered him. "What did you think might happen to us?"

He glanced away before answering. "Probably nothing."

Something told her that he wasn't being honest with her but she couldn't imagine why.

He took her hand. "Will you promise me one thing?"

"What might that one thing be?"

"Will you promise me that you will not go out again today? You and your sister, that is."

What an odd thing to ask. "Why?"

"Will you allow me to simply say that there are things I know about Genoa and the people here that I cannot share?" He squeezed her hand. "And most of those things you do not want to know."

She raised a brow in question. "More secrets?"

He shrugged one shoulder and grinned unrepentantly. "Just a few more." His eyes pleaded with her to understand.

"Does this have anything to do with the Romano family?"

After a second of surprise, his expression blanked. "I'm afraid I cannot say."

It only took a moment of internal debate for her to ask the question she had long been pondering. "Did you have anything to do with Signor Romano's death?"

"No."

There had been no hesitation in his answer. Should she believe him? Nothing in his expression made her think he was lying to her. Yet, still. What did she really know about him? After all, she knew man standing before her by a different name. That alone should give her reason to doubt everything he said.

Yet her gut said he told her the truth.

She took a deep breath. "Very well. I promise to not go out again. And I will do everything I can to keep Sophia inside as well."

She didn't realize how stiffy he had been holding himself, waiting her answer, until she saw it drain from him.

"But…"

He froze.

"You owe me an explanation as soon as we both return to London."

He gave her a brisk nod. "Very well."

"Perhaps I will allow you to escort me to the Pink Rose one afternoon."

One of his brows arched in question. "Isn't the Pink Rose a tea room?"

"It is."

His lips twitched into a grin. "I suppose I owe you at least that much."

"I believe so."

"Until then." He held her gaze as he raised her hand to his lips.

Her mouth went dry. She felt the kiss he pressed just above her fingers sent tingles all the way up her arm to the back of her neck.

When he lifted his head his eyes twinkled as if he knew exactly how he affected her. "Safe travels."

"And to you."

He squeezed her hand one last time then headed for the gate. He turned to look back at her just as he put his foot on the step of the carriage. With a lift of his chin he told her, "Get back in the house before you get chilled."

She gave him a wave to let him know she heard then started toward the front entrance.

At the door she paused. When she looked back she found him watching her from the carriage. Their eyes met. Even across the distance of the garden she felt a connection deep inside of her.

She would see him again. Somehow she was certain of that.

The question was when.

11

THE rest of Phoebe's afternoon and evening was spent packing and finalizing the details of their travel. Despite the flurry of activity, Phoebe went to bed that night with Vernon at the forefront of her thoughts. Where she at home, she might have gone to her mother for advice just to calm her mind. Perhaps she would when they returned home. In the meantime she needed to get what rest she could and ensure Sophia didn't leave the villa.

Vernon might not have shared any information with her but he seemed sincere in his concern for their welfare.

She refrained from saying anything to Sophia. Outright forbidding her from leaving the house in order to see Romano would have only encouraged her to do so. She also didn't have proof that they were in danger. And everyone in the family knew how she felt about rumors.

Surely she could keep an eye on her sister for a little while longer.

She fell asleep to troubled dreams. Dreams of people and dogs chasing her through a series of tunnels. She managed to stay ahead of her pursuer, but only just.

When she woke, her heart was pounding in her chest. She lay in bed in order to calm her racing pulse and to allow the sun to sneak over the horizon.

Even after she rose, washed and dressed, the sense of being watched stayed with her. She hurried to the kitchens to make a pot of tea in hopes that the warmth would drive the chill away. Despite her insistence that she could manage on her own the cook shooed her from the kitchens.

Phoebe had just finished her tea and toast when Aunt

Gladys made her appearance in the breakfast parlor. "Good morning, dear."

"Good morning. I trust you slept well?" Phoebe asked her aunt.

"I did, thank you." Aunt Gladys took a seat at the table. "Are you ready to return to England?"

"I am." Phoebe added a dab of preserves to her plate. "I have enjoyed our visit to Italy. But I do miss home."

Her aunt nodded. "Even I miss sleeping in my own bed."

"So it isn't just me?"

"Of course not. Travelling abroad, while exciting, can also be exhausting. And it usually gives one a deeper appreciation for home."

"I see that."

"Did you check to see if Sophia out of bed yet? She really ought to have a something to eat before we begin loading trunks."

"I did not check as I passed her room. Although in truth, I am surprised she hasn't shown yet."

Her aunt went to the sideboard and added a couple slices of toast to her plate. "You know she is not an early riser."

"I do know that. But I thought I heard her up and about this morning while I was dressing."

Aunt Gladys paused her perusal of the food to glance at Phoebe. "Well that is a surprise." She added an egg to her plate then returned to her seat. "When I spoke to her late last night, she did seem be excited to be going home today."

"Did she?" Phoebe snorted. "I thought she was still distraught over leaving the city in which her beloved Agapito resided."

"Perhaps she changed her mind after receiving that letter."

Phoebe was just about to take a sip of tea when her aunt's statement registered with her. "What letter?"

"I'm not certain." Aunt Gladys spread butter across her toast. "I was just leaving the sitting room when the footman accepted it."

"You didn't read it?"

"Of course not." Glacys seemed affronted by the suggestion. "It wasn't addressed to me."

"Of course." Phoebe pushed her chair back when she stood. "I think I'll just go and check on Sophia."

Aunt Gladys took a sip from her own teacup then added as an after thought, "Tell her I believe it would be in her best interest to eat a light fare this morning."

"I will tell her you said so."

A sense of unease teased the back of Phoebe's mind as she headed to the wing of the villa that she shared with her sister. There was only one person in all of Italy that would be writing Sophia. What could Agapito possibly need to say to Sophia in the midst of everything he must be dealing with after his father's untimely death? Surely he and Sophia had not grown so close that he would be worrying about their return to England more than his family's grief.

She gave her sister's door several quick raps. "Sophia? Are you awake?" When there was no response, Phoebe turned the nob and pushed the door open. The room was still dark. Obviously the maid had not opened the drapes yet.

"Sophia?"

Phoebe drew one curtain panel back letting the light spill into the room. A dirty hand towel sat next to Sophia's washbasin. The gown Sophia normally slept in lay over the back of the dressing table chair. And the dress and shoes Sophia planned to wear were missing.

It appeared Sophia had gotten up and dressed. But Phoebe had not passed her along the way. So where was she?

Phoebe hurried to the library to see if Sophia had gone there instead of the breakfast room. But she wasn't in the library. Nor was she in the sitting room.

Phoebe then returned to the dining room. Her aunt and Lady Charlotte were chatting about something to do with hats when she interrupted them. "Did Sophia come in?"

Both ladies looked at her in surprise. "No," Lady Charlotte answered.

"Was she not in her room?" Aunt Gladys asked.

"No." Phoebe frowned. She nibbled on her thumbnail as she tried to think where else in the house she might look.

"Perhaps the library?" Lady Charlotte asked.

"I already looked there and the sitting room."

Her aunt turned in her chair so that she faced Phoebe directly.

"Are you sure she wasn't in her room?" Aunt Gladys asked.

Phoebe nodded once. "Quite."

Lady Charlotte set her teacup aside. "Might she have gone to your room for something?"

Phoebe's mood lifted. "I hadn't thought of that. I'll be back shortly."

Phoebe practically flew to her room. When she found the door open she hoped it was a good sign. "Sophia?" she called out as she turned the corner.

The maid who was gathering the dirty linens from the bed looked up. "*Si, Signora?*"

"I'm sorry. I thought you might be my sister."

"Ah." The maid bobbed her head and continued with her duties.

"I don't suppose you have seen my sister this morning, have you?"

"I'm sorry, Signora, but I have not."

Disappointment and worry set in again. "Thank you."

"Signora? You could ask Valentino if he has seen your sister."

Phoebe nodded. "I will do that. Thank you."

Since she was close to Sophia's room she returned to take another look. Just in case. The one window covering was still pulled back but it didn't look as if the maid had been in to clean yet. Phoebe opened the lid of Sophia's trunk. It appeared to be untouched from where Sophia had packed her things last night. The bag Sophia planned to carry with her on the train sat open on the chair near the trunk. Sophia's book and personal items were still inside.

It didn't appear as if anything were missing. But where was Sophia?

Phoebe moved toward Sophia's side of the bed. On the bedside table she found an envelope with a broken seal. Phoebe hesitated just as she reached to take the letter. She glanced toward the open bedroom door. There was no one in hall. Even if Sophia caught her reading the letter Phoebe felt she could justify her snooping. After all, she had no idea who had written it.

Firm in her conviction, she pulled the paper from the envelope and began reading. The large, messy scrawl appeared to be written by a masculine hand. The note simply instructed Sophia to meet the author in the front garden, just after daylight. But to tell no one and come alone.

Phoebe's heart pounded against her ribs.

The little fool. She likely did just as the writer asked.

Phoebe ran back to the dining room, letter in hand.

"Lady Charlotte, could I get Valentino to go out to the garden with me?"

"At this hour? Whatever for?" Lady Charlotte asked.

"Why do you need to an escort to go to the garden?" Aunt Gladys' chimed in.

"Because I think Sophia met a man out there this morning." Phoebe thrust the letter into Aunt Gladys' hands.

Lady Charlotte dropped her fork and rushed to Gladys' side. They both scanned the note then Lady Charlotte called out to the maid. "Rose, would you please ask Valentino to escort Miss Phoebe out to the front garden. And call for Angelo too. But caution him that we may have an uninvited visitor."

"Thank you." Phoebe rushed to the front entrance and pulled the door open. She wanted to run as fast as she could into the garden but wasn't so foolish. She looked as far as she could into the gardens while she waited on the step for Valentino but couldn't see Sophia or anyone moving about.

Thankfully Valentino did not dawdle. "Here, Signora." Valentino handed her one of Lady Charlotte's wool wraps.

Phoebe tossed it around her shoulders as she rushed out to the garden. She paused at the first pathway long enough to ensure Valentino had followed. "Sophia!" Each time she peered down a row she held her breath hoping to find her sister. Her concern even overrode the chill that slowly crept through her shawl. Still, she kept moving on. By the time she reached the far side of the garden, her fear had become mixed with anger.

What if Sophia had run off because she knew they would have told her not to? She could have walked to the stables without telling anyone. She may have even borrowed a horse and ridden into town. Or she could simply be hiding behind one of the many topiaries in order to steal a kiss from Agapito or who ever had written that note.

"Signora?" Valentino hurried to her side. "I do not think your sister is here."

Phoebe's gaze scanned the shrubs and statues around them. "I am afraid you are right."

"Come. You should return to the house. The men will go and look for her."

She pulled her wrap tighter. Regretfully, she cast one last glance behind her then nodded and followed Valentino back to the house.

Valets and errand boys were still coordinating efforts in the main entryway when Phoebe and Valentino returned. Valentino joined them after she assured him that she would remain at the house. It seemed Signor Bianchi and Lady Charlotte had made it a priority to find Sophia.

Phoebe went immediately to the library in hopes of locating Aunt Gladys. She found her aunt pacing in front of the fireplace.

"Please come and sit, Gladys," Lady Charlotte pleaded. "I'm sure Sophia will turn up directly. You'll see."

"She must be found." Gladys twisted her handkerchief in her hands. "I just don't know what I would tell Margaret if something happened to her."

"I'm sure it won't come to that," Lady Charlotte assured her.

Both ladies turned as Phoebe approached.

"There you are." Aunt Gladys rushed to take Phoebe by the hand. "Your fingers are like ice. Come warm yourself by the fire."

"No luck finding her?" Lady Charlotte asked.

Phoebe shook her head. "No." It was becoming harder to hold her emotions at bay. Part of her wanted to scream in frustration and the other part struggled under the weight of her fear for her sister.

"Where could that girl have gone? Surely she knew she would worry us." Aunt Gladys fretted. "Running off so close to our departure time. What was she thinking?"

Phoebe blinked. *What had Sophia been thinking?* Now that Aunt Gladys pointed it out, this truly wasn't like Sophia. She might be a little self-absorbed at times, but not to the extent of deliberately hurting her family. "I wasn't surprised to learn Sophia had snuck out into the garden to tell a gentleman farewell. But I struggle to believe that she left the estate without saying a word. And she certainly would not have jeopardized our return home. She just wouldn't. Despite all her theatrics over not seeing Agapito again, she really was ready to go home." Phoebe looked first at her aunt then at Lady Charlotte to emphasize her point. "Something feels very wrong about this."

Aunt Gladys dropped into the nearby chair. "Oh, dear." She closed her eyes and pressed her fingers against her temple.

"I think I will have Rosa bring us some tea." Lady Charlotte got up and left the library.

"Your mother will never forgive me for this," Aunt Gladys mumbled.

Phoebe glanced away from the dancing flames that she had been staring into. "Mother won't blame you for Sophia's inconsideration."

"She will. And rightfully so. You girls are my responsibility and I fear I have been lax in my duties."

"No, you haven't." Phoebe went to her aunt and took her hand. "You've been wonderful. Sophia would have done this even if Mother and Father had both been here. If anything, I blame Agapito."

"You had concerns about his character from the start." She squeezed Phoebe's hand. "Perhaps I should have listened to you."

"That's not important." Phoebe took a seat near the fire. "All we can do is pray she is found quickly."

"Indeed."

The rest of the morning was spent in flurry of servants coming and going making reports of where they had searched and what they had learned. Phoebe's fear grew as the parameter of their search grew wider. It was no surprise when Aunt Gladys cancelled their plans to return home. Seeing Signor Bianchi make the trip into town to personally oversee efforts to find Sophia only amplified Phoebe's worries. Without a doubt something was very, very wrong.

She had made several trips out into the gardens but Aunt Gladys refused to let her go farther than the garden walls. And never without one of the valets as an escort. Even though she knew she wouldn't find any new clues to Sophia's whereabouts her anxiousness simply wouldn't let her sit still for long.

In a desperate attempt to do something, she penned a note to Vernon, telling him about Sophia's disappearance. She gave one of the errand boys a few coins and asked him to deliver it. While she had no idea where Vernon was staying she felt certain one of the gentlemen's clubs in town would know how to contact him. While she had no desire to expose her family to possible ridicule, her sister's safety came first. He might be a rogue, but he might also have connections in Genoa that Signor Bianchi did not. Saving her sister was worth any embarrassment they might later face.

By bedtime, a somber pall had fallen over the household. Signor Bianchi's late return home empty handed and with no information on Sophia was the last straw on Phoebe's emotional dam. She retired to her room physically and emotionally exhausted.

In a fog she readied herself for bed without the assistance of a maid. After brushing out her hair and pulling on her warmest nightgown she turned down the covers of her bed.

There she found a note had been slipped under pillow. She grabbed her glasses from the bedside table and slipped them on so she could read what was written.

Your missive was received. We have extended our efforts to search for Sophia. Take care until I see you tomorrow. ~V

The tears Phoebe refused to shed during the day fell onto the parchment as she read the note again and again. Finally, she collapsed onto her pillow and poured out her fear and anxiousness through her sobs. But when her tears dried she realized that a tiny portion of her worry had eased.

She held Vernon's note to her chest and said a silent prayer not only for her sister's well-being but also of thanks for the efforts everyone was making to find Sophia. Most especially for Vernon.

Strange that just the thought that he too was out there looking for Sophia made her feel just a little better.

 12

AFTER having spent the better part of the night working, Vernon rose earlier than he would have liked in order to pay a visit to Phoebe that morning. She was probably worried sick over her sister's disappearance and he felt compelled to see her.

Most of Vernon and Lawrence's evening had been spent looking through shipping records they had helped themselves to, courtesy of another locked, yet easily picked, window. But after receiving Phoebe's note, Vernon made a few discrete inquiries into Sophia's disappearance. By midnight he had at least eliminated the possibility of the girl being at the Romano estate as a properly invited guest. Still, he set an additional man on watch at the estate in case she turned up through nefarious means.

While he didn't have any news to comfort Phoebe with, he at least wanted to check on her. He only briefly allowed himself to wonder why he needed the assurance that she was safe before he dismissed the thought.

All of the information they had gathered on the missing women in the area weighed heavily in the back of his mind. He couldn't shake the idea that Sophia's disappearance might be related. Despite her being English.

As he rode toward the Bianchi estate he debated how much to tell Phoebe. He wanted her to be cautious for her own safety but didn't want to cause her more worry. She struck him as a steady sort—one never given to vapors or hysterics—but people often reacted differently under duress.

The rocking of the carriage when it came to a stop at the Bianchi estate pulled Vernon from his thoughts. He spoke briefly with the driver before approaching the house. A younger, muscular man greeted him at the door.

"Good morning." Vernon kept his tone neutral. "I came to pay Miss Phoebe Ashdown a call. Is she receiving visitors this morning?" Vernon pulled one of his calling cards from his pocket and handed to the man.

The man glanced at the inscription on the card. "I'll ask." For a moment Vernon was surprised the man had closed the door without at least inviting him into the foyer out of the cold. But given the circumstance, the man's rudeness could be overlooked in favor of securing the household.

A moment later the man who Vernon thought to be the butler opened the door. "My apologies, Signor Bennett." He stepped back to allow Vernon entrance. "The ladies will receive you in the sitting room." After taking Vernon's hat and gloves, he gestured toward one of the connecting hallways. "Please follow me."

Before he could even step through the door Phoebe rushed to greet him. "Mr. Bennett. It's so good of you to come."

There were dark circles under her eyes hinting that she hadn't slept well. But otherwise, she was calm and poised. He kissed the top of her hand and gave it a comforting squeeze. "I would have come yesterday when I heard the news but didn't want to intrude."

"It was a bit chaotic." She gestured toward the couch where her aunt and Lady Charlotte sat. "You remember my aunt, Lady Gilbray, and Lady Charlotte?"

Vernon dipped his head. "Good morning."

They both mumbled their greetings.

"Do have a seat Signor Bennett," Lady Charlotte motioned toward one of the chair across from where them.

"So you have heard of our...situation then?" Lady Gilbray asked as if the thought pained her.

"Of Sophia's disappearance?" he asked to clarify.

Lady Gilbray cleared her throat still her answer came out somewhat strangled. "Yes."

"I did."

"Has word spread so far then?" Lady Charlotte asked.

"Actually, I sent him a note yesterday asking for his assistance in the search." Phoebe's admission both surprised and pleased him. He had been prepared to attribute his knowledge to local gossip, but her quick ownership of her actions spoke of integrity not often seen in the ton.

"Phoebe," her Aunt exclaimed. "What were you thinking?"

"That I want Sophia home as soon as possible."

Phoebe's declaration immediately deflated any argument her aunt might have offered.

"Please be assured of my discretion." He glanced at Phoebe to check her reaction to the conversation. Other than her unusually stiff spine, her expression remained the same. "My business partner and I are in a unique position to assist, at the moment. We have been keeping close watch on local gossip." Vernon shrugged. "You would be surprised how often business deals are made or broken because of idle talk."

"I see. And have you heard anything related to Sophia?" her aunt asked hopefully.

"Unfortunately, nothing yet. But I made several discreet inquires last night that I hope will prove helpful." Vernon directed his next words to Phoebe. "I was truly sorry to hear about Sophia. I do hope you are faring well under the circumstances."

"As well as can be expected, Mr. Bennett." For the slightest of moments her mask of calm slipped. "I just pray she returns to us safe and sound."

To Lady Charlotte he asked, "If I may be so bold, what has been done to locate her?"

The older ladies exchanges glances, then Lady Charlotte looked to Phoebe.

"Mr. Bennett is a friend," Phoebe assured them. When her gazed returned to him he was surprised to see a hint of warmth and trust. "I believe he can be trusted and am confident he will be discreet about Sophia's disappearance."

"Very well." Lady Charlotte folded her hands in her lap. "Obviously the estate has been thoroughly searched. More than once. Signor Bianchi has made many inquires in town.

You would have to ask him the specifics on that. But I do know he paid the Romanos a visit yesterday."

"He did?" Phoebe asked, obviously surprised by the revelation.

Lady Charlotte cast an apologetic look at Phoebe. "He told me after you had both retired for the night." She shrugged. "He learned nothing of any value. Both Signora Romano and Agapito assured him they had not seen Sophia."

"Did he tell them she had disappeared?" Phoebe asked.

"No, of course note. Carlo simply asked a question in passing so as to not distress the already grieving widow."

Phoebe frowned as she nodded. Clearly, she didn't like the answer any more than he did.

"Mr. Bennett, would you like tea?" Lady Charlotte gestured to the tray sitting on the table between them. "I can have Rosa refresh the pot."

"No, thank you. I do not mean to stay long."

Phoebe's express fell a little further. While he hated disappointing her, there were a couple of leads he needed to follow up before meeting Moretti.

"It would not be a bother," Lady Gilbray reassured him.

"No, truly. I am sure you have things to attend to and I have no wish to disrupt your household further. I would however like to extend my assistance to Signor Bianchi. If you wouldn't mind passing word to him, I can make myself available in whatever capacity he deems fit."

"Thank you for your offer." Lady Charlotte smiled. "I will be sure to tell him you said so "

"He can send word to Il Falco Rosso. They know how to find me," he added.

Lady Charlotte dipped her head in acknowledgement.

"Now I believe I must take my leave." Vernon turned to Phoebe. "Would you be so kind as to walk me to the door?"

He wasn't sure if Phoebe was surprised by his request or that he felt he had to ask. "Of course."

"Ladies, it was nice to see you again. I am sorry it isn't under happier circumstances." Vernon got to his feet. "Please do let me know if I can be of assistance."

"We will," Lady Charlotte assured him.

Lady Gilbray offered her hand to him. "Thank you for stopping by, Mr. Bennett. Perhaps we will see you again after this dreadful situation is resolved."

"And hopefully that will be soon." Vernon bowed over Lady Gilbray's hand, then quickly released it as soon as he realized his formal manners were showing. "Good day, ladies."

He gestured for Phoebe to precede him toward the door.

As soon as the door closed behind them, he lowered his voice, "I had hoped to have a moment of privacy with you, if you don't feel that would be too forward of me."

"Is it about Sophia?"

"Yes."

"Let me get my wrap and I'll walk out outside with you."

He glanced at the nearby doors but dismissed them as options. As much as he didn't want her getting cold, he couldn't be certain they wouldn't be overheard inside of the house. Reluctantly, he nodded his agreement.

As soon as they set foot on the pathway leading from the house to the gate near the road, the muscular man who had met Vernon at the door stepped around one corner of the house. He made no effort to hide the fact that he was watching them.

In French, Vernon asked, "Do you speak French, by chance?"

"*Oui.* Yes, I do."

"*Bien.*" Good. He continued their conversation in French. "I cannot be certain who might be listening."

Phoebe responded in French as well. "Ah. I understand."

"When I came here today I wasn't sure how much to tell you." She started to say something but he held up one finger to beg her patience. "Please understand that I am limited on what I can say because of the reasons I am here. But after seeing you, I believe I can share a little of what I know."

"Please. I would appreciate anything you know at all."

"We have traced Sophia as far as the piazza Corvetto. We

have witnesses that say she got into an unmarked steam carriage of her own accord here on the estate. At the end of the lane just there." He glanced toward the area he meant. Phoebe followed his gaze. "A carriage similar in description was spotted pulling up to a home we have been watching for some time. But no one in the area saw your sister enter the house."

"You're sure she got into the carriage freely?" she asked.

"The first one, we believe so."

"Was it Agapito?"

He grimaced. "We cannot be certain."

"He sent her a note asking her to meet him in the gardens the morning she disappeared.'

Vernon's brows rose. "He did? Do you have the note?"

"Yes." She pulled a wrinkled note from the folds of her gown and handed it to him.

A surge of energy flowed through his veins as he scanned the note. If Agapito did write the note and Sophia did turn out to be one of the victims, it would tie him to the disappearances. "May I keep this?"

She shrugged. "I suppose. It is doing me no good except to give focus to my frustration."

"Then I am glad to relieve you of it."

She opened her mouth as if to say something then bit her lip and frowned.

"What is it?" he prompted.

"Is Romano involved in this?"

He could tell she was torn about what to believe and very likely what to hope for as to her sister's wellbeing. Unfortunately, he couldn't relieve that indecision without violating his mission's need for secrecy. "I cannot say."

"Cannot or will not?"

He sighed. "I will tell you that we have been keeping a close eye on his estate but your sister has not been spotted there nor have we seen anything there in the last few days to alarm us."

"But you told me at the ball that he was not to be trusted."

"I stand by that."

"I'm confused."

He took her hand. "I understand." He squeezed her hand reassuringly. "There is more going on in the shadows of Genoa than I can divulge."

"Why can you not tell me?"

"Because I am not at liberty to do so." Her frown deepened. The urge to kiss it away startled him with its intensity. "I must once again beg your discretion. Just know that I will do what I can to locate your sister. But in the meantime, please trust that Signor Bianchi and I will do everything we can to find Sophia."

She nodded. "What should I tell my aunt?"

"Nothing."

"Why?"

"Because this is bigger than you, me, and I hate to say it, but even your sister."

"How?" She jerked her hand away as tears of frustration pooled in her eyes. "How can this be bigger than the life of an innocent girl? And how can I believe you when are aren't telling me what you do know?"

His own frustration rose with hers. He knew his mission. He had his orders. Those orders included telling no one his true objective for being in Genoa. For the first time since he agreed to join the Royal Intelligence Office, he considered disobeying his orders and taking her into his confidence. But the truth would likely only heighten her fear for her sister. After all, no gently raised young lady needs to hear the disturbing realities of slave trade. "You have absolutely no reason to be believe me. And I wouldn't blame you if you didn't." He gentled his voice. "But I wish that you would."

She searched his eyes then finally let out a sigh. "Very well."

"Thank you." He took her hand.

She met his gaze. "Your annual Christmas letter to me had best be detailed and informative."

He smiled. "When this is all over, and you and your sister are back in London, I will be happy to read that letter to you in person."

"I look forward to it."

"Now, I must go. I cannot be late."

She nodded her understanding.

"I promise I will send word if we learn anything about Sophia."

"Thank you."

With a jerk of his head, he gestured to the front entrance. "I will not leave until you are safely on the other side of that door though."

She nodded then hurried away. Over her shoulder she gave him a sad smile then stepped inside and closed the door behind her. Vernon looked at Signor Bianchi's hired man. As expected the man was still keeping a close eye on him. Vernon touched the brim of his hat in a salute then made his way down the path to the gate.

The hackney he had hired waited for him just outside of the fence. He gave the driver his next destination then climbed into the cab. Once the carriage was in motion he pulled the letter Phoebe had given him from his pocket. The parchment was a quality paper. Certainly nothing a commoner would use. He couldn't be certain it had been written by Agapito without comparing it to some of the other documents they had. But the flourish on the A appeared to be the same.

It was one more piece of evidence to add to their rapidly growing collection.

 13

PHOEBE barely made it to afternoon tea before the urge to climb the walls became unbearable. Signor Bianchi had learned nothing new about Sophia's disappearance. Or at least nothing he was sharing. The local magistrate stopped to ask the family a few questions. However, based on the man's attitude Phoebe had little reason to believe their concerns would be given much, if any, real attention. It made her want to scream in frustration.

"Phoebe I do wish you would come and sit with me," her aunt pleaded for the fourth time since luncheon.

"I simply cannot sit still." Phoebe continued pacing between the large windows of the sitting room. Every time she reached one she would look out, hoping to see her sister winding her way through the bushes and lifeless flower beds. "I wish there were something I could do to find Sophia."

"Perhaps we could take a ride into to town?" Lady Charlotte offered. "Just to take a look around."

Phoebe came to a halt. "Could we?"

"Oh, Charlotte, I don't believe I am up to that," Aunt Gladys bemoaned.

Phoebe's heart sank. "Oh, please, Aunt Gladys." Phoebe rushed to her aunt and grasped her hand. "I'm going mad with worry. I must do something."

"I know, dear." Aunt Gladys patted her hand. "But I'm not sure that your going for a ride into town will accomplish anything."

"Maybe not," Phoebe admitted. "But at least then I could tell myself that Sophia isn't just wandering the streets cold and alone."

Her aunt grimaced.

"I don't see what harm a ride into town would do, Gladys," Lady Charlotte offered.

"But what if you suddenly disappeared as well?" her aunt asked Phoebe.

"I won't let it happen, Aunt. I can take one of the valets. And I promise to stay in the carriage. We'll just drive through town looking. That's all."

"Oh, I don't know," her aunt pressed her handkerchief to her brow.

"If Signor Bianchi has a small pistol, I could take that with me as well," Phoebe suggested.

Both ladies gasped.

"Phoebe, why ever would you suggest such a thing? Do you even know how to use one of those things?" her aunt asked in outrage.

"I do." Phoebe didn't think it possible for her aunt to be more shocked.

"Does your mother know that?"

"Yes." Phoebe shrugged. "Of course she and Father had words over the fact that he wanted to teach me in the first place."

"Your father taught you?" Phoebe couldn't tell from Lady Charlotte's expression if she were shocked or impressed.

"Yes."

"Oh, my stars." Aunt Gladys slumped further in her seat.

"Are you proficient at it?" Lady Charlotte asked.

"Oh, Charlotte. Why on Earth would you ask something like that?" Aunt Gladys waved her handkerchief as she spoke.

"Just curious."

"Actually, Father says I'm a better shot than my brother."

"I dare say, I'm impressed," Lady Charlotte said.

Aunt Gladys groaned.

One of the maids came in, drawing their attention. "Excuse me, Signora, but the Signor has returned and would like to speak to you in his study."

"Thank you, Rosa." Lady Charlotte got up. "Do stop

moaning, Gladys. You know full well you would have learned to shoot a gun if your father had been willing to teach you."

Her aunt sat up. "Mother would have never allowed such a thing."

"Oh, poo. When did that ever stop you?"

Aunt Gladys harrumphed.

To Phoebe, Lady Charlotte added, "I will speak to Carlo about your going into town."

Phoebe smiled gratefully. "Thank you, Lady Charlotte."

"Wait here. I'll return shortly."

Phoebe turned to her aunt. Her complexion did seem pale. "Are you sure you do not wish to go into town? The distraction might do you some good."

"You're probably right but I am afraid to leave in case someone sends word of Sophia."

Phoebe nodded. "I suppose one of us should be here."

"As much as it pains me to admit, I do understand your need to take action. I will worry about you every minute that I cannot see you, but you go ahead and do what you need to do. Just be safe and hurry back."

"We don't even know if Signor Bianchi will give his blessing."

Aunt Gladys waved the thought away. "If Charlotte believes you should go, there's very little that Carlo will say to disagree."

"Do you really think so?"

"You'll see." Her aunt pointed to one of the bookshelves. "While we wait, would you be a dear and fetch me that book I was reading? The green one there on the middle shelf."

Phoebe did as her aunt bid her. "Shall I read it to you?"

"That would be lovely." Her aunt beamed at her.

Taking the chair next to her aunt, Phoebe settled her skirts around her. She began to read aloud starting at the page where the marker had been left in the book. Her nervous energy barely allowed her to sit still as they waited but being forced to pay attention to each word did help. While it seemed like an eternity until Lady Charlotte returned, Phoebe knew it had not based on the number of pages she had turned.

Lady Charlotte clapped her hands together. "All right my dear, everything is arranged. The carriage will be brought around and we have asked Paolo to ride up top along with Renzo."

"Is that the steam carriage, by chance?" Phoebe asked hopefully. "Not that it matters," she added hastily.

Lady Charlotte smiled knowingly. "I believe it will be."

Phoebe giddiness was only dampened by her worry for her sister. "You and the Signor are good to us. Thank you so much."

Lady Charlotte made shooing motions. "If you need to change your dress, you had best hurry."

Phoebe glanced down at what she was wearing. "I think this one will do. After all, I'm not planning to call on anyone." She hurried out the door. "I just need my paletot from my room. I'll only be a moment."

In her room she took a quick glance in the mirror. Her hair wasn't as neat as she would have liked but it would do. Her gaze landed on the hat she had left next to her trunk. It would cover most of her hair and it matched her jacket. She snagged both then hurried back to the sitting room.

Lady Charlotte met her in the foyer. "Do not tell your aunt I gave you this." She offered Phoebe a small derringer. "This is what I carry when I go into town alone."

Phoebe looked up in surprise.

"I would go with you but I don't want to leave your aunt alone. Sophia's disappearance has disturbed her deeply. I must admit that I am worried about her health."

"I did think she looked rather pale," Phoebe admitted.

"I understand why you feel you must do something. It's almost cruel to be expected to sit still and pretend to be helpless."

Phoebe nodded her agreement.

Lady Charlotte pressed the weapon into Phoebe's hand. "This only has two bullets. But hopefully that is all you would need to get away or to get someone's attention."

"Thank you." Phoebe slipped the gun into her skirt pocket

then pulled her paletot on and buttoned it up.

One of the valets came in through the front entrance. "The carriage is ready, Signora."

"Thank you," Lady Charlotte told him. She faced Phoebe again. "You had best tell your aunt goodbye. I will do my best to keep her entertained while you're away."

Phoebe squeezed Lady Charlotte's hand. "Thank you again. I promise to return shortly."

"You had best. Or I will never hear the end of it."

After saying her farewells to her aunt, Phoebe raced out to the waiting carriage.

"You just wanted to drive through town, miss?" the valet asked as he handed her up.

"Yes, as slowly as possible without drawing attention."

"Hoping to find the young lady that went missing, are you?" he asked.

"I am."

He nodded sadly but Phoebe refused to let his lack of faith in their endeavor dampen hers. She sat back against the leather cushion and focused on the marvel that was Signor Bianchi's steam powered coach. Despite her fascination with the machine she kept her gaze on the view from her window. After all, there was a slim possibility they could pass Sophia as they drove into town.

When they reached the main part of the city, Phoebe checked every woman they passed who had pale blonde hair. The number of bonnets and caps did hamper her efforts but she still felt as if she had checked all that she could. With each street they finished, her hope sank lower. Finally, the valet jumped down from his perch and rapped on the carriage door.

"That's all of the main roads. Everything beyond this square are private homes. I'm not sure it would do for a young miss like yourself to be seen lurking about. Shall we return to the villa?"

Phoebe frowned. While she agreed with his concerns, she wasn't prepared to give up just yet. "Perhaps we could make a quick pass near the port?"

He frowned. "The port, Signora? Are you sure you want to go there?"

"It's the last place we went with Sophia," she explained. When she thought he might argue with her she added, "I just cannot bear the thought of giving up so easily."

He sighed. "All right, Signora. We can take the long route home."

"Thank you."

The carriage tilted a bit when the valet climbed back into his place on top. With a cough it lurched forward. A few minutes later, the driver stopped near the front entrance of the port.

Phoebe climbed down before the valet could intercept her.

"Miss, I thought you were going to remain in the carriage," he protested as he scrambled down from his perch.

"Do not worry yourself. I just want a quick look."

"Renzo, you heard me tell her she ought to remain in the carriage, didn't you?" the valet groused to the driver.

"Yes, yes. We both did."

Phoebe held her hand up to shield her eyes from the sun's glare. When she did, she spotted a petite blonde hurrying through the doorway of the building at the far end.

"Sophia?" Without a second thought, Phoebe raced after the woman.

"Miss! Where are you going?"

Phoebe didn't even bother answering. She kept her eye fixed on the door the woman had disappeared through. She mumbled apologies as she brushed past two groups of girls coming out the door she wanted to enter. When she finally made it to the other side she looked all around for her sister. "Sophia?"

The ladies tending one of the stalls nearby paused and looked at her in question.

"Did you see a woman about this tall..." Phoebe held her hand out to demonstrate how tall she meant. "She was wearing a blue dress. And she has light hair."

"Ah. Yes." The woman pointed to their right. "There was a

girl. She went that way."

"Thank you." Phoebe hurried away in the direction the woman had indicated.

She looked down each row she passed until she spotted the girl. "Sophia!"

Phoebe's heart sank when the girl did not respond, still she ran after her. Since she couldn't get a clear look at the girl's face around her bonnet, she had to be sure it wasn't Sophia.

She managed to catch up to the girl on the next row. "Sophia?" Phoebe asked as she grabbed the girl's arm.

"*Cosa stai facendo?*" What are you doing? The girl faced Phoebe and Phoebe's heart sank.

"I'm sorry." She let go of the girl's arm. "I thought you might be someone else."

The girl frowned at her in suspicion.

Phoebe remained frozen in place even after the girl continued on her way. She didn't want to believe that she hadn't found her sister. Even though the rational part of her mind knew it had been extraordinary for her to do so.

Tears clogged her throat and threatened to spill over as she watched the girl make her way to the end of the building.

"Miss, can I interest you in a bit of handmade lace?" Someone asked.

Phoebe blinked away her melancholy. "I'm sorry. What did you ask?"

"We have some very fine lace you will like. Right this way." A thin man with yellowed teeth and foul breath attempted to steer her to the next row.

Phoebe pulled away. "No. Thank you. I'm not interested." She turned to go back the way she had come but found her way blocked by a much larger man. "Excuse me." She tried to step around the man but he once again blocked her.

"Why the rush?" His deep voice rumbled through her making her skin crawl.

Phoebe stiffened her spine. "My driver is waiting for me. Please let me pass."

"Oh, your driver is waiting for you." The larger man taunted as he took a step closer.

Phoebe heard the thin man snickering from behind her as she stepped back.

"Yes, and I'm sure they will come looking for me shortly." She put her hand in her pocket. "Now please step aside."

The larger man leaned forward. "I don't see why I should."

The stale smell of sweat and smoke made Phoebe lean away just so she didn't gag while panic threatened to cloud her thoughts.

"The lady asked nicely." The cocking of a pistol echoed around them. "I won't be nearly as nice."

The larger man pivoted to the side. Phoebe's knees went weak with relief when she saw Vernon pointing a gun at the man's heart.

14

VERNON motioned Phoebe forward without taking his eyes off the oversized sailor he had been tracking through the market. The fury that had washed over him when he saw the men attempting to corner Phoebe still had not dissipated.

Phoebe started forward but as Vernon feared the man grabbed her then wrapped his muscled arm around her neck and used her as a shield. "I don't think so mate. I need to speak privately with the lady, so how about you just run—"

A gun went off, cutting off the sailor's words. His eyes widened in shock then contorted in pain. Phoebe staggered free as the man clutched at his leg.

Vernon grabbed Phoebe's hand and pulled her behind him. Vendors cried out in alarm. Some peeked around stalls, others ran for the exits. "Are you hurt?" He shouted at Phoebe as he searched the area for the shooter.

Her voice cracked as she pushed her spectacles back into place with her free hand. "No."

"You're sure you weren't shot? I have no idea where that bullet came from." He backed them toward the exit as he scanned the shadows for the assailant. He had no idea who might be helping them. Lawrence was on the other side of town. And while they did have hired men in the area, he couldn't think of one that would be that good of a shot.

"It was me. I shot him."

He whipped his head around in surprise. "You shot him?"

She pulled a small pistol from her pocket and showed him. About the same time the injured sailor roared in outrage and lumbered after them.

"Let's go." Vernon grabbed Phoebe by the hand and raced

for the doors. He took a winding path through the market but every turn he made seemed to run into one of Romano's men. He foolishly thought he had been tracking them but now he wondered if they had been following him instead.

"What are you doing here?" he asked over his shoulder.

"Looking for Sophia."

"In the market?"

"I thought I saw her from the carriage."

"You did?" He cringed. People often saw what they wanted to see. Especially during times of stress.

"Yes, but it was just someone who looked like her."

At the end of a row he stopped behind a stack of crates. He pulled Phoebe up against his side then peered around the corner to see if any of Romano's men were waiting there.

He spotted one that he felt certain was one of Romano's. He calculated the odds of sneaking by him without incident. Were it just him, getting past would be no problem. But with Phoebe in tow...

"Are you going to tell me how just happened to be here?" She tugged on the sleeve of his ill-fitted jacket. "Dressed as a...a dock worker, no less?"

"I'd rather not." He searched the structure for other possible exits. The idea of going back the way they came didn't appeal to him since he felt certain they had been followed. And he needed to make a fast decision before the sailor she'd shot caught up to them.

"The number of secrets you are trying to keep seems to be growing."

"Every day," he mumbled. "Okay, here is what we're going to do." He had just pushed her back a step when the wood next to his head splintered from another gunshot.

"Run." Keeping his hold on her hand he took off for the exit. Despite the difference in their strides she managed to stay in pace with him.

Romano's man stepped forward to intercept them but became distracted when Phoebe pointed up in the air and shrieked. Vernon used the opportunity to hit the man in the jaw. A small measure of satisfaction washed through him when the man dropped like a stone.

"What did you see?" he asked Phoebe as he pulled her along behind him.

"Nothing. Just wanted to distract him so you could hit him. Just like you did."

"How did you know to do that?" he asked incredulously.

"I have brothers."

Despite the danger around them, she managed to make him laugh.

He ducked behind a wagon so he could check their surroundings. There was one man still following them.

"I need you to do exactly as I say." When she nodded, he continued. "You see that door there?"

She glanced in the direction he pointed. "Yes."

"When I shoot at the men following us, I want you to run inside. Understood?"

She nodded again. "What about you?"

"I will follow you as soon as it's clear again."

"Just making sure."

He checked his gun to see how many bullets were left. "Okay. Go." He fired two shots. The first he aimed at the man's leg. Based on the way the man grabbed his thigh, Vernon felt certain he had at least grazed him. The second he fired at the crate the man ducked behind, just to keep him out of line of sight.

After Phoebe made it through the doorway, he sprinted after her. Once inside, it took a moment for his eyes to adjust to the change in lighting.

Phoebe whispered, "Vernon. Over here." He spotted her peering around the corner of the stair landing above him.

"Don't go up—" Vernon's protest was cut off when two men burst through the door Vernon had just closed. "Bloody hell." He grumbled as he hurried to the stairs. Last thing he wanted was to get separated from Phoebe.

He grabbed her hand and pulled her up the stairs behind him. At the top he shouldered his way through the door then assessed what they had to work with. Being stranded on the upper floor with an unknown number of assailants flowing in behind them was not how he would have liked this to go. But at least it appeared there was only one entrance.

There were stacks of crates along one wall and hay bales along the other, making an L-shape. A desk, bookshelf, and two chairs were pushed up against the wall closest to them. The rest of the floor was simply a wide-open space.

"Hide behind some of those crates over there," he gestured to the stacks. Much to his relief, Phoebe hurried to comply. He pushed the desk in front of the door even though he knew it wouldn't hold them then followed her.

"I need to reload," he mumbled as he checked his second gun.

The door rattled as the other men pounded against it.

"Give the guns to me," she urged.

"What? Don't be ridiculous."

Wood scraped against wood as the men forced the desk back.

"I'll reload. You worry about them." Phoebe pointed at the men shoving their way through the door.

Vernon barely had time to dig a handful of bullets from his pocket before the first man charged at him. He dropped the ammunition onto the floor and lunged forward in order to meet his attacker.

While Vernon took on the larger of the two men with his fists and a rather large knife, Phoebe scooped up the ammunition Vernon had dropped. She said a prayer of thanks that either the men were out of ammunition or they didn't carry guns.

A thin, greasy-looking man leered at her as he slowly moved closer. "Hey, pretty lady what 'ave you got there? I don't think you ought to be playing with men's toys." He pulled a revolver from his coat and shook it at her.

She rushed behind a crate so as to not distract Vernon from his fight and calmly reloaded both weapons. Thankfully she was familiar with one of the two and the second wasn't hard to figure out.

The greasy man rounded the corner of the crates just as she finished snapping the camber of the second revolver into place. His eyes widened in surprise when he found her pointing not one, but two guns at him. One leveled at his crotch, the other at his head.

"Toss the weapon out the window behind you or I will dismember you." Keeping her breath slow and steady as her father taught her to do while hunting, she made sure neither her hand nor her voice quivered in the least. It was critical that the man believe she meant what she said.

She contained her surprise when he actually tossed his gun away. She truly thought she would have to shoot him to get him to believe her. She had just been debating where to put the bullet.

"Now, if you would be so kind as to take several steps back." She smiled as if she had just asked him to pass her a plate of biscuits.

Once again, he complied. However, his oily grin made her realize the man was simply humoring her. Little did he realize that she was a far better shot at long distances. And the truth was, she didn't want to get blood on her clothes if she were forced to pull the trigger. Aunt Gladys would be most displeased and likely never let her out of the house again.

Without taking her eyes off the greasy man before her, she aimed the gun she held in her left hand at the man Vernon was fighting. "Now tell your friend to stand down."

The greasy man yelled, "Hey, Gino. This lady says you should stand down." He chuckled but Phoebe wasn't sure if he was laughing at her or the situation. Not that it mattered much.

"What are you—" From the corner of her eye, Phoebe saw Vernon pause, distracted by what was happening between her and the greasy man.

That small delay gave his opponent an opportunity to lunge forward.

Without a second thought, Phoebe shot Vernon's opponent in the knee. The man howled in outrage and pain.

The greasy man took a step in her direction but she halted him with a stern look. "In case you are wondering, I did not, in fact, miss. I chose to not kill him. But I could just as easily choose to kill you. Now back away."

Vernon rushed to her side. Without taking her eyes off the greasy man, she handed Vernon the second gun.

Phoebe gestured to the floor with her weapon. "Now that I have thought about it, I'd rather you got down on your knees."

The greasy man complied while glaring at the two of them.

"Are you okay?" She asked Vernon as he went to check the man she had shot.

"I'm fine." Vernon picked up the knife the man had dropped and used it to knock the injured man out. The man crumpled the rest of the way to the floor. Next, Vernon searched the greasy man for weapons and ordered him to sit on his hands next to the crates. Using a length of rope he found in the desk, Vernon bound the hands of both men.

Once the two of them were out of commission, Phoebe lowered her weapon. Almost immediately a shiver racked her.

Vernon approached and gently grasped her shoulders. "Are you all right?"

She closed her eyes and nodded.

"You were amazing."

She met his gaze. The warmth and sincere admiration in his eyes pleased her more that it likely should.

He smiled. "We have agents who would not have handled that situation as well as you."

His praise cut bolstered her sagging strength. "Thank you."

"As much as I hate to say it, we're not out of hot water just yet." He rubbed her arms. "But we will make it out of here."

She took a deep breath. "Yes, we will." She lifted her chin. "I am determined to not let a couple of ruffians stop me from finding Sophia."

His smile faltered. "We will talk about you searching for your sister later. But I'm glad you are handling this so well."

She lifted his gun, with the barrel pointing downward. "I

believe this is yours."

"Since you obviously know what you're doing with it, why don't you hang on to it for now?" He gestured to the men he had tied to a hay bale. "I will take theirs."

While he checked and secured his weapons, she inspected the condition of her skirts. One side was singed around the hole from the gunpowder, but the pattern in the gray wool helped disguise it. She left Lady Charlotte's pistol in the pocket with the hole. Vernon's revolver went into the other. If it hadn't been for her corset, she would have put it in the waistband of her skirt the way he had with his trousers.

For the briefest of moments she contemplated the purchase of a holster she could wear under her skirts. Then it occurred to her that if she were lucky, she would never be in a position to need a weapon again.

Vernon once again reached for her hand. This time he paused and gazed into her eyes. "I—" He pressed his lips together and shook his head. "That will wait. Let's get you out of here."

"Very well." His strange behavior only made her curious about what he would have said.

He led her to the window but motioned for her to stay out of sight. He peered down onto the streets below them as well as each direction. "I don't see anyone watching the building but that doesn't mean they aren't there. We still need to be cautious."

When they approached the door he stopped and motioned for her to stay where in place. Then, his weapon at the ready, he checked the landings.

"It's clear." He motioned her forward then grasped her hand.

Every time he touched her she felt a fluttery sensation in her belly. Seeing him stealthily creep forward with such confidence and, if she were to honest with herself, lethal intent, impressed her in a way that would have shocked her aunt, much less her mother. Admittedly, it was possible all of the new feelings she was experiencing came as a result of the heightened sense of danger. But now was not the best time to ponder it.

They made it to the ground floor without incident then, instead of going out the way they had come in, he led her around the crates and partially loaded wagons to the doors on the other side. There, he released the latch on one of the doors and peeked out.

A tilt of the head was the only notice he gave her before he pulled her through the door open. Outside, he set a brisk pace and stayed in the shadow of the building as much as possible.

Trusting that he knew where he was going she refrained from asking questions. They hurried from building to building in similar fashion. It didn't take long for her to realize that he was using the buildings and his own body to shield her.

When they turned into the market he snagged a shawl from a booth and handed it to Phoebe. "Put this on over your head and shoulders," he ordered as he tossed a few coins to the woman selling the goods. The woman gave him a toothless smile and waved her thanks.

Several booths later he told Phoebe to select a bag of fruit while he watched the crowd. After paying for the fruit he steered her deeper into the market. Along the way he switched his hat out for another without saying anything to anyone. Phoebe frowned at him but didn't comment.

When they turned the corner to enter the next building, a large man barreled past Phoebe causing her to stumble and drop two of her apples. The man's glare turned into surprise just before he reached a meaty paw out to her. Vernon quickly pulled her out of the giant's reach and rendered him unconscious with little effort. He tipped the unconscious man behind a stack of crates and tugged her along as if nothing happened.

She looked around to see if anyone noticed what had happened but was surprised to find no one watching.

When they drew close to the main entrance, he pulled her aside and positioned her up against the wall. He then blocked her in by leaning his hand on the same wall, shielding her from view. To a stranger, they likely appeared to be a couple sharing an intimate conversation.

"Do you see the carriage you came in out front?" he asked in a lower tone as he took one of the apples from the bag she carried.

"Yes. It's the horseless one just there." She indicated the direction she meant by touching his chest. She frowned. "But that isn't Renzo, the driver."

He glanced to where her finger still lingered on his chest. Then slowly he looked to the side and mumbled a curse. "That is one of Romano's men. The two smoking near the wagon behind yours are also Romano's men. Guess that explains why we didn't run into any more of them."

"But what happened to Renzo?"

He grimaced. "He could have been paid to get lost for a little while."

Phoebe's heart beat a little harder in her chest. Based on his expression, she doubted Vernon believed that. "So what do we do now?"

Vernon pulled his watch from his pocked and cursed again. "I planned to get you back to the Bianchi villa before my appointment but I am quickly running out of time."

"You have an appointment?" she asked incredulously.

"Yes." He tucked his watch away. "And unfortunately it is one that I cannot miss."

He wrapped his arm around her shoulders and steered her toward a shaded area where a group of boys were playing a game. Vernon asked the boys if they knew of anyone who might be willing to give them a ride into town. One of the boys nodded eagerly and ran off. The boy returned a moment later with a young man in tow. It didn't take Vernon long to negotiate a ride for them. Thankfully the lad's wagon was not far and he knew how to navigate around the bustling crowd at the entrance.

Still, Phoebe didn't begin to relax until the port fell from her line of sight.

15

VERNON directed the young man to the end of the park situated just behind the villa he and Moretti were leasing. He helped Phoebe climb down then passed a handful of coins to their rescuer and waved him off.

"Your appointment is in the park?" Phoebe asked.

"No." He took her hand and led her around to the back of the row villas. "Keep your head covered. I hate to do this to you but I honestly have no other recourse."

"What exactly are you doing to me?"

"We are going to sneak in through the kitchens at the place I have been staying. I will show you to the study then run up and change clothes." He grimaced. "Unless you can come up with a better plan in the next two minutes, I am afraid this is unavoidable."

She pulled her shawl a little lower over her head. "Why exactly do you need to change clothes?"

"Because I cannot appear at my appointment dressed as a dock worker."

"After you change clothes, will I need to refer to you as James Bennett or something else entirely?"

"So long as I am in Genoa, I am James Bennett."

He opened the door to the villa and hurried her inside. Thankfully their valet was nowhere to be seen. He checked out the glass to ensure they had not been followed then gestured for her to follow him to the study.

"Help yourself to some wine, if you're so inclined." He pointed to the bar along one wall. "And there is a wash closet just near the kitchen if you wish to freshen up. I should only be a few moments."

"Vernon," she said just as he reached the door.

He turned to look at her in question.

She smiled. "I was curious if you still answered to that name."

He went to stand in front of her. "It is dangerous for you to know that. Dangerous for me and even you. There are men in this country who would kill both of us if they knew of my mission. Please do not take this lightly."

Her eyes widened in surprise.

To lighten the sting of his reprimand, he brought her hand up to his mouth. But instead of kissing the top as she likely expected, he turned it over and placed a lingering kiss on her wrist. All while maintaining eye contact.

Had he not been watching so intently he might have missed the faint tremor that rippled through her. She might be a proper lady, one that managed well under fire, but it pleased him enormously to know he could get to her. With a grin, he released her hand and hurried away before he was tempted to pull her onto the settee and kiss her senseless.

As promised, he made fast work of washing his face and hands and donning clean clothes. His dockworker's clothes were so ill-fitted that they were easily stripped off. For the sake of time he looped his tie around his collar but left it unknotted knowing he could fix it in the carriage.

As he armed himself, Moretti burst into his room. "Who is the girl in our study?"

Vernon holstered the revolver he held. "Good day to you, too." He pulled his jacket on.

"The girl?"

"A friend." Vernon buttoned his jacket. "No time to explain, but I'm glad you're here. You can drive us to Pereira's."

"Pereira's?" Lawrence's tension turned to interest. "I assumed you met with him already. That's why I stopped by. Hoped to find out what you learned."

"I was about to leave. But if we don't hurry I'll be late." Vernon straightened his lapels. "You can drive us, can't you?"

Moretti grumbled as he headed for the door. "Why not?" He paused. "But I expect an explanation for why you brought a woman into our domain. Temporary though it may be."

Vernon waved him on. "Later."

When Vernon returned to the study he found Phoebe had also taken the time to straighten her clothes and neaten her hair. "Are you ready?" he asked.

"Since I am not sure what I should be ready for, I suppose so." She gestured to the desk. "I didn't know what to do with your revolver so I left it there."

"Ah, yes." He retrieved the weapon and dropped it into a drawer then used one of the keys he always carried to lock the desk. "I assume you still have yours?"

"Of course." She patted her pocket.

"Good." He gestured to the front door. "My driver will bring the carriage around."

"Wait." He paused, fearful that she would protest being seen leaving the villa. Not that he would blame her but he didn't see a way around that. Being seen sneaking out the back way would draw far more attention in his estimation.

She came to stand in front of him. "You forgot to fix your neck tie." She reached for the loose ends.

Her nearness distracted him momentarily. "I had thought I would do it in the carriage."

"Don't be silly." She proceeded to tie the fabric almost as competently as his valet. "There. Now you are presentable."

He touched the neat bow she had made at his throat. "Thank you." He cleared his throat. "How is it that you know how to do that?"

"My father's valet is horribly inept at the latest styles, but he's such a dear old man that none of us have the heart to correct him. So Mother and I always fix my father's and my brothers' because they rarely notice."

"Ah." He stirred uncomfortably at the warm feelings their rather domestic scene created inside of him. "We should go."

"Very well." She followed him to the door. "I assume you'll explain if I need to do anything along the way?"

"Yes." He waited for Moretti to pull the carriage to a stop at the walk before opening door for Phoebe. Once he handed her up he settled himself into the seat next to her. "I should probably explain my situation."

"Indeed."

"You have likely already worked out that I am not visiting Genoa for entirely personal reasons."

"I have."

"While I cannot disclose my purpose, suffice to say that I am acting on behalf of others for the good of crown and country."

She studied him for a moment. "Very well."

"The man I am about to meet supposedly has information related to my purpose. But due to the dangerous situation his father was in, and likely killed for, he and I cannot be seen exchanging anything outside of a normal business transaction." He gestured to Phoebe. "As much as I do not want you involved, your presence would provide me a good cover."

She frowned. "How so?"

"I am meeting him at one of the boutiques in town. One that specializes in ladies accessories."

"That seems an odd choice for a clandestine meeting."

"His father owned the store," Vernon explained. "My contact is here to sell the remaining inventory before leaving town. I originally planned to use the excuse of buying a gift for a lady friend. But with you there, I won't need an excuse at all."

"I could ask what information you are hoping to get but I suspect that you wouldn't tell me."

Vernon dipped his head. "You would be correct."

"Will you answer me one question?"

He cocked his head and regarded her cautiously. "If I can."

"Is this related in any way to Sophia's disappearance?"

He turned his head away so she wouldn't see his frown. He couldn't tell her anything about his mission but nor did he want to lie to her. Despite having worked behind lies and deception for several years. "Not directly."

"Hmmm."

He took a deep breath. "This could be my one and only opportunity to obtain the information we need. It's crucial that my contact doesn't become frightened or feel threatened in any way."

She inclined her head. "Very well. What do you need me to do?"

Her agreement allowed him a small measure of ease. "Mostly be calm, act as if nothing unusual is happening or has happened. You are simply a young lady out on a shopping excursion with a gentleman friend. Look at the goods around the store as you would if you were with your aunt." He held up one finger. "But whatever you do, do not draw unnecessary attention to yourself or him."

"I think I can manage that."

He intertwined his fingers with hers and looked her in the eye. "I feel confident that you can."

Her cheeks turned a pale shade pink that he found delightful. The urge to kiss her swelled again. If he didn't need to be in the right frame of mind to handle Pereira, he probably would have.

The rosy hue of her lips kept distracting him. While great for his chosen persona, she was quickly becoming dangerously distracting.

When the carriage came to a stop at the end of the block, Vernon stepped out and checked for Romano's men. He had deliberately chosen a busy time of day so he would blend in with the usual crowd. But since they were late, he would need to hurry Phoebe along.

He reached for her hand and helped her down from the carriage. He immediately placed her hand on his arm to ensure she remained close. As they strolled, he whispered, "We need to go to the store that is three doors down. Do you think you could make a bit of a show and pretend it's your idea instead of mine?"

Phoebe tilted her head up at him and gave him a dazzling smile. "Darling, would you mind terribly if we stopped in one of the shops just up ahead? Aunt Gladys bought the prettiest wrap the last time we were here and I think I should like to have one as well." The little minx even batted her eyelashes at him.

It was so out of character for her that he was somewhat taken back. "Not at all, my dear. Which store was it?"

"The one just there." She vaguely gestured ahead of them just as she turned her head to look at something in the window they were passing. "Oh, but that is pretty as well."

"I am afraid that we only have time for the one stop. Which place you would like to go?"

She pouted prettily and paused as if to consider his words. "I do like the wrap my aunt bought. So I suppose we can skip this one."

She reminded him of his younger sister. Perhaps all the years of observing her own sister's behavior was the reason she could put on such a believable performance.

Once inside Pereira's shop, Vernon steered her around the perimeter looking for Miguel, his contact. Miguel had just finished assisting an elderly matron with a package when he spotted Vernon. Miguel's smiled faltered slightly but gave him a brief nod before disappearing through a curtain.

Vernon waited anxiously to see if Miguel had panicked and run away or if he would return. Meanwhile Phoebe prattled on about the various ribbons on display before them. He asked her what the ribbon was made from, but failed to hear anything she said. Even though she tried to be nonchalant she did take several peeks at the curtain his contact had vanished through out of the corner of her eye.

Finally, the man reappeared and came to assist them. "Good afternoon. May I assist you with anything?"

"Yes, I wondered if you had any wraps the lady might like."

"I do believe I have two left." He gestured to the left side of the store. "If you would follow me?"

Vernon took Phoebe by the elbow and followed the storeowner to a sparsely filled set of shelves. He made a production of showing them the two wraps he had.

"Which do you prefer, my dear? Pink or green?"

"Hmmm." She touched the side of her face as if thinking deeply about her choices then smiled brightly. "The green, I think."

"An excellent choice, Signora. Will there be anything else?"

"Darling, you seemed rather interested in the ribbons they had, why don't you get a few of those as well. It will be my treat."

"You are so good to me." Once more she batted her eyelashes at him then sauntered over to the ribbon table.

Miguel turned his back to the store windows while he folded the lengths of the wrap neatly. "I assume you came for my father's journal?" he whispered.

Vernon kept his eyes on Phoebe. "Yes, if you are still willing to part with it," he whispered back.

"I have no need for that cursed thing. Perhaps some good will come of it in your hands."

"I certainly hope so. Is there anything else you can tell us? Perhaps whom your father was working for?"

The man shook his head. "The only other thing I can give you is a name I found on a few invoices." He dropped his voice even lower. "Marco Vittorio."

Vernon frowned. The name was familiar but he couldn't recall where he had heard it before.

"Here we go," Phoebe said brightly as she returned carrying three or four lengths of ribbon.

"Is that everything then?" the store owner asked.

"I believe so," Vernon answered.

"One moment while I tally your goods and wrap them you."

After the store owner walked away Phoebe gazed up at him in concern. "Everything go well?" she asked softly.

"Yes." He brushed a stray lock of hair behind her ear and whispered, "You are doing very well. Just a moment longer."

She nodded.

The man returned with their neatly wrapped package. Vernon handed him several banknotes for their purchase as well as a little extra for his trouble. The shop owner started to protest, but Vernon waved him off. "Keep it for your trouble.

You've made the lady very happy with her purchase."

"*Grazie, Signor.*"

"Come along dear." Vernon tucked the package under one arm and ushered Phoebe toward the door with his free hand. "I believe I can just get you back to your aunt before my promised time." He opened the door and allowed Phoebe to sail through then with a touch to his hat for the shop owner, he followed quickly on her heels.

At the carriage he whispered instruction to Moretti before helping Phoebe into the carriage. Still, he didn't draw an easy breath until he had settled next to her and they were heading away from the shop.

 16

"**DID** you get the information you were hoping for?" Phoebe asked as soon as Vernon pulled the door to the carriage closed.

"He gave me a name."

"That's it?" She had trouble believing that was the all-important information he needed.

Vernon tapped the package that lay between them. "And this."

She cast him a questioning glance but didn't ask more. Even though she really wanted to.

After their carriage rolled away from the main square Vernon opened the package. Almost absently he slid the shawl and ribbons to her side of the seat while he inspected some kind of book. As soon as he opened the pages he muttered a curse.

"What's wrong?" she asked.

"I cannot read it," he grumbled and flipped through more pages.

"Messy hand writing?" She guessed.

"No." He kept flipping pages. "It isn't written in Italian. Or English." He let his head fall back against the wall of the carriage with a thud. "Or even French."

"You're certain?"

"Quite."

"What did you hope to find in the book?" she asked.

"I never knew for sure." Vernon rubbed his head as if it pained him. "Miguel only said that his father kept of all of his off-the-books transactions recorded in this." He tapped the cover of the journal.

"Why would that be important?"

"Because we believe the late Signor Pereira was providing supplies for the people running the slave ring in the city."

Phoebe gasped in surprise. "A slave ring? But the shop looked like a respectable business. One that most anyone of the ton might frequent."

"It did." Vernon nodded. "Which makes it the perfect front for ugly activities."

"So why is Miguel helping you?"

"The previous owner, Miguel's father, recently died. Quite possibly, was murdered. Miguel wants nothing to do with his father's former activities. He only returned to Genoa to sell off the business and settle his father's legal affairs. We were lucky to have made contact with him. While he doesn't want to be involved in helping or hindering the criminals, he doesn't mind turning over what little evidence he stumbled across in his father's possessions. Especially if it means bringing down the men we believes were blackmailing his father, and very likely, killed him."

"Oh, I see."

"Since the notes are written in another language it might be days before we learn what it says much less whether or not it of any value to us at all." He scowled down at the book.

Phoebe leaned closer and looked at the page. "Unless I am very much mistaken, that is Portuguese."

He frowned. "It is?"

She tugged on the book until he let her take the book from him. She peered closer, interpreting a few words here and there until the language came back to her. She turned a few pages, looking at a few other sections, then declared with certainty, "Yes." She nodded as she handed the book back to him. "Definitely Portuguese."

"And you can read it?"

"I can."

His expression indicated he didn't know what to think of her. "Where did you learn Portuguese?"

"Our governess was from Braga. She taught us."

He closed the book and slipped it back into his pocket even

as he stared at her thoughtfully.

When the carriage stopped in front of the Bianchi's villa, one of the servants rushed out to greet them. Her aunt stood on to the porch clutching what appeared to be a handkerchief.

Vernon helped her down from the carriage and asked the driver to wait. He escorted her to the door.

"There you are," Aunt Gladys declared. "When Paolo returned without you I thought my heart might burst."

Phoebe hugged her aunt. "I'm sorry to make you worry. I got turned around in the market and when I finally found my way out again, I didn't see Paolo or the carriage."

Lady Charlotte hurried through the door. "Oh, thank goodness." She glanced at Vernon before embracing Phoebe. "You gave us all quite a fright, my dear."

"I didn't mean to worry any of you." Phoebe gestured to Vernon. "If it hadn't been for Mr. Bennett I'd likely still be wandering through the market."

"Paolo said you thought you saw Sophia?" Aunt Gladys asked hopefully.

"I thought so, too." Phoebe grimaced. "But when I caught up to the young woman, it wasn't. I must have been seeing what I wanted to see." She smiled sadly. "I dare say she thought I was quite mad chasing after her like that."

"Did she look so much like Sophia?" Lady Charlotte asked.

"From the carriage, yes. But the closer I drew to her, the more I began to question my own mind."

Her aunt asked, "I don't suppose you learned anything at all about Sophia today then?"

Phoebe glanced at Vernon. He gave a slight shake of his head.

"I'm afraid not." Her aunt's hopeful express fell making Phoebe add, "But we haven't given up trying."

"I know it doesn't offer much in the way of comfort but I assure you that we are doing everything we can to find your niece," Vernon told her.

Her aunt clasped her handkerchief to her chest. "I just don't know what I will tell your mother."

Phoebe hugged her aunt again and ushered her into the house. "Let's hope we don't have to tell her anything."

"Oh, how I pray you are right."

Vernon hovered at the back as Phoebe settled her aunt into a chair in the sitting room. He gestured for her to return to the foyer with him. She nodded she understood. "I'll be right back, Aunt Gladys. Do you want me to bring you some tea? I could certainly use some refreshment."

"Nothing for me, dear, but do ring for some for yourself." She looked back at Vernon. "And you too, dear boy. You are certainly welcome to stay."

"Thank you, but no. I have things I need to attend to."

"Yes, of course." Aunt Gladys waved him off. "You young men always have something to keep you busy."

Phoebe was torn between demanding to go with him and staying for her aunt's sake. "I'll see you out."

When they reached the front entrance Vernon whispered, "I do need to follow up on a few things. Will you be all right?"

"Yes, of course. I'll be fine."

"And will you promise me that you will not go looking for your sister again?"

"I cannot promise to sit here and do nothing. I simply cannot."

He grimaced. "If I promise to return for you tomorrow will you at least stay in tonight? Going outside of these walls without adequate protection may be putting yourself needlessly at risk."

She shuddered.

"I don't mean to be an alarmist but you need to take care."

"I want—I need to find my sister." She had no words to describe how much the thought that Sophia might be in danger weighed on her.

"I understand. But Genoa is far more dangerous than you realize. I do not want you stumbling across things you are better off not knowing about."

She crossed her arms over her chest and let out an aggravated breath.

"Promise me. Please."

His concern fractured her stubborn resistance. "Promise what exactly?"

"That you won't take foolish risks? That you will stay inside, with your family, or at least with people you trust, until we have a few more answers."

"I promise I won't take foolish risks." That was a relatively easy promise to make. After all, she wasn't a nincompoop.

"And you will stay here, inside, with your family, at least for tonight?"

She sighed. "Very well. I promise to stay in for the rest of the night."

"Thank you." He took a breath. "Now, I need to go."

"You will be back tomorrow?" she asked hopefully.

"Yes. I will be back tomorrow."

Finally, she smiled. "Then I will see you tomorrow." She stuck out her hand as if to shake hands with him.

He looked at her hand then raised a brow. The smolder in his eyes said that a handshake simply would not do. Her heart skipped a beat in her chest.

He held her gaze as he brought her hand to his lips. And just as she feared, but—if she were completely honest—secretly hoped he would do, he turned her hand over and placed a lingering kiss against the inside of her wrist.

Her breath caught in her throat and she wondered if her corset had somehow shrunk.

"Until tomorrow." He released her hand and sailed out the door.

As soon as the door closed behind him, Phoebe took a ragged breath.

She stood in the entryway debating the wisdom of returning to the sitting room. She felt certain her cheeks were flushed. And her thoughts were scattered in a hundred directions. If her aunt weren't so distracted with worry, she would undoubtedly pick up on her distraction. Phoebe simply wasn't in the mood to answer all of the questions her aunt was likely to ask.

But nor could she slip off to her room without a word.

She allowed herself a moment then hurried to the kitchen under the guise of arranging for a pot of tea. When she returned she found Lady Charlotte speaking in hushed tones with her aunt. No telling what the two of them were plotting. Hopefully it nothing to do with her, but one never could tell.

"I brought tea," Phoebe announced as she sat the tray on the table nearest to them.

"Oh, thank you dear." Her aunt rearranged herself so that she could reach for a cup.

"That was rather fortunate that you ran into Mr. Bennett today," Lady Charlotte said.

Phoebe poured for her aunt and Lady Charlotte before helping herself. "Indeed, it was."

"And do you expect to see Mr. Bennett when you return to London?" Lady Charlotte asked.

"I should think so," Phoebe told them. "While he may not receive all of the same invitations, we do share several mutual acquaintances."

"I see." Lady Charlotte cast a sideways glance at her aunt while she sipped her tea.

"If I might pry, for a moment," her aunt prompted. "What are your expectations for a husband?"

Phoebe lowered her cup. "I had rather hoped that I might find a gentleman who shared the same interests as myself, and if we suited well enough, I might consider matrimony." She shrugged. "However. I would also be content with being the eccentric aunt to all of the nieces and nephews that I feel certain my brothers and sisters will provide."

"So you do not have any aspirations on the handsome Mr. Bennett then?" Lady Charlotte pressed.

Phoebe felt her cheeks grow warm. "I—" She cleared her throat. "He is most certainly handsome enough to catch any girl's eye. But I'm not sure he is the man for me." She reached for one of the biscuits that cook had added to the tray.

"Why ever not?" her aunt asked.

"Well because…" Phoebe glanced from her aunt to Lady Charlotte and tried to think of a single reason why she wouldn't be interested in him. "I—"

Lady Charlotte's brow rose in question. "You?"

Phoebe lifted her chin. "I can't think of a single reason why not, but I know it wouldn't be a good idea."

"Are you not attracted to him?" her aunt asked.

"She already said he was handsome," Lady Charlotte false-whispered to her aunt.

Aunt Gladys nodded to her friend. "She did, didn't she?"

"Is he not intelligent enough for you, perhaps?" Lady Charlotte asked.

"No, no." Phoebe shook her head. "He is quite intelligent, actually."

"Has he been unkind to you?" Aunt Gladys asked, somewhat alarmed.

Phoebe's frustration rose. "Oh, no, not ever. He's always been a perfect gentleman."

Lady Charlotte's brow rose in question, almost smugly, as if she knew full well, Phoebe was very nearly trapped by their questions. "Well then why do you not find him a suitable match?"

"Other than the fact that he may or may not be returning to England any time soon?" Phoebe threw out the last valid argument she could think of.

Without missing a beat, Lady Charlotte answered, "Yes. Other than that minor issue."

Phoebe struggled to find a legitimate reason to give them. After all, she couldn't very well tell them the truth. That he was, in fact, a gentleman's son, working under a false name, for some secret purpose. And despite her early objections to him based on what she believed to be ill treatment of her friend, she had learned new information about him. Especially about his character. Deep in her heart, she found her answer. "I suppose I don't object to him at all," she whispered.

The two matrons practically beamed at each other.

"There." Lady Charlotte patted her on the knee. "That wasn't so hard to admit, now was it?"

Phoebe's hand shook as she put her cup on the tray. "That

doesn't mean that he has any aspirations of acquiring a wife."

Lady Charlotte waved her hand. "Every man thinks they don't need a wife until they find the woman they cannot do without."

Phoebe stared into the distance as she contemplated what it must be like to have a man think that way of her. Not just any man. Specifically, Vernon. Someone wanted to be with her because he enjoyed her company, not because of who she was related to. Someone whose touch made her long for more.

She grew warm and her belly felt as if there were a dozen butterflies set loose inside.

Vernon fit each of those requirements. But what should or could she do about that?

Aunt Gladys let out a long-suffering sigh. "It is a shame that he doesn't hold a title though."

Phoebe bit her lip and looked away.

"He seems to do well for himself even if he isn't titled," Lady Charlotte said. "His clothes were well tailored and his manners were just so. Do you know who his parents are?"

"I can't say as I know them, no." Phoebe's fib was just a tiny one. While it was true she had never met Vernon's father, she had been briefly introduced to his mother at a garden party the summer before. So brief, in fact, that she doubted the woman even remembered her.

"You should learn what you can when you return home," Aunt Gladys advised.

"Absolutely," Lady Charlotte agreed. "While he may be perfectly charming and widely accepted by society, you don't want to be blindsided by any unpleasant connections down the road. Think of your children."

Phoebe leapt to her feet. "I think I will retire for the night."

She said her goodnights and hurried to her room so she could think. Along the way, she tried to categorize all of the thoughts bouncing through her head. Many were related to Sophia and everything she knew about her disappearance. A few related to the mental stability of women as they grew older. Others about the condition of her gown and how she would explain it to her maid. At least one was a passing regret that she had not snagged a biscuit before storming out of the room. But, hardly surprising, the most pressing thoughts were of Vernon.

In her room, she sat on the foot of the bed and dropped her head into her hands. She rubbed the sides of her head in hopes that it might calm the whirlwind of her mind but it didn't help. Perhaps if she wrote everything down?

She rummaged through her bag until she located her journal. By the time she found a pen and ink as well as a blank page, she had come to the conclusion that there was little she could, or would, write. Because what did she really know? And what was she willing to admit on the page, where anyone could read it? After spending several minutes staring at a blank page, she slapped the cover of the journal shut and dropped her spectacles on the bedside table.

Dwelling on a topic that was better left untouched would do her no good at all. But with nothing else to occupy it, her mind wandered back to her most pressing problem. Sophia's disappearance. At this point she believed in her heart that even if Sophia had left of her own accord, she was likely being held against her will. Even at her worst, she would not have wanted to cause Aunt Gladys undue worry. She would have sent a note telling them where she was, or at the least assuring them she was well. Someone else had to be involved in her disappearance.

Romano, of course, was the first name that sprang to mind. She had every reason to believe the note written to Sophia had come from him. But what did he have to gain by holding keeping her?

She shuddered. At least nothing worth dwelling on, anyway.

As she paced the confines of her room, her thoughts grew darker. She couldn't help recalling Vernon's comment about the former owner of the shop they stopped at being involved in a slave ring.

Her breath caught in her chest. What if Sophia had been taken because of it? She sank onto the foot of her bed.

No, no, no. Not Sophia. That couldn't be her sister's fate.

The ache in her chest grew. Her thoughts spun, making her light-headed.

All of the gossip and shunning she had imagined would come as a result of a reckless elopement paled in comparison to what she now feared for her sister.

What made it worse was her inability to right the situation. Whispers and idle chatter she could manage. But this...

She couldn't even wrap her mind around the horrors women might be subjected to in a slave ring. And she didn't want to know.

All she did know was that she had to get Sophia back. And it seemed Vernon was her best chance of doing so.

Tomorrow she would find a way to get Vernon alone and demand answers from him.

In the meantime, she would grieve and pray for her sister's safe return.

 17

BACK in their own villa, Vernon poured himself a drink then went in search of Moretti. When he failed to find him, he let himself into the room they used to store their important documents and weapons. After using it for the past month he finds he rather likes having a hidden room below the main floor. When he returned to London he would very likely begin looking into the possibility of having one built into his townhouse.

He turned the crank to ignite the cog lamps that hung from the stone walls just inside the door. Traditional oil lanterns were fine, but the cog lamps burned brighter and it was nice to not worry about a flame or scot.

At the desk he made himself comfortable and began flipping through the journal the shopkeeper's son had given them. He still couldn't decipher anything written on the pages but he had hopes that something might jump out at him. Even something as simple as the dates or figures might provide a clue.

Hopefully Moretti would be able to read it or know someone who could. He really didn't want to ask Phoebe to do it. There was no telling what might be recorded in the book. Allowing her to translate it would pull her deeper into their investigation. And that would place her in even more danger.

Putting Phoebe in danger was simply unacceptable.

He retrieved the list of passengers they had ripped from Signor Romano's log and scanned the book for possible matches. He didn't know what he was looking for, but he felt the need to do something while he waited.

It didn't take long for Moretti to join him. "What are you

working on?"

"The journal Pereira's son gave me. I was hoping to match some of the entries up against our list."

"Find anything?"

"Not so far." Vernon looked up from the book. "You don't happen to know Portuguese, do you?"

"No, why?"

"Because that is what this…" Vernon held up the book. "Is written in."

Moretti took the journal and glanced at multiple pages.

"Know anyone that can read or write it?" Vernon asked.

Moretti shook his head. "Afraid not."

Vernon cursed.

"Do we need to have it translated?" Moretti asked.

"Yes." Vernon grimaced. "Maybe."

"Why? What do you think is in it?"

"Miguel said his father recorded all of his off-the-book transactions there."

"Damn. Then yes, we probably do need it translated." Moretti tapped a finger on the table in annoyance. "It might take me a while to find someone who could do it though."

Vernon sighed. "I know someone."

"Then why didn't you get it to him already?" Moretti pushed the book back across the desk.

"Because I don't want her any more involved than she already is."

Moretti's brow rose in question. "Her?"

"Phoebe Ashdown."

"Is that the young lady you took to the store earlier or have you been collecting all the English women you come across?"

Vernon shot his partner an annoyed glance. "There's more." He slumped in his chair. "Her sister went missing two days ago. I've been following leads on it while searching for ours."

Moretti frowned as he pulled a chair out and straddled it. "Tell me."

Vernon recounted everything the family had told him and

all that he had learned since.

"Describe the sister to me."

"Young, pretty, inexperienced." Vernon gestured to his own face. "Fresh complexion Blonde hair."

Moretti pulled out a sheet of paper and set it on the desk. "That's the third woman matching that description that has gone missing." He pointed to three names that had been marked with a star. "Is she gentry?"

Vernon answered absently as he read the list of names. "She is."

"These others—" Moretti pointed to two more names. "—while not necessarily titled, were raised in good households. They would have had gentle upbringing. Manners. Polish."

Damn. Worst-case scenarios for those girls flashed through Vernon's head making his gut burn with indignation. "We have to put a stop to this."

"We would have to find them first," Moretti reminded him. "You said the sister was taken two days ago?"

"Yes."

"These two went missing three weeks ago. This one two months ago."

"That's long enough for any number of ships to sail to any number of ports and return."

"My guess is that they aren't taking them one at a time," Vernon said. "And they certainly cannot take multiple people from the same city. Families would notice and the authorities would be forced to get involved."

"But if they are collecting one or two, maybe even four or five from various places, and bringing them together here. They could be shipping to their final destination from here."

"My sources say Genoa is the origin city."

"As do mine," Moretti agreed.

"But where?" Vernon pulled a map of the city from their stack of documents and slapped it on the table.

"We've searched the entire port." Moretti swiped his hand across the map. "I've had men on board every ship that has come in over the last month. None of the ships match the description or the information we have."

"And I haven't turned up any signs of prisoners aboard the few ships I have searched either." Vernon dropped into his chair in frustration. "You simply can't hide a group of people for long without other people knowing it. At least not in a busy city."

"Could they be hiding them outside of the city then?"

"Perhaps." Vernon folded his arms and leaned back, balancing the chair on its rear legs. "But they would still have to transport them to the ship and get them on board without anyone seeing them."

Moretti got up and paced the room while they tossed more ideas around. Finally, he declared, "We could speculate for hours on this. I think we need to have your lady friend work on that journal and see what she can tell us."

Vernon let his head drop against the back of the chair. "She wants to help find her sister anyway."

"Well now she can. How much does she know about this mission?"

"Nothing. She knows I'm not here just on a whim but not why."

"But she knows you," Moretti pressed. "Away from RIO, correct?"

"Yes."

"And you trust her?"

That question gave him pause. His training and his instincts warred with each other. It forced him to take a hard look at what both were telling him. Still his answer remained the same. "I have no reason not to."

"Despite her sister's connection to Romano's son?"

"That connection appears to be a young, naive girl's infatuation with a suave foreign gentleman. And I strongly suspect, if he is behind her disappearance, that he likely used that connection to obtain her."

"Your lady friend doesn't have the same features as her sister though, correct?"

"No. Her hair is darker. They have the same fair

complexion, but Phoebe has a few freckles and wears spectacles. And, from what little time I spent with the sister, Phoebe is definitely the more intelligent of the two."

Moretti considered him. "I see."

"You see what?"

Moretti shrugged one shoulder. "I was merely speculating whether or not she matched the descriptions of any of the other women on the list." He held up his hand. "She doesn't. So unless she boasts some trait or skillset we have yet to discover this group is interested in, she should be reasonably safe."

Some of the knot in Vernon's gut eased. "I admit I wondered whether this group would be interested in Phoebe as well as her sister. The last thing I want to do by asking her to interpret that journal is to put her in any more danger than she may already be. But I believe she may be the fastest and most reliable source we have at our disposal."

"Agreed. So you'll talk with her then?"

Vernon took a deep breath. He felt certain Phoebe was capable of translating it for them. Likely in a speedy manner. Especially if they told her it may help find her sister. Normally he wouldn't hesitate obtaining assistance wherever they had a need. But the idea of her being exposed to the things he often was, much less the danger, made his gut churn. Yet he didn't see a better alternative. Since all of the evidence indicated the previous attacks involving Phoebe had been due to her being in the wrong place at the wrong time, he relented. "Yes."

Moretti nodded his approval. "Meanwhile I will continue to gather information on the missing people. Including the sister. The docks are being watched closely. My men have gotten good at finding ways to board ships so we'll continue to check any incoming."

"Short of kicking in Romano's door and beating answers out of him, I'm not sure what else we can do."

Moretti pointed at Vernon with his glass. "I am not opposed to that idea."

"Nor am I, but I don't want to have to write the rather

lengthy report later explaining how and why I became involved with an international incident with a man still grieving the loss of a much-beloved father."

Moretti snorted. "Grieving." He tossed back the rest of his drink and slammed the glass on the table. "Agapito most likely hired the man who killed his father. The only thing that bastard is grieving is the time he lost arranging it."

 18

VERNON arrived shortly after breakfast the next day. Not that many in the house had been in the mood to eat. Phoebe's tea and toast sat like a lump in her stomach but knew going without food wouldn't help anyone.

When the maid came to tell her that she had a visitor, it took all of her will power to not run to the door. Would Vernon have new information about Sophia? After all, it had been more than twelve hours since she last saw him.

Her excitement had nothing to do with the fact that she'd spent half the night thinking more about him and that unsettling kiss than planning how to she might find her missing sister. She forced herself to slow her steps and take a calming breath before entering the front parlor. All of her pre-planned greetings and questions vanished when she found a man she did not know looking out the front window. Alarm skirted up her spine until Vernon stepped into her line of vision. "Good morning." Seeing him alleviated most of her concern but not all.

"Good morning." She glanced at the other man. "I didn't expect to see you this early."

"I do hope we didn't catch you at a bad time?" Vernon asked.

"Not at all."

"Good." Vernon gestured to the man by the window. "Allow me to present my associate, Mr. Moretti."

The man moved from the shadows toward them. Like Vernon, he was dressed in a black wool jacket and dark trousers. His broad chest and shoulders, however, required a bit more fabric to cover them adequately. "Miss Ashdown."

Sunlight streaming through the glass glinted off the coppery threads in his hair when he dipped his head in greeting. "Vernon told me about the situation with your sister. You have my sympathy."

"Thank you, Mr. Moretti." She waived them toward the seating area. "Please. Have a seat. I can ring for tea if you'd like."

"No tea for us, thank you." Vernon waited until she sat on the sofa then took the spot at the other end while Mr. Moretti stationed himself away from the windows. "We're here, actually, to ask a favor of you."

"Of me?" She glanced between the two men to try to determine if they were serious or not. What could she possibly do for them?

Vernon pulled the journal he had showed her the previous day from his pocket. "You said you could read this, correct?"

"Yes."

"We need you to tell us what it says."

She blinked surprise. "Everything?"

"Not word for word," Mr. Moretti reassured her. "Just anything that might be pertinent."

Her gaze swung to Vernon. "Pertinent to your...business dealings, you mean?"

"Yes," Vernon answered.

"Does this book have anything to do with Sophia's disappearance?" She had to know the answer even though she dreaded it at the same time.

The men exchanged solemn glances.

Vernon answered. "We don't have proof, but yes. We believe it's possible. Your sister matches the description of other women who have disappeared in the area."

Phoebe's blood ran cold enough to make her light headed but she swallowed her panic. "Then by all means, I'd be happy to help." Her hand shook when she reached for the book. Vernon, however, didn't release his hold of it.

"There's one catch," Mr. Moretti interjected.

"We need the information right away," Vernon added.

"How quickly?" she asked for clarification.

"Today, if you could," Vernon answered.

She bit her lip as she considered how quickly she could work. "I am not sure I can promise to finish translating everything today. But I can commit to doing as much as possible. Aunt Gladys might ask questions but I could always lock myself away in my room claiming a headache."

"I wondered if you might be willing to come with us—or at least me—today," Vernon said with a touch of hesitation.

Her heart skipped a beat. "Why would I need to come with you?" The idea of spending time with Vernon after the heated dreams she had of him last night made her more than a little unsettled.

"It's not that we don't trust you, Miss Ashdown," Mr. Moretti said. "We don't trust everyone else and would prefer that the journal did not leave our possession."

Phoebe turned to face Vernon's companion. "I don't wish to offend you, Mr. Moretti, but I don't know you. Why would I go anywhere with you? For all I know you could be one of the men responsible for my sister's disappearance."

Vernon smirked at his companion. "I told you she was the smart one."

Mr. Moretti tipped his head in acknowledgement. "Well put. And I applaud your caution." He leaned forward in his chair, resting his elbows on his knees. "What can I do to put you at ease?"

"Where are you from, Mr. Moretti?"

A flicker of surprise flashed across his face. "What makes you think I'm am not from Genoa?"

"Aside from your physical characteristics, your Italian, while quite good, does not have the same lilt as Signor Bianchi or any of his servants. All of whom I know to be native."

"You have quite the ear for languages." Mr. Moretti glanced at the open door. "Where I hail from is unimportant." He lowered his voice. "But I admit to being neither English nor Italian."

Phoebe swung her gaze to Vernon. "You can vouch for Mr.

Moretti and his intentions?"

"I can. He and I have been working together for some time. Our reasons for being in Genoa are the same."

She looked deep into Vernon's eyes. Her heart told her she could trust him. In truth, despite the lethal edge she sensed in Mr. Moretti, she didn't feel he posed a threat to her. As a matter of fact, she suspected she would be safer with them than with all of the men within the Bianchi's household.

"Very well. I will go with you." She stood, prompting Vernon to rise also. "I just need a few minutes to change and let my aunt know that I'll be going out."

"What will you tell her?" Mr. Moretti asked.

"That we're looking for information to Sophia's disappearance and that I should return by supper."

Vernon looked dubious. "Perhaps we should speak to her."

"I don't think that will be necessary. I doubt Aunt Gladys will mind."

"Don't think I'll mind what, dear?" Aunt Gladys said from the door.

All three of them turned as Aunt Gladys and Lady Charlotte sailed through the door.

"We were just speculating on whether or not you would permit Miss Ashdown to accompany us into town to tour the music theater with us." Vernon grimaced. "I had rather hoped to distract her for a bit from the distressing situation your family is experiencing."

"I don't believe the theater is open during the day," Lady Charlotte said with a frown.

"It isn't. But I recently made the acquaintance of the theater owners. They promised to give me a tour of the building any time they were rehearsing." He gestured to Phoebe. "I thought today would be as good a day as any."

"And your companion?" Aunt Gladys asked, with a pointed look toward Mr. Moretti.

"I do beg your pardon." Vernon gestured to Mr. Moretti. "Lady Gilbray, Lady Charlotte, this is a friend of mine, Mr. Moretti. I thought that given the circumstances you would feel more comfortable if she were to be accompanied about town by more than just myself."

Mr. Moretti tipped his head. "Ladies."

Aunt Gladys took in Moretti's appearance then turned to Lady Charlotte. "What do you think, Charlotte?"

Phoebe stifled the urge to roll her eyes. Neither of the ladies would dare say no to such a request. After all, they were not in London proper. And it was her aunt's greatest wish for her to find a suitable husband. Vernon passed all of her aunt's requirements within minutes of meeting her for the first time.

"Well…" Lady Charlotte considered both men. "I should think our Phoebe would be safe with these two healthy looking gentlemen. I know I would feel adequately protected in their company."

"I agree." Aunt Gladys nodded her head at Phoebe. "Very well."

Vernon's smile widened. "Excellent."

Phoebe returned his smile. "As I was saying before, I just need to change into something a little warmer. It will only take a moment or two."

"Take your time dear," Aunt Gladys said. "We'll entertain your guests."

Phoebe shook her head as she headed to her room. Those two were likely to talk Vernon's ear off. And they were very likely to question him about all the things she had been unable to answer about it. She chuckled to herself. Hope he was used to being interrogated. They might even get the seemingly stoic Mr. Moretti to reveal a thing or two.

Phoebe changed her dress and returned to the sitting room, as promised. Since she was unsure what to expect for the day, she chose a dress suitable for walking and a jacket that allowed ample room to hide Lady Charlotte's pistol. After all, she didn't want to depend entirely on the gentlemen for protection.

When she returned to the sitting room, she found Vernon entertaining her chaperones with a lively story about some escapade he and Moretti had gotten into while in France. She quietly retook her seat so as to not interrupt.

"Are you ready?" Vernon asked Phoebe when he finished answering her aunt's latest questions.

Phoebe smiled at the pleading look in his eyes. "Yes."

"Enjoy your outing dear, but do take care," Aunt Gladys said from the sofa.

"I will." She let Vernon help her into her wrap. "I'll send word if I will be late for supper."

The two matrons waved them off with a sad smile. Vernon helped her into the carriage then settled into the seat beside her. Moretti gave the driver instructions then climbed in as well.

Once they were rolling Vernon handed her the journal.

"Would you like me to write the passages somewhere or just read aloud?"

"Just read it for now," Vernon told her.

She opened the book to the first page. "Whoever the author is, references a meeting with a Signor Vittorio. There is an order placed for merchandise he doesn't normally carry and he worried it might take too long to secure." Her finger skims most of the way down the page then halts and jumps back up a couple of rows. "Here he says four of the five items will be delivered the following day."

"Does he say what the merchandise is?" Mr. Moretti asked.

She shook her head. "No." She turned the page and began reading again. "I'm not certain, but I think a little time has passed before this next note."

"Why do you think that?" Vernon asked.

"Difference in the ink and the nib width as well as the condition of the paper." Her finger danced across the page. "Now the author says he is expected to fill one order every month. He makes a comment that it is the same type of merchandise."

"What else?" Mr. Moretti asked.

She skims over the next few pages, flipping back and forth to be sure. "These all seem to be the same types of entries. There's a note here that says the orders may be increasing soon as well as a question about increasing what he charged." She points to a different note. "Here he says his customer agreed to the increased prices so long as he delivers on time."

She turned another page or two. "Here he says his customer asked him to hold the merchandise until they contact him. He's worried he may end up with more corn meal than he needs or can off load in a timely manner."

"Corn meal?" Vernon looked at Mr. Moretti.

Mr. Moretti shrugged.

"The author either became worried about missing something or he became paranoid. He switched from a diary type entry to straight lists. This is an order for women's dresses in three different sizes as well as what seems to be clothes for children. Pants and shirts. There are various sizes of serviceable shoes included too."

"Maybe he was asked to buy clothes for these people?" Moretti asked.

Vernon frowned. "Certainly sounds that way."

"Are there any descriptions?" Moretti asked Phoebe.

She shook her head. "There are some kind of markings next to the items, but I'm not sure what they mean."

"Like what?" Vernon looked over her shoulder.

She pointed to the small letters next to the words.

"Color perhaps?" Vernon speculated.

"Maybe," she murmured. "If we're talking about clothing, I would think measurements would be far more relevant."

"A good point."

Despite the gravity of the situation, his nearness still managed to make her pulse race. While she was disappointed to not have time alone with Vernon, she was also grateful. So long as Mr. Moretti was with them, she wouldn't have to worry about doing something to embarrass herself.

Something like staring at his lips hoping he might kiss her.

 19

CARRIAGE traffic picked up when they reached the outskirts of town. Moretti kept watch out the window but Vernon's gaze kept wandering back to Phoebe. He tried to tell himself it was because she held the journal and he needed to ensure its safety. But a nagging voice in the back of his head said he was lying to himself.

This woman simply appealed to him on a level he had not previously experienced. And it alarmed him. People in his line of work couldn't afford distractions. Distractions got you killed. Or worse, they got you taken, interrogated, maybe even tortured before being killed.

He forced his eyes to stop tracking the way her delicate fingers slid across the pages like a caress.

Suddenly there was loud crash followed by a grind of metal. The carriage rocked on its axles. The window he had been looking out went dark as another carriage scraped against the side. All three of them were thrown to one side as their driver attempted to regain control.

Vernon used the bench in front of him and the carriage sides to brace himself and, as much as he could, Phoebe. The inevitable second crash came far too soon.

Vernon shook off his shock and reached for Phoebe. "Are you all right?"

"I…" She touched a place on her head. "Yes, I think so."

"Moretti, I assume that little bump didn't even phase you."

Moretti had already had his weapon drawn. "Not a bit. You?"

Vernon brushed the pieces of glass from his lap. "I'm fine." He told Phoebe, "Grab the journal. We need to get out of here."

Wide eyed, she retrieved the book from where it had fallen onto the floorboard then stuffed it into her skirt pocket.

"I'll take Phoebe with me. Standard protocol in place?" Vernon asked Moretti in a low voice.

"Yes." Moretti eyed the scene outside the carriage. "I'll go first."

"Good luck."

Moretti shouldered open the door on their right and shouted at the driver to ascertain how he fared.

"What is—" Vernon silenced her question by holding up one finger while he listened to everything going on outside. In a whisper he told her, "We're going out this side." He pointed to the door on the left. "Stick close to me. Don't look back. And whatever you do, hold on to that book."

She nodded she had heard.

"Ready?"

She swallowed. "Yes."

He checked for immediate threats outside the carriage. Then as soon as it sounded as if Moretti had the attention of anyone nearby, he opened the door and jumped down. Their side had not taken as much damage and faced away from the street. He helped her down and wrapped his arm around her waist and hurried her toward the alley across from them.

He looked ahead and behind them frequently to see if they were followed. As they approached the end of alley, two men stepped out to block their path.

Phoebe gasped in surprise. He turned to go back the other way and found one man coming their way. Dread settled in his gut.

This was about to get messy.

He turned, putting Phoebe behind him, so he could see both threats and backed the two of them into a small cove.

He triggered the device on his wrist to spring one of his smaller guns into his palm. In a low tone he told Phoebe, "Reach under my coat and get the gun I have holstered in the middle of my back. But do it without making it noticeable."

He felt her hand searching under his coat and he hoped she appeared to be cowering behind him. Despite the distraction her hands caused he kept his eyes on the approaching men.

The two closest to them stopped a few feet away effectively blocking the way.

Vernon looked them in the eye. "Gentlemen."

"Give us the book."

"What book?"

"The book you took from the shopkeeper."

Vernon faked confusion. "I have no idea what you're talking about."

Light reflected off the metal of the knife the man now held. "We know you have it. Turn it over and perhaps we will let you and the lady live."

"Now, now." Vernon told them with deadly calm. "You shouldn't lie to a lady."

The man's lip lifted in amusement.

Instead of waiting or attempting to reason their way out, Vernon shot the man holding the knife and then his friend.

Phoebe let off another shot, this one aimed at the third man who had just closed in on them. That man grasped his hand after dropping his weapon and took off down the alley in the direction he had come.

"Let's go." Vernon grabbed Phoebe's free hand and pulled her farther down the alley.

At the end, he paused to check around the corner for new threats. A few people watched their hasty retreat did nothing to help or hinder them. They ran down the block, turned another corner, and crossed the street before slowing to a fast walk.

Vernon paused long enough to check Phoebe. He cheeks were pink against her now pale complexion but her eyes were bright and alert. "Are you okay?"

"All things considered, yes." She answered in a breathless rush.

He chuckled. The thrill of the chase had always been a bit of a high for him, but fear for Phoebe had dampened it considerably. "Tell me if you need to stop to catch your breath. But I would rather put as much distance between us and that area."

"So would I."

He wound her through various streets, making their path as twisted and unplanned as possible. All the while he kept an eye out for new threats.

Finally, they reached one of the taverns he frequented. He led her into the alley then through the back entry. He motioned for her to remain quiet as he led her up the narrow back stairway. At the top he used his key to let himself into the room he had secured for moments such as this.

He made it a habit to arrange for alternate living quarters in every city he worked. When you had people chasing you, it was good to have a hiding place that your enemies knew nothing about.

The room was sparsely furnished. There was a cot, washstand, and a mismatched desk and chair. The rug on the floor was faded but clean.

He gestured for her to have a seat while he slid the bolt into place on the door. He also added one of his mechanical security devices to the upper corner of the doorframe.

"We'll be safe here while I figure out our next move. Just keep your voice down."

She nodded her understanding then paused as she looked between the bed and the chair.

"Make yourself comfortable. I am not about to hold you to some ridiculous social standard when we've just been running for our lives."

"I guess that's true." She cautiously went to the bed and sat down on the end. Her back remained stiff even as she sat. "It's surprisingly warm in here."

"These rooms are located over the boilers." He pointed to the section of brick that ran up the center of one wall. "The owner said this chimney vents one of them. Heat radiates off of it all day."

"Fine for the winter, but I bet that makes this room

unbearable in the summer."

"Most likely." He shrugged. "But I don't plan to be here when the weather gets warm again."

He went to the larger window to see if they had been followed. He positioned himself against the wall and pulled the curtain back only far enough that he could peer down at the street. Almost immediately he spotted two of Romano's men on the corner. From their gestures and the way they watched everyone passing by, he felt certain they were still looking for him and Phoebe.

"Is this where you've been living since you arrived in Genoa?" She asked. "It's pretty bare."

"No." Taking care to not draw attention, he let the curtain fall back into place. "The villa we stopped at yesterday is where Moretti and I are staying. This is one of my bolt holes in case I need a quick escape."

"Like today?"

"Indeed." He tried to ignore her sitting on what was technically his bed, even though he had only slept there a few times when he first arrived in the city. He retrieved the locked chest he had stashed beneath the bed and set it on the desk. The lock still held and layer of dirt he had coated the top with remained. He used the key he had hid behind one of the loose boards to unlock the case.

He took off his jacket and then the spring-loaded pistol hidden beneath his sleeve. He reloaded the device and added a few extra bullets to the leather case he carried in his pocket. He took one of the knives from the chest and glanced toward Phoebe. She had taken off her coat and was looking through the journal.

He considered the jacket that lay folded in the chest. It had a special liner that would stop some bullets and even smaller knives. It was too bad that he didn't have one that Phoebe could wear. His was far too large and likely to heavy for her to wear. Still unsure whether he should take it, he lay it over the back of the chair.

"Here." He held the knife out to Phoebe. "Do you know

how to use a knife?"

She looked at the weapon then up at him. "I know how to use one at the dinner table but I cannot say that I've ever used it to defend myself." Her nose scrunched up in an adorable way. "I'm not sure that I could."

"You might be surprised what you could do when you're confronted with the possibility of being killed."

She cringed.

He gestured for her to take it. "I'd rather you have it than not."

With a sigh, she took the weapon from his hand but paused, as if she didn't know what to do with it.

"I would recommend putting it either in a pocket that you could easily reach or strapped to your leg. Not to be forward, but I don't suppose you are wearing a garter, are you?"

Her cheeks turned pink. "Yes, as a matter fact I am."

"I've been told that is one place that makes it easy to hide a weapon if you're wearing a full skirt."

"Really?" She looked up in surprise. "But how would I secure it?" She pulled the side of her skirts up, exposing a span of her cream colored thigh.

He swallowed hard.

"If I just slip it under my garter it would likely just slide into my stocking."

"I'm not certain, but I think ladies run the ribbon through the loop of the sheath." Somehow he managed to keep his voice steady.

She turned the holster over. "Oh, I see."

She untied her garter and made a few adjustments to the material of her stocking. Then she pulled some of the ribbon free and threaded it through the loop. Then she retied the ribbon, securing everything to her leg once again. She stood and let her skirts drop back into place and checked the way everything looked. When she looked up, she was frowning. "Like that? That doesn't seem right."

"No. That's more likely to show through your skirts. Here, let me help you." She pulled her skirts out of the way allowing him access to an area that he felt certain no one other than her mother and perhaps a physician had ever seen. His hand shook as he rearranged the knife and retied ribbon. "I think it would work better here." His voice had a catch to it. "See how this extra layer of skirting hides it?"

"I, uh… yes, I that makes more sense."

He looked up at her. Her eyes were wide and the pupils dilated. Slowly he rose from where he had knelt in front of her.

"I really want to kiss you right now but I don't think that would be smart."

"Why wouldn't it be?" Her voice held a breathy edge to it.

"Because you might think I was taking advantage of you and our situation."

"I don't think you would do that." She reached out and touched his chest. "If nothing else, this situation makes me realize how valuable these moments are and that we might not get another one."

"Are you sure?"

"Quite." She rose up on her toes and pressed her lips to his without giving him a chance to think about it further.

He grasped her about the waist and pulled her against him even as he took control of their kiss. He reveled in the taste of her lips and the feel of her delicate curves as she slumped against him.

The slow burn he'd felt in his chest ever since he'd seen her on the dance floor at the ball burst into a raging inferno. The small part of his mind that still functioned properly cautioned him to go slow and not overwhelm her. She was inexperienced. Not the kind of woman he often encountered while investigating the seedier side of the world.

He fisted his hands into her shirt and skirt. Her hands splayed out across his chest then slid up to his shoulders.

He paused their kiss and rested his forehead against hers. "This is madness. You should push me away and tell me all the reasons why we can't do this."

She tipped her head back and looked him in the eye. "Vernon, I may not be experienced in this arena, but I do understand how it works. And I know the consequences. I have always been the cautious one." She touched his cheek. "But right now I want this moment with you because if the people who keep chasing us get their way, we may never get another one."

He groaned. "Don't say that." He captured her lips in a punishing kiss. "I don't want to think about you not having a thousand moments. You deserve them." He searched her eyes looking for an answer to a question he didn't know how to ask. "You also deserve better than this. You deserve better than me. But damn if I can help myself." Like a starving man, he drank in her passion and gave more in return. With the tip of his tongue he teased the edges of her lips, encouraging her to open to him. Her compliance and trust were very nearly his undoing.

Desperate to taste every inch of her, he dragged his lips along her jaw until he reached her ear. He traced the curve of her ear with his tongue then dropped kisses along the sensitive area along her neck. She whimpered and clung to him drawing him further into a passionate haze.

With her still wrapped in his arms, he walked her to the edge of the bed. Then he pushed her back until they both tumbled onto the bed. To ensure she wasn't squished, he caught them before he fell on her and slowly lowered his weight onto her. The metal springs groaned beneath them.

Almost frantically, she tugged the edge of his shirt from his trousers and slipped her hands underneath. The cooler temperature of her fingers did nothing to dampen the fire raging inside of him. All he could think of was how good it felt to hold her in his arms and to taste her untapped passion.

When he managed to pull the edge of her skirts up, he ran his hand across her thigh and up to her hip. She squirmed beneath him, inadvertently bringing him closer to where he really wanted to be.

Needing another taste of her, he captured her lips as he shifted to lay beside her. There were still far too many layers of fabric between them. After moving more of her skirts out of the way he loosened the ties of her pantaloons and slid them down as far as he could reach.

She broke free from his kiss and told him in a breathless rush. "My boots."

He looked down and realized he hadn't even considered that obstacle. "I'll get them." The bed squeaked as he crawled to the end. He untied each of her boots and worked the laces loose so he could tug them off. They made a hollow thud when they hit the floor beside the bed. While he was still sitting up he worked the buttons of his vest and his shirt free then pulled them off.

Kneeling beside her, he took in the sight of Phoebe's flushed cheeks and lustful gaze. She was a heady mixture of innocence and enthusiasm. He leaned forward and ran his hands up the length of her legs. When he reached the top of her thigh she instinctively tried to keep them closed. Instead of fighting her instincts, he gave her a moment to adjust while he loosened the ribbons on her garters and slipped the knife they had just secured there beneath the pillow. Then he slid her stockings off along with her pantaloons.

As he held her gaze, he slid his hands back up her legs, parting them as he moved. Even though he craved a peek at what he had uncovered, he took her lips again in a searing kiss. He wanted her relaxed, he wanted her open and needy.

Slowly, reverently, he slid one hand to the apex of her legs. Even though she momentarily tensed, his fingers parted her folds with ease. Her dampened center let him know she was indeed enjoying his attentions. With his thumb, he found the sensitive bud that would bring her the most pleasure and worked it until she squirmed beneath him.

Reluctantly, he gave up kissing her when she became lost in sensation and her breath came in short pants. Besides, he wanted to watch her when he sent her over the edge for the first time. He worked her nub until she whimpered and clung to him desperately. To add yet another sensation, he dipped one finger into her channel to mimic the ultimate act.

"Vernon, I…" She panted. "It's too much. I don't know what…"

"I have you." he whispered. "Just let go. Let it happen."

She rocked her hips against his hand until finally she stiffened and let out a gasp of pleasure. He pumped two fingers in and out her channel and held her as she rode out the rest of her orgasm.

The expression on her face was one of the most beautiful things he had ever seen.

He nuzzled and kissed the side of her face and neck until she returned to her senses and kissed him back. When she opened her eyes and smiled up at him he felt his heart expand.

"That was surprisingly pleasant," she said with a touch of awe.

"You liked that, did you?"

"Very much." Her cheeks were flushed with passion and perhaps a touch of shyness.

"I'm glad." He kissed the corner of her lips. "There's so much more though."

"I thought there might be." She bit her lip. "You didn't, um…"

He chuckled. "No. I didn't experience fulfillment but I very much enjoyed watching you."

"What can I do to make sure you enjoyed it as much as I did?"

He groaned as his erection strained against his now too-tight pants. "There is so much you can do but this really isn't the best time for it."

"Why?"

"Because I need to protect you, first and foremost, and I cannot do that if I'm lost in you." He motioned to the room behind them. "And this is not what you deserve for your first experience." He brushed his palm across her cheek, pushing a stray lock of hair away. "You deserve silk sheets and a mattress made of the finest down. And a lover who will give you hours of pleasure. Not a heated moment while running from armed gunmen."

Her already flushed cheeks turned a deeper shade of pink. "I suppose it is an awkward time to be thinking of such things."

She sat up and patted her hair, obviously unsure of what to do.

Vernon felt like a heel and a fool for turning her down. But the protector in him knew this wasn't right. This was the wrong time, the wrong place, and in truth, he was probably the wrong man. After all, what he could offer her? He had no title, no fortune he could call his own. Yes, he might be connected because of his father, but what did that say about him as a man?

Not a thing.

He rolled off the bed and stood, then offered his hand to Phoebe. "Let me help you."

"I can—"

"I insist."

She finally lay her delicate fingers on his palm and he helped her scoot to the edge of the bed. Then he knelt in front of her and helped her with her stockings, garters, as well as her knife. When she stood, he straightened her skirts just to have another excuse to touch her. "I'm afraid I'm at a loss as to how to assist with your hair. But I believe there is a glass on the inside of that cupboard there." He pointed to the door he meant.

"Thank you." She gave him a shy smile that did strange things to his insides.

What was this woman doing to him?

 20

AFTER Phoebe re-pinned her hair she felt a little more in control of herself. Yes, she was still a little embarrassed for engaging in such activities with a man who was not her husband, but otherwise, she did not regret what she had learned.

Vernon of course, didn't need long to make himself presentable. It felt a little odd to dress while sharing a room with a man, but the logical part of her mind reassured her that he had seen her most intimate parts so why should it matter if he saw her putting clothes back on?

He had even pinned the strands of hair she had missed in the back. He would make some lucky woman a fine husband while she... well, she would most likely make a fabulous aunt to her siblings' children.

She ignored the ache in her heart and focused on their mission. Finding her sister was her first priority.

"So what's next?" She asked.

"For me, protocol. For you, that book." He took a sheet of paper from the desk and scribbled a note.

"You mentioned protocol to Mr. Moretti in the carriage. But what does that mean?"

He used some kind of device to seal the notes he had penned. "I won't give you the specifics, but it's a course of action Moretti and I planned when we began working together. If our missions were compromised or our identities were discovered, it's the way we would reconnect as soon as it was safe to do so."

"Ah. I guess that is smart. But also kind of scary that you have to think of those things." She frowned. "May I ask what it is that you do? Surely you didn't wake up one morning and decide that you wanted to look into a slavery ring in a foreign country."

He sat next to her on the bed. "What I'm about to tell you is not common knowledge. And so long as we are away from home, it is also dangerous knowledge." His voice came out just above a whisper. "Do you understand what I'm saying to you?"

She met his gaze. "I believe so."

"I work for an organization called the Royal Intelligence Office. Our orders come directly from the Queen or the Prince Regent. Our assignments always have some impact on the well-being of the country and often ensure the security of the crown."

So her father and his friends had been right. This intelligence thing did exist. She frowned. "How did you even learn about this Office?"

He smirked. "They made contact with me during my last year at Cambridge."

"Did they know who you were?"

"Of course."

"What did your father have to say about it?"

Vernon snorted. "My father doesn't know." He intertwined their fingers. "He believes I am just a wastrel, traveling abroad to sow my wild oats while living off my monthly allotment."

"Does anyone in your family know you're here?"

"Not specifically where I am. But one of my brothers knows I'm involved with the RIO."

She tipped her head slightly. "Rio?"

"Royal Intelligence Office. RIO."

"Ah." She nodded. "So you were given an assignment to come to Genoa. Because of a...slave ring?"

He shrugged. "More or less."

She waited, hoping he would elaborate. She wanted to understand not only the situation she had found herself in but also more about the man before her.

"Our hope, ultimately, is to cut off the flow of slaves into London proper. We believe Genoa to be one point of origin."

"And you think Sophia may have been taken by the same people involved in this ring?" she asked.

"It's definitely a possibility. Moretti found a pattern in some of the kidnappings. Young women who matched your sister's description had been taken in at least five instances over the couple of months."

"But why?" Her mind raged against the notion that there was such evil in this world. She knew that primitive man took what he wanted but in a civilized society that simply wouldn't do.

He grimaced. "I would rather not speculate on that. And you would do well to not dwell on it either. I know it seems like a long shot, but we are doing everything we can to find your sister. I can promise you that not one ship has left the harbor without our men searching it. So if this is a point of origin, they are either leaving some other way or all of our information is wrong. And I truly don't believe we are wrong."

Some of her anxiousness eased at his words. She still carried a great deal of worry for her sister but at least she knew Signor Bianchi wasn't the only one who trying to get Sophia back. He was a dear man, but his resources were limited.

"Since we're waiting, tell me what else is in the book," Vernon prompted her.

She retrieved the journal and flipped to where she had left off. As she read, he looked over her shoulder. It felt odd having a man taking up so much of her thoughts and, quite frankly, space around her. Even her father and brothers never cuddled with her. Perhaps as a child, but certainly never as an adult. Her sisters sometimes did but this felt completely different.

She rather liked it.

"What does it say?" He prompted her.

"Oh. Yes." She cleared her throat. "Um... this is just summarizing the ordered items. It appears to be more of the same. Ladies dresses, shoes, and one item that I'm not sure about."

"Which one?"

She pointed to the word.

"Any ideas?"

"No." She frowned at the word as if staring at it might make the meaning magically pop into her head. "It could be a locally used word that I never learned."

"Hopefully it's not important. But I'm going to flag that page in case we need to come back to it." She nodded her agreement as he bent a small corner of the page down.

"Anything else?"

"No." They went through several more pages of similar information before finding something new. "This indicates the merchandise will no longer be picked up. His customer now wants him to deliver the items."

If she hadn't been sitting so close to him she might have missed the tension that rippled through him. "Does it say to where?"

"The name is partially scribbled out, but it looks like Caffè Fiorio."

"I think I know where that is." His free hand tapped against his thigh. "We'll need to investigate to see how it's connected though."

"Do you want to go take a look?" she asked.

"Yes. But not right now."

She twisted to better look him in the eye. "Why not? We're not doing anything else." To press the issue, she added, "And I wouldn't mind a cup of tea and perhaps a biscuit."

He grinned unrepentantly. "Did you work up an appetite?"

Her cheeks grew warm. "I may have."

"Then we were doing something right." The kiss he gave her was slow and lingering and warmed her insides in a way that a fireplace never could. She sank against him, memorizing the feeling.

"My God, you are addictive," he murmured against her lips.

His words warmed her further. "So are you," she admitted shyly.

"If I had my way, I'd whisk you away somewhere safe where I could spend the rest of the night teaching you everything there is to know about love making."

Her heart skipped in her chest.

He ran his finger down her cheek then lifted her chin, forcing her to look him in the eye. "But we can't."

"I know." She ran her fingers through his hair. "You need to find bad guys and I need to find my sister."

He eased away.

"Shall we investigate the cafe?" she asked.

He sighed. "As much as I don't want to put you in danger, I fear you already are." He glanced down at the book she held. "And we really need to know what is in there."

"So, tea then," she suggested.

"Yes." He checked his pocket watch. "We need to get moving."

"Okay. I just need to lace my boots and put my coat back on."

"While you do that I need to dispatch my notes."

Her eyes widened in alarm at the thought of him leaving without her. Mr. Moretti wasn't here to watch his back. He could be attacked in the tavern and she'd never know about it.

"Don't worry. I'll lock the door behind me and a bell will alert me if anyone tries to come in without a key." He retrieved the spring-loaded pistol from the desk where he had laid it. "Just in case, I'm sure you know how use this." He handed her the device and dropped a quick kiss on her lips. "I'll be right back."

She blinked in surprise and watched him disappear through the door. It took almost a minute for her to remember what she needed to do. She pulled both boots on and laced them up. Then she adjusted her skirts and make sure her blouse and hair were presentable. Being without a full-length looking glass made it more difficult, but as long as she didn't draw unnecessary attention to herself or to Vernon, her appearance didn't really matter.

She had just taken a seat in the chair when she heard the lock rattle. She slid the pistol into her lap and covered it with her jacket and waited to see who was coming in. When Vernon appeared, she let out the breath she had been holding.

He closed the door behind him. "Are you ready then?"

"Yes." She set the pistol on the desk so she could pull her coat on.

Vernon raised his brow in question. "Did someone try to get in while I was gone?"

"No. Just thought it couldn't hurt to be cautious."

"True." He checked the device, then loosened his sleeve and strapped it to his inner arm. After rolling the sleeve back in place he shrugged his coat on over it.

"That's a unique device."

"It has been rather useful on occasion."

"May I ask where you found it?"

He smirked. "I have a friend who likes to dabble in, shall we say, unique tools of the trade."

"I see."

"He is always coming up with new gadgets for me to try out." He grimaced. "Although some work better than others."

"I would expect so."

At the door he paused. "You have the book, correct?"

She patted her skirt pocket.

"And the knife?"

She patted her leg where they had strapped the blade and holster.

He nodded his approval. "The gentlemanly thing would be letting you go ahead of me, but in this case, I'd rather go first."

"I'm following your lead. I would rather you worry about keeping the two of us safe instead of offending me somehow."

He pulled her in for a kiss that sent tingles down her spine. "Thank you for trusting me."

She smiled up at him. "You've made it a rather easy thing to do." He kissed her once again then released her.

She shrugged aside her disappointment. This was no time for tender feelings. People were trying to kill one or the other of them. And her sister was out there somewhere. She needed her mind clear to focus.

At the door, he looked in both directions, then gestured for her to move through the doorway. He locked the room and slipped the key into his pocket. He took her hand and led her down the hall instead of using the stairway they had entered through.

At the end of the hall, he opened the window and looked down. Seemingly satisfied by what he found he closed the window and took her hand again. This time he led her into a narrow stairway that was likely used by the workers or servants.

He held one finger up to his lips telling her to be quiet then pointed to the floor. She nodded she understood then followed him down the dirty wooden stairs as silently as possible. It was difficult to walk on her toes, but it was the best way she knew to prevent the heels of her boots from striking on the flooring.

When they reached the bottom he opened a door that led to the outside. Once again, he checked the area before gesturing for her to follow. The chilled wind hit her in the face and made her breath catch. The temperature dropped enough to make her wonder if a storm had blown in.

Vernon led her to the end of the alley then stopped. He checked the area as if expecting something or someone to appear. Finally, he must have spotted what he had been looking for. "Okay, here we go." He took her hand, pulled her next to him, and then lay her hand over his arm.

They strolled to the end of the block where he hailed a carriage. He told the driver the name of the cafe then helped her up. When he settled into the seat beside her he prompted her to continue reading.

"Like the other pages, he listed what merchandise was ordered and delivered. And there are some of the same odd markings next to certain items "

"Hmmm." Vernon fell silent as she scanned the pages. Each time she flipped a page she let him know if the content was the same.

"Here's a new entry," she was finally able to tell him.

He turned his attention from the passing scene to the place where she pointed in the book.

"All the other entries were for serviceable, pinafore dresses. This one is for a silk gown."

He frowned. "A ball gown?" He leaned closer to look at the page. "Is there a date for that entry?"

"Yes." She pointed to where a date had been hastily scribbled.

"Remind me to ask Moretti about it in case there is anything significant about it."

She nodded.

She was able to read through a few more pages before the carriage slowed. She peeked out the window on her side. There were a number of people milling about making it more difficult for carriages to make much progress. But eventually they rolled to a stop in front of a marble fronted building with large glass windows. The name of the cafe was displayed in copper above the windows. Ladies and gentlemen passed on the street. A few entered the establishment while others hurried away with small bags of goods.

For the time of day it was hardly surprising.

Vernon paid the carriage driver then helped her down to the street. He placed her hand around his arm and escorted inside. Despite the number of patrons, they managed to find a table near the back of the room that would be suitable to their purposes.

Normally she preferred to be near the front windows so she could observe the people coming and going. But today, knowing someone out there wanted the item she had concealed in her skirts, she was perfectly content to seek shelter near the back.

They ordered tea and something to eat. While they waited, they took in the ebb and flow of customers, the merchandise served, as well as doors the staff used to access the kitchens and back rooms. By the time they finished consuming the items they'd ordered they were no closer to answers than before.

"I see nothing out of the ordinary here," Phoebe remarked.

"Nor do I." His tone hinted his disappointment at not finding anything.

"Perhaps this was just a meeting place?"

"Maybe." Vernon frowned. "What I would really like to do is to walk through the back."

She raised a brow. "Now?"

"Ideally. But I would settle for coming back after they close."

She shook her head.

"Excuse me, Sir. You are Mr. Bennett, correct?" One of the serving staff asked.

"I am," Vernon confirmed.

The server set a package, tied with twine on the table. "Your cousin sends his regrets that he cannot join you."

Vernon smiled. "Thank you."

Phoebe raised her brow in question but held her questions and waited for Vernon's lead.

He made a show of inspecting the box, which held several baked goods. After she declined his offer to sample them, he retied the string and asked, "Are you sufficiently refreshed?"

"I am."

He stood and offered his hand to assist her. "Then perhaps we could take that tour of the theater while we are in the area?"

"I, uh... certainly." She got to her feet. "That would be lovely." She smiled through her confusion.

After leaving coins on the table for their server Vernon escorted her out to the busy sidewalk. Like two people on a leisurely stroll, he led her down the block and around the corner. The paused occasionally and gazed into a few shop windows. All the while, he kept up a steady stream of unimportant conversation.

Vernon tensed when a carriage rolled to a stop just beyond where they stood until someone stuck his head around the edge and whistled to them. Because of the hat and goggles that he wore, it took a moment for her to realize that it was Moretti driving.

"Hurry." Vernon rushed her to the carriage and very nearly tossed her up into the cabin. He jumped in behind her just as Moretti whipped the vehicle into motion.

"Slouch down a bit," he told her just as a shot rang out.

She gasped as something burned across her arm.

The ping of metal hitting metal echoed above them. Then the carriage lurched forward quickly picking up speed.

"Hold on," Vernon cautioned her. "This will likely be a bumpy ride."

 21

VERNON pushed his foot against the seat across from them to brace himself. He grabbed the bar attached to the window frame with one hand and with the other he held onto Phoebe as best he could. He prayed she didn't become ill from the way the carriage bounced and swayed as Moretti sped through town. In truth, he would count himself fortunate if he managed to hold down the scone he had eaten in the cafe.

Eventually the road straightened and the traffic around them lightened. Vernon suspected they were out of immediate danger, but he was reluctant to release his hold of Phoebe. He did however release his foothold on the seat across from them.

"Oh, dear," Phoebe murmured as she examined her own arm.

"What's wrong?" He couldn't see what she was looking at since he was sitting on her other side.

"I…" She held up a bloodstained finger. "I think I may have been shot."

Alarm washed through him. He switched to the seat across from her so he could better see her. She twisted, giving him access to that side. Sure enough there was a tear in her jacket and dress.

He pushed the torn fabric aside so he could inspect her injury. As best he could tell, the bullet had grazed her arm. While it wasn't life threatening at the moment, he knew it probably burned like the devil.

"Are you all right?" He asked as he pulled a handkerchief from his pocket.

She nodded. But one glance at her face and he could see that she had lost nearly all of her color.

"I think it's just a scratch. I don't think the bullet actually went into your arm."

She bit her lip and nodded again.

"I'm going to use this." He held up the white fabric. "To put a pressure on it until we can get somewhere I can clean it. Let me know if I tie it too tight."

"Okay." Her voice waivered just a bit.

He folded the square into a narrow band then tied it around her arm. She only cringed when he tightened the knot.

"Where are we going?" She asked, almost weakly. Perhaps she was simply looking for a distraction for the evening.

"I'm not certain." The landscape did not look familiar, but it whirled past his window at a faster pace than he normally saw. "If I know Moretti, he has a plan though." He returned to her side of the carriage and wrapped his arm around her shoulders.

Phoebe leaned into his side. "You must trust him quite a bit."

"Yes."

"How long have you known each other?"

Vernon shrugged. "A few months." It was probably closer to a year but while he may trust Phoebe with the information he couldn't make that assumption for Moretti.

She blinked up at him in surprise. "Only a few months?"

He nodded. "When you're on assignments like this, you quickly learn who you can and cannot trust. If you don't, your likelihood of being killed goes up significantly."

"That..." She swallowed. "That is a little frightening."

Again, he shrugged. "It's the way it is." Perhaps he had grown a little desensitized to the cat and mouse game he and Moretti played so often. To an outsider it probably did seem harsh.

The carriage slowed, then turned onto a narrow lane. A dense overhang of trees and vines that blocked not only their view but also a great deal of the light covered the lane. Phoebe stole frequent glances at him as if gauging his reaction to where they were going.

Taking care to avoid her injury, he rubbed her arm to reassure her.

The view finally cleared at the end of the lane. Moretti turned the carriage and came to stop in front of old, long forgotten barn.

"What a ride!" The carriage bounced as Moretti sprang from his place in the driver's seat.

Vernon snorted as he unlatched the door and let the step down. He too leapt down then held his hand out to help Phoebe ascend. "I assume we weren't followed?" Vernon asked Moretti.

"Of course not." Moretti held his hands out to either side. "Isn't this a great location?"

Vernon and Phoebe exchanged glances.

"Um. Yes. It's lovely," she said hesitantly.

Moretti faced the half-decrepit building and rested his fists on his hips. "I'm thinking about buying it."

"Really?" Vernon asked.

"Maybe." He faced them again and shrugged. "Did you bring my biscuits?"

Vernon waved toward the coach. "They're somewhere in there."

"Good. I'm hungry." Moretti leapt through the open door.

"After getting bounced all over the carriage, they're probably just crumbs," Vernon shouted to Moretti's retreating back.

"Do you have any idea where we are?" Phoebe whispered to Vernon.

"I'm pretty sure that we're west of town." He tried to gauge which direction the sun was setting to be sure. "There was one turn in the road that might have thrown off my sense of direction but I don't think so." He turned Phoebe so that a band of sunlight illuminated her injured arm. He untied the knotted handkerchief and inspected her wound.

"How does it look?" she asked.

He frowned. Why did the fact that she was bleeding make him simultaneously hurt and want to punch someone? "We need to clean it."

Moretti returned with the open box and a mouthful of food. "These are rather good." He paused just before stuffing another biscuit in. "What's wrong?"

"She was shot." Vernon retied the handkerchief.

Moretti frowned as he peered closer. "How bad?"

"More than a graze but I don't think it damaged anything. I can't tell if it needs to be stitched though."

"You said it was just a scratch earlier," Phoebe protested.

"I didn't want you to panic." Vernon felt a little guilt for lying to her. But only a little. It had been for her own good after all.

"Harrumpf."

Vernon flicked his thumb to their coach. "Where did you find the horseless carriage?"

"I borrowed it from Romano's collection," Moretti told him with a touch of pride.

Phoebe's eyes widened. "Borrowed?"

Moretti shrugged. "Stole. Borrowed. It's all the same."

"You can't be serious," Phoebe said incredulously.

Vernon shook his head. "He probably is."

"Won't that make him mad?" she asked.

"I'm counting on it," Moretti said around a mouthful of biscuit.

"What's your plan?" Vernon asked.

"I don't have it completely worked out yet." Moretti popped another partial biscuit into his mouth. "I wanted to wait to see what you might have found out."

"We have read a little more than half of the journal," Vernon told him.

"Did you learn anything?" Moretti's words were muffled due to his mouth being full.

"A little." Phoebe pulled the journal from her pocket. "There are markings that we feel certain mean something but we haven't pinpointed exactly what."

"And there was a change to the orders that we wanted to run by you," Vernon said.

"Why me?" Moretti wiped his hand on the side of his overcoat.

Vernon shook his head at his friend's lack of manners. "Because you have the lists of the disappearances and when they occurred."

"Perhaps we should go inside to discuss this."

"Inside?" Phoebe asked with a squeak.

"Don't worry." Moretti grinned. "I made sure it's structurally sound." He practically leapt across the rickety porch. "You'll want to avoid that one board there, though." He pointed to one board that had split down the middle yet held its place thanks to one last nail.

The main door opened with one long squeak.

"No one will be coming through that door without everyone in the house knowing it," Vernon muttered.

"A bonus," Moretti called out gleefully as he led the way further into the aging manor.

Someone had attached mechanical lights in the foyer and hall, which made it easier to find their way. Vernon kept his hold of Phoebe's hand so he didn't have to worry about where she might be.

Gesturing at the first door they passed, Moretti told them, "The sitting room is a wreck, so best avoid it." He opened the next door they came to. "The study is habitable and so are the rest of the rooms on this floor. Raffaele just hasn't cleaned everything."

"Raffaele?" Vernon asked.

"The man of the house."

"I thought you were thinking of buying this."

"I am."

"Then what about Raffaele?"

Moretti waved the question away. "He comes with the house."

Vernon and Phoebe glanced at each other in question.

"Let's go to the dining room," Moretti suggested. "It's the cleanest. And there's water in the kitchen not far from there."

"Very well."

The dining room was, like the other rooms they had seen, dilapidated. The wall coverings and drapes were faded and tattered. And what little furniture remained, while reasonably clean, was certainly worn with use.

The table was pushed against the wall instead of centered in the room. Scratches covered the once glossy surface. An empty chain hung limply from the ceiling where a chandelier probably once hung.

The arms of the candelabra on the table were coated with multiple layers of candle wax. Based on the size of the stack of newssheets in the corner, Vernon suspected this room was occupied far more often than the study.

"Have a seat." Moretti gestured to the chair next to the table. "I'll fetch a pitcher of water and see if Raffaele has any clean bandages."

Vernon pulled the chair out for Phoebe. "Here." He dusted off the cushion before she turned to sit there.

"Thank you."

He gestured to her. "You should probably take off your jacket."

"Oh. Yes." She tugged at the first button. "That would probably be best."

The sight of her peeling away even one layer of clothing mesmerized Vernon. He knew what lay beneath those prim layers of cotton and wool and he wanted more. No matter what the logical part of his mind tried to tell him.

He turned away in order to discreetly adjust his crotch as images of her writhing with pleasure flashed through his mind.

"What about my sleeve?" She pulled at the fabric below her wound. "Won't it be in the way?"

"Yes. But we can work around it." He jerked his head toward the door Moretti had disappeared through. "I feel certain you would not be comfortable removing your dress. And I know for sure I don't want anyone else seeing you less than fully dressed."

Her cheeks turned pink.

Vernon busied himself with lighting candles and

familiarizing himself with how the house was laid out. Anything to resist the temptation of pulling Phoebe into his arms and kissing her senseless.

Moretti sailed into the room carrying a pitcher. A bottle of some kind of liquor had been tucked under his arm. "Here is the hot water." He held up a fist of linen strips. "Raffaele gave me what he had as well as a needle and thread."

"Good." Vernon took the strips and set to work cleaning Phoebe's wound. His hand quivered just before pressing the alcohol soaked cloth against her arm.

She hissed in reaction but didn't cry out. The muscle in her jaw twitched even as she turned her face away.

He hated being the one to hurt her further but it was necessary. Even the smallest of wounds got worse if not properly tended. "You okay?" he asked when he dabbed the last part.

She nodded but didn't answer.

"That needs to be looked at again later but I think it will do for now."

"You-You're not going to use that?" Phoebe pointed to the needle and thread.

"No." He wrapped one of the bandages around her arm. "I don't think the cut is deep enough to need it."

Phoebe slumped against the back of her chair. "Thank you."

"You're welcome." His response came out gruffer than he intended. The knot in Vernon's gut loosened as he gathered the things he had used but had not dissipated. Cleaning a wound never bothered him before. It shouldn't have bothered him now. So why did it?

He shook off his questions and focused on his task since he wasn't sure he wanted to know the answers.

 22

VERNON had a strange expression on his face when he glanced her way. Almost as if he were angry about something but Phoebe couldn't imagine why.

He had been gentle with her when he cleaned her wound. But he also acted as if it bothered him to do it. She would have taken care of it herself if she had known what to do. However, it was her first gunshot wound so she was at a bit of a loss.

She picked at the tattered edges of her sleeve. There would be little point in mending it. It was wide enough that everyone would notice the stitching. She would have to get rid of her dress. Her aunt—and probably Lady Charlotte, too—would likely faint when they learned she'd been shot. She hated to think what her mother would say if she ever found out.

"Are you able to talk about what you learned?" Moretti asked.

"Yes. Of course." She patted her pockets looking for the journal and her spectacles.

"Here." Vernon held the book out for her to take.

She sighed with relief that she hadn't misplaced it. "Thank you." She put her glasses on and opened the journal.

"You said earlier the orders changed?" Moretti's demeanor turned serious.

"There was a change right around..." Phoebe flipped through the pages until she came to the one with the corner turned down. "Ah. Here it is." She showed Moretti the page.

"What's different?" Moretti asked.

"This." She pointed to the order for a satin ball gown. "Previously he had been asked to supply basic pinafore dresses. I'm curious why they would suddenly need an expensive gown."

"It could be nothing, but I agree that it's worth looking at." Vernon pointed to Moretti's pocket. "Your list was the first thing I thought of."

Moretti pulled a few sheets of paper from beneath his coat and handed it to Vernon. "Go ahead and take a look." Vernon put Moretti's list and the journal side-by-side, on the table.

While Vernon studied the two documents, Moretti offered her a glass of what she hoped was just water. "What were you looking for at the cafe?"

She pointed to the book. "We found an entry in the journal that mentioned that cafe and wanted to see it for ourselves."

"Did you find out anything?"

"No." She crinkled her nose. "Everything looked pretty normal."

"No women being carted out the back door against their will?" Moretti asked.

Phoebe flinched. "No. Thankfully."

"Well if all you saw was the public view, you likely wasted your time."

"Maybe," Vernon admitted. "At a minimum we eliminated small questions."

"Do you think the location is important enough to make an after dark visit?" Moretti directed his question to Vernon.

"Perhaps," Vernon told him. "But I am willing to wait and see what else we find in that book."

Moretti dipped his head. "Fair enough."

"Did you figure out anything from the list?" Phoebe asked.

"Maybe." Vernon pointed to Moretti's list. "The entry we found about the ball gown does correspond to a disappearance. It's two days off, but that's still pretty close. And..." He shifted the list so they could see the first page. "The other interesting thing is that I think this may be the first time that a woman from a wealthy family went missing."

Phoebe leaned closer to see the list better. "So up to this point the women who went missing were poor or lower class?"

"As far as I can tell." Vernon looked to Moretti. "Do we

know that for certain?"

Moretti took his list back and re-read it. "I believe that is an accurate statement."

"Interesting," Vernon mumbled.

"Does that mean the merchandise listed in the journal represents the women who went missing?" Phoebe asked.

"I think it might," Vernon said grimly.

"Oh, dear." Phoebe drew her hand away from the book. She felt dirty just having held it.

"Are you okay?" Vernon asked.

"I...uh. Yes." She took a breath. "The idea that multiple women and children had been taken from their homes, from their families, didn't seem real before. But now that I have been reading about them over and over without even knowing it. I just..." She wrapped her arms around her middle and walked away.

Vernon handed Moretti the book and followed her. "It's a harsh reality, isn't it?"

She nodded.

"And you're worried about your sister." He didn't bother asking it as a question.

She sniffed. "Yes." She glanced back at Moretti. "I mean if all those women disappeared without being found, what are the chances that Sophia will be?" She couldn't bear the thought that her sister might not be found, safe and sound.

"Better than for those women."

"Why do you say that?" The part that was clinging to the last shred of hope perked up at his words.

"Because we're working on it now. We weren't then."

When she looked up at him, her vision had blurred because of unshed tears. She willed him to tell her everything would be okay even though she knew he couldn't promise that. No matter how much she wanted him to.

She stiffened in surprise when he wrapped his arms around her. But it felt so nice having someone to lean on that she melted against him and returned his embrace. A small voice in the back of her mind reminded her that she shouldn't get used to the feeling because it wouldn't last.

But for a just a moment she wanted to let her guard down and lean on someone. She would be strong again. For her sister. In a minute or two.

She inhaled his scent and committed it to memory. After all, she might not have another opportunity to be this close to him.

He kissed the top of her head. "Some of the entries in that journal are more than a year old. Sophia has only been missing for two days. There is a very good chance we can still find her."

She loosened her hold of him and looked up into his eyes. "And if we can't?"

"Don't think of that. All we can do is focus on here and now." He wiped the tear from her cheek. "Like my grandfather used to say, it's expensive to borrow trouble."

She nodded. "Okay." She took a deep breath. "I'm sorry. I didn't mean to break down."

"Don't be. I'd be more surprised if you hadn't at some point." They both glanced back at Moretti but he had returned to the kitchen. Most likely to give them a bit of privacy. "I should take you back to Casa Bianchi."

She shook her head. "I'm fine. Really. I want to help."

"What if I tell you that I really don't want you here?"

She started to pull away but he held on to her and wouldn't let her retreat.

"What I mean is that we are more than likely going to ride back into town to do more investigating. Which means being in proximity of people who don't want us there and who will kill to protect whatever they are doing wrong. I don't want you to be harmed. It would be safer if you weren't with us."

"But…"

"But my gut says we need the information in that book and right now you're the only one who can give it to us."

She held her breath, afraid to say anything that might make him insist she leave.

He touched her cheek. "I will do everything in my power to protect you. But I need your promise that you will do as I say.

That includes running like the devil is chasing you if I tell you to. Okay?"

She nodded. "All right."

He touched his lips to hers. That gentle kiss both soothed and inflamed her. How did he manage to evoke so many feelings in her when none of the dozens of eligible suiters her mother paraded before her could produce even a spark?

Phoebe slipped her hand into his. She needed to be careful. She enjoyed his embraces far too much. And she was no simpleton to expect any attachment from him. After all, the life he had chosen involved mystery and adventure. She doubted he would even consider taking a wife. And in truth, if he did, she would never be happy being left at home while he traveled the world.

"All right, Moretti," Vernon shouted. "Now that you've driven us all the way out here, what is your plan for getting us back into the game?"

Moretti returned, wiping what appeared to be crumbs from his lapel. "I think we all agree that we need to finish review of the ledger." He took his list from the table, folded it, and slipped it inside the front cover of the ledger. "Then I would like to get a closer look at the cafe. If there is any connection to our den of thieves, I want to know what it is and how deep it goes."

"Agreed," Vernon said with a nod.

"After that, I need to check in with my men down at the docks to see if there have been any recent sightings." Moretti handed the book to Phoebe. "If your sister is newly taken, then they would need some way of transporting her." He raped his knuckles on the table. "Someone should have seen something. It's impossible to move captives through a busy port and not be spotted."

"You would think," Vernon mumbled. "So far no one has or at least they aren't admitting to it."

"That just doesn't make sense," Phoebe said.

"No, it doesn't," Vernon agreed.

"Something definitely stinks about this whole thing and it's aggravating me that I can't find the one clue I need to solve it," Moretti grumbled.

"Standing around here isn't getting the job done," Vernon pointed out.

"Yes, of course." Moretti said. "You're right." He straightened his collar. "Follow me."

Vernon and Phoebe exchanged glances but marched after him. He led them through the kitchen, out a back entrance, to the barn.

"You stole more than one of Romano's horseless carriages?" Vernon asked with just a touch of humor.

"Yes," Moretti said unrepentantly. "But this one isn't his. I won this in a game of cards last week from a gentleman who lives a couple towns over."

"At least you've been staying busy," Vernon mumbled.

Phoebe shook her head. Men, it seemed were fundamentally the same. More than once she had heard her brothers and their friends tease each other in a similar fashion.

She climbed into the carriage when Vernon opened the door for her then settled into the seat while Vernon and Moretti finished discussing details. As before, Vernon climbed in with her while Moretti took the driver seat up front.

He gestured to the journal she still held. "Why don't you keep reading while we head back to town? We agreed that a winding route and arriving from another direction would be the best course of action."

"Seems logical." Phoebe adjusted her spectacles then opened to the page where she had left off. "Do you want me to read you the highlights? Or just let you know if there is anything interesting?"

"Perhaps a little of both. Just let me know what each entry was about and if you see anything of significance, let me know."

"Very well." The next few entries were much like the previous, with the exception of the ball gown. Similar orders had been placed. Similar timings during the month as well as quantities.

"Do you think they might have a limit to how many they can carry at one time?" She asked after giving him the summary.

"Maybe. I'd had much the same thought." He looked at her. "Why do you ask?"

"Well...I'm not sure but it feels like there is some kind of pattern to these entries. I just haven't put my finger on it yet."

"You said it's the same merchandise, right?"

"Yes, but it feels more than that."

"Like what?" he pressed

She shook her head and frowned. "Like it is part of a cycle or something. I don't have more to go on than that, it just feels very...regular somehow."

He nodded. "Don't force the thought. I've found if you let it come on its own you'll figure it out sooner rather than later."

"I guess I can try that," she mumbled. Perhaps he had more success than she when trying to calm wayward thoughts. Most of the time she felt the need to write things down. But that wasn't possible while bouncing along in the back of a coach, at least not one being driven by Moretti.

She summarized another page or two before finding an entry that gave her pause. "Here's another one that includes a ball gown."

"Pass Moretti's list to me." Once she complied, he unfolded the page and asked, "What's the date of that one?"

She read it.

He frowned. "It is close to when a girl from one of the more elite families disappeared."

"That's not good." Her heartbeat sped up as she flipped through the pages to the end.

Vernon put his hand on hers to still her actions. "Don't."

"I need to look."

"You won't find anything about Sophia in there."

She pulled the book away. "You don't know that. There could be something."

"There won't be."

"How do you know that?"

"Because Pereira was killed before your sister was taken. Likely before you even came to Genoa."

"Oh." She deflated. She really needed to find some clue to her sister's disappearance. Even if it horrified her. She needed to know something. Anything. The not knowing was killing her.

"I'm sorry."

"Don't be." She took a breath and stiffened her spine. "It's not your fault."

He grimaced. "Sometimes I wonder."

Her head jerked up so she could see his expression. "Why do you say that?"

"Because I've been here for almost three months and have very little to show for it." He looked out the window instead of at her. "If I had handled this investigation the way I wanted to, instead of adhering to protocol and avoiding any kind of political scandal, your sister might not have been taken."

"How would you have handled it?" she asked quietly.

He drummed his knuckle on the window ledge. "I've had no less than three chances to kill not only Agapito Romano but also his father." He grimaced. "But I didn't."

When he faced her she could see his anger and frustration. Possibly even guilt.

"I was ordered not to take action on anything we found. For the sake of diplomacy and the mission." He told her.

"But if you hadn't followed orders, would you have been able to live with yourself?" she asked quietly.

"Maybe." He grimaced then turned away and looked out the window again. A moment later he added, "No. Probably not."

"Then I'd say you did the right thing." She intertwined her fingers with his. "It can't be an easy thing to take a life."

"No," he admitted. "But I'm willing to bet that neither Romano blinked an eye when they ordered people killed. Or to be ripped from their homes." Anger and indignation burned in his eyes. "And it is likely that Agapito will never spend any time in prison. I'd be surprised if he is even accused of any wrong doing."

"Surely not." The idea that someone could get away from such crimes was unfathomable to her. In her perfect world if you did something wrong, you were caught and punished. But she was realistic enough to know that it wasn't always the case.

"The Romano family has a controlling interest in the biggest bank in Genoa. They own a lot of land because they have foreclosed on people's property. People fear him and what he can do."

"I have to believe that karma will eventually catch up to him."

"God, I hope so."

She let Vernon return to his own thoughts as she read more from the journal. Occasionally she reported what she'd found. Just as she noticed the scenery had changed outside their windows, she asked, "What is a Vallisneria?"

"I believe it's a plant," Vernon told her, after some deliberation. "Why?"

"I'm seeing that word more and more."

Vernon frowned. "Why would Pereira suddenly be supplying them with plants?" He peered over her shoulder at the book. "Where did you see it?"

She pointed out the instances where she had found the word. "The first time was scribbled in the corner of the page. The other times simply state that delivery was expected to be made at Vallisneria." She looked up at him. "Is there a location by that name? Some kind of tavern or shop, perhaps?"

Vernon's frown deepened then he shook his head. "The name doesn't ring any bells."

"Do you think it could be a ship name?"

"I don't know why anyone would—" Vernon blinked and stared off into the distance for a moment. "Son of a—" He beat on the ceiling of the carriage.

The carriage swerved as Moretti slowed their pace. "What's wrong?"

Vernon poked his head out the window. "Phoebe found something."

"Something you wanted me to stop the carriage for?"

"Yes."

Moretti pulled on the break handle, making a loud clicking sound, until the carriage came to a stop. "You do realize that we're almost to town?"

Vernon snatched the book from her then jumped out of the carriage while Moretti climbed down from his perch. Phoebe stuck her head through the door Vernon had left open so she could hear what they were saying.

"What do you know about Vallisneria?" There was a hint of excitement in Vernon's question to Moretti.

Moretti frowned. "Nothing. Why?"

"It's a plant."

Moretti's brow rose. "That better not be the reason you wanted me to stop."

"It is. Just listen." Vernon's gestures became more pronounced in his excitement. "Vallisneria grows in the water."

"So?"

Vernon pointed in her direction. "So Phoebe said it has been mentioned in the notes multiple times. We both think it might be a ship name."

Moretti looked down at the journal to the page they had marked. "I guess that's possible." He didn't sound convinced of the idea. "But I have never seen that name on any of ship registrars. And I've looked through them more than once."

"The unique thing about Vallisneria is that unlike most aquatic plants it grow entirely under water." Vernon looked at Moretti as if waiting for him to react.

Moretti blinked once. Then his face lit up. "I'll be dammed."

 23

EXCITEMENT coursed through Vernon's veins. It happened every time he caught the trail of his quarry. "We've spent days looking for a ship that would hold captives and cargo," Vernon explained to Phoebe. "Maybe even one with special rigging to make it look different somehow. But we never found anything to make us think it might be the ship."

"Were looking in the wrong place?" Phoebe guessed.

"We didn't know exactly what to look for. We were just looking for something different. Something...." Moretti widened his eyes and wiggled his fingers in the air as if trying to look eerie. "Ghostly."

"Ghostly? Why?" Phoebe asked from the carriage.

"There are rumors all over town about a ghost ship," Vernon waved his hands in the air.

"One that slips in and out without anyone seeing it." Now both Moretti and Vernon were over-animated.

"A ghost ship?" Phoebe clearly had no idea what they were talking about.

Moretti pointed at her. "Yes." His voice rang with enthusiasm.

"And you believed that?" Phoebe directed her question at Vernon who was grinning like a loon.

"No, I didn't." Vernon tapped her on the end of her nose. He wanted to kiss her but it was neither the time nor the place for that. "But I do now."

"You can't be serious." She looked at each of them as if they had lost all good sense.

"Oh, but we are," Moretti said.

Both men closed in on her.

163

"It's the perfect way to smuggle people in and out," Vernon said.

"What is?" she asked.

"The Vallisneria," Moretti told her.

Her gaze hoped from one of the men to the other. "You said that was a plant."

"It is," Vernon confirmed

"Well, that's where the name came from anyway," Moretti clarified.

She continued to look between the two of them, as if waiting for one of them to make sense.

"You were right," Vernon accented his words by pointing at her.

"About what?" She asked

"About it being a ship name," Vernon answered, barely containing his excitement.

"It is?" She seemed even more confused.

"Yes," Vernon told her.

Moretti held one finger up. "But not just any ship."

Her brow arched in question.

"A ship that can travel under the water," Vernon said in a hushed voice. Giddiness bubbled inside of him at the notion of what they were likely chasing.

She frowned. "Is there such a thing?"

"Well..." Vernon and Moretti exchanged glances. "We've never actually seen one. But I do know of several scientists and inventors working on the idea. And I've heard that some of them have gotten close to a working model."

Moretti nodded. "That's right. And if someone has actually made that work, it would explain why we haven't been able to find them."

Phoebe turned pale. "Oh, God. That just makes it even more terrifying for those poor women."

"Maybe." Vernon put his hand over hers where it rested on the window ledge of the carriage needing to reassure her. "It's also possible that they have no idea their ship is underwater."

"On larger ships, more than half of the structure is below

deck. Most of which is below the waterline," Moretti reminded her.

"I guess that's true," she admitted.

"We need to get back to town and re-start our search," Vernon told Moretti.

"Agreed. Now that we know what we're looking for."

"Do you though?" Phoebe asked.

"Of course," Vernon said confidently.

Moretti shrugged. "Mostly anyway."

"What are you going to do?" Phoebe asked. "Just hop in the harbor and start walking around under the boats? The water is far too cold for anyone to be out there in it."

"She has a point." Vernon raised a brow. "I'm not planning on swimming at this time of the year."

"What do you suggest we do then?" Moretti asked.

Vernon scratched his head, knocking his hat askew. "If there really is a ship that can maneuver under the water, there must be a way to get on board below the water too, right?"

Moretti shrugged. "We certainly haven't found anything above the water so maybe."

"Then perhaps we should start looking for a way to get down to sea level or below. Where they might be."

"Like under the docks?" Phoebe asked.

"Maybe." Moretti shook his head." But I would think that would be too congested with normal sea traffic. They would risk having a big ship running right over the top of them."

"Where else might they be?" Vernon asked.

"There is a lot of shoreline so the possibilities are plentiful," Moretti said.

"Well, wouldn't it need to be somewhere the water would be deep enough for the ship to still float yet not seen?" Phoebe asked.

"Yes." Moretti drew out his answer.

"That eliminates the shallow parts of the coastline," Vernon said. "Those with beaches."

"It also eliminates any areas that have rocky areas." Moretti shook his head. "I'm not sure what this thing is made of, but I wouldn't want to risk running onto rocks if I were driving it. It's scary enough trying to navigate a normal ship around rocky outcroppings."

"Agreed," Vernon said with a grimace.

"Some of the men at the port could probably help narrow down those options," Moretti told them.

"True." Vernon slapped Moretti on the shoulder. "Let's get to town and start looking for more clues. In the meantime, Phoebe can keep working her way through the journal to see if anything else jumps out at her."

"Agreed," Moretti said.

"Yes," Phoebe smiled. By her expression, she was thrilled to still be included in their plans.

Vernon stepped up into the carriage to ride with Phoebe while Moretti went back to his place at the front. Vernon had barely settled into the seat when it lurched forward.

Phoebe grabbed the side of the carriage. "I guess he's in a hurry?"

"This is the first solid lead we have gotten in weeks."

"I'm not complaining, mind you," Phoebe quickly assured him. "Just surprised by how animated he is."

Vernon shrugged. "I think he's anxious to go home. It is almost Christmas you know."

She tipped her head. "Aren't you anxious to be home for Christmas?"

He shrugged and looked out the window. "I suppose."

"I'm sure your parents would be happy to see you. Your brothers and sisters, too. Right?"

"Perhaps my mother. I doubt my brothers will even notice I'm missing." His pasted a neutral expression on his face before facing her again. "There are seven of us, after all. More now that the eldest have married and come with spouses."

Her eyes widened. "That many?"

He nodded.

"I knew you had a couple of older brothers. And one sister that was close in age to my oldest. Where do you fall in the list?"

"I'm the third son but fifth child. What about you?"

"There are six of us in total. I'm the fourth child."

"You speak fondly of them." He had no idea what a close family would feel like. While he and his siblings got along well enough. Theirs family gatherings were always seemed formal and strained. "Would you be sad if you were unable to spend Christmas at home?"

"Yes. But I would not be able to leave without Sophia no matter what holiday was around the corner." She grimaced. "I can't even begin to imagine what Mother, or Father, for that matter, will do when they learn of her disappearance."

He reached for her hand and squeezed. "Don't give up just yet. Maybe we found the clue that we needed in order to find her."

"I hope so."

He shifted and wrapped an arm around her shoulders and pulled her against his side. He rather liked having her cradled next to him. As a matter of fact, the more time he spent with here the more he liked her. If things had been different, perhaps he would have courted her.

But none of that mattered. He made a commitment to serve. No matter what else happened, he was determined to resolve this case. The women, and families, being torn apart by one man's greed needed help. He wanted to do everything in his power to find justice for them.

How had someone not realized what a wonderful woman she is?

Likely because none of the dandies that haunted the London ballrooms bothered to look beyond the shine of her glasses to see the intelligent woman staring them in the face. More the pity for them.

As tempting as it was to hope that she would still be unmarried whenever he gave up his role in intelligence acquisitions, he would never do that to her. She deserved far better.

 24

MORETTI drove them directly to the villa that he and
Vernon shared. Phoebe appreciated their efforts to make her
arrival as inconspicuous as possible. Once inside, they even
drew all of the curtains so that no one passing on the street
would spot her. Not that she was terribly worried about a
neighbor recognizing her. But then again, she didn't want to
risk embarrassing the Bianchis since they were her hosts.

Vernon even made a spot for her at the desk—complete
with chair, pen, and paper—so she could finish interpreting the
journal.

"I don't suppose it would be possible for me to freshen up
and maybe even make a pot of tea before I get started?" she
asked.

"Yes. Certainly." Vernon left the items on the table he had
been clearing away. "My apologies. I'm afraid we get caught up
in the work and forget that ladies have different needs." He
gestured for her to precede him from the sitting room. "There
is a guest room you can use that has an adjoining wash room.
Will that do?"

She smiled her thanks. "Yes, thank you."

When they reached the door he opened it for her and let
her pass. "I believe there is a comb and brush on the vanity if
you need them. Help yourself to the linens."

She nodded. "Thank you." She took in the space around
her. Much like the room she had been using at the Bianchi villa,
this one had floral patterns on the walls but simple bed
coverings and drapes. Comfortable yet lacking personal
touches.

"I'll go put a pot on for tea and meet you back in the sitting room." He hesitated. "Can you find your way back?"

"I believe so. It wasn't far." She found his concern touching.

"Very well." He lingered. "I wondered—"

"Yes?"

"To hell with it." He muttered as he closed the distance between them. The unexpected kiss he gave her made her toes curl. Her body became flushed with warmth and all thought flew from her head. He slowly ended the kiss but kept his hold of her. If he had let go, she felt certain she would have sagged to the floor in a heap. "I've been wanting to do that all afternoon."

She blinked up at him, torn between the need to kiss him again and to maintain some shred of propriety.

"I should let you freshen up. Otherwise I'll be tempted to forget about this dammed mission and steal you away to my room for the rest of the day. Maybe even two or three."

"I…" Two or three days? Was that even possible?

He jerked his head toward the washroom. "Go."

She bit her lip in order to hold back the yes she wanted to give him. Her sister's life could be at stake. It would be selfish to give in to her desires right now. She took a step back, testing how steady her legs were, then rushed into the washroom. She closed the door and leaned against it to fortify her decision. Only after his footsteps retreated did she make a move to take care of her personal needs.

After washing her face and hands she tidied her hair. Every time she lifted her arm the bandage around her arm pushed against her wound making her wince. If she could have managed it on her own, she would have retied the bandage. Perhaps she could ask Vernon to re-wrap it later.

She started to pinch color into her cheeks as she normally would have but a glance in the looking glass revealed she didn't need to. Her skin was still rosy pink. Likely from the kiss she shared with Vernon.

Just recalling it raised her color even more.

She lingered in the bedroom for a moment in order to

collect herself before returning to the study.

As she made herself comfortable at the writing table in the study, she realized that she was alone in the room. Where might they have gone? Surely they wouldn't leave her here alone. Her pulse quickened as she pondered the possibilities.

Only when Vernon returned carrying a tray with refreshments did it calm again. "Where's Moretti?" he asked.

"I don't know," she said with a shake of her head. "He wasn't here when I returned."

Vernon grunted. He set the tray on the table near her chair. "Help yourself. There is tea as well as meat and cheese. I may know where Moretti disappeared to."

After pouring herself a cup she settled into the chair at the desk. She only managed to read a single page when the men returned. Moretti carried a large roll of paper. Vernon scrambled ahead of him to clear a place at the desk. The roll turned out to be a map.

She tried very hard to pay attention to her own work, but she couldn't help but listen to their conversation as well. They pored over the document pointing our various places of interest. They shared what they knew about the various areas and debated which might hide an underwater ship.

By the time they finished, she had only read another dozen pages. In truth, she didn't recall any groundbreaking information in any of them, but given how often her thoughts returned to Vernon, she couldn't swear that she had been thorough.

"The men can cover these." Moretti set an ashtray on the paper covering several places on the map.

"I can take these." Vernon moved a pen over his picks.

"And I'll take these." Moretti scooted a spoon over his.

"That only leaves this one."

Phoebe got up from her chair and moved to where they were working. "I don't mind taking a look at one if you tell me what I'm looking for."

"Absolutely not," Vernon said emphatically.

Moretti raised a brow at Vernon's outburst, but he didn't

argue.

"Why not?" She asked.

"Because we don't know for certain that you don't fit their list of requirements for the women being taking." He held up one finger. "And…" He held up two fingers. "You've been spotted assisting us. If they are willing to kill us over that journal, they will kill you, too." His gaze dropped to her bandaged arm.

She flinched.

"He's right," Moretti agreed.

"But I want to help," she protested.

"You have already helped us a great deal," Vernon reassured her. "The primary thing you can help with is find to more clues in that book."

"As a point of question, what do you plan to do with her while we go and search these areas?" Moretti asked.

"I hadn't really worked that out," Vernon admitted. "I don't think it would be a good idea to leave her here without us."

"Nor I."

"Excuse me gentlemen, but do I not have some say in this?" She asked.

"But I also don't think it would be a good idea to take her back to the Bianchi villa," Vernon crossed his arms and leaned his hip against the table as he considered her. "Mostly because she knows where we will be looking and I wouldn't put it past her to head there on her own."

"That would be problematic." Moretti also crossed his arms and leaned his hip against the table.

"Did it not occur to the two of you that you're discussing my welfare while I am standing next to you, listening to everything you have to say?" she protested.

Both men acted as if she hadn't said a word.

"Should we tie her to a chair and leave her in the cellar?" Moretti asked.

Her eyes widened in alarm. Surely they were not serious.

Vernon shook his head. "I'm not certain this place isn't being watched."

"True." Moretti unfurled his arms and shrugged. "We may have to take her with us."

Vernon took a deep breath. "I don't see that we have a choice."

Moretti grunted.

Both men looked at her. She crossed her arms and gave them a withering look.

"I suppose you get to come along for another ride," Vernon told her grudgingly.

"So I gathered," she said stiffly.

"Now that I think about it, this may be a bad idea," Moretti interjected. "She's going to stand out like a red flag." He waved his hand up and down in her direction.

Vernon raised one brow. "You just now thought of that?"

"No. But I had dismissed it until now."

"What do you suggest?" Much to her irritation, Vernon asked Moretti instead of her.

"Do you think we could disguise her as a boy?" Moretti asked.

Phoebe's mouth hinged open in surprise.

"I don't suppose you have any trousers you could wear, do you?" Moretti finally asked her directly.

"Certainly not here," she protested.

"I suppose we could borrow something from Armilia," Moretti suggested. "She is probably about the same size as Armilia's son, don't you think?"

"I doubt that." Vernon's frown deepened.

"I think it will be close enough. Why don't you dig up a coat and cap for her to wear? I'll go see about the trousers." Moretti headed for the door, but stopped and gestured at her. "You may need to find a belt for her too."

"Fine." By his tone of voice, Vernon wasn't happy with the idea.

"Oh." Moretti paused at the door. "I may be awhile." He grimaced. "The last time I saw Armilia she became quite cross with me. I suspect I'll have to sweeten her up a bit."

"Since you're heading to the quarter, could you round up a

few of the men in case we need them?" Vernon asked.

Moretti nodded. "Probably a good idea."

Once Moretti disappeared around the corner Vernon reached for Phoebe's hand. He pulled it loose from where she stood defensively. "We didn't ask you first. I know. But despite his lack of tact and diplomacy, I agree with Moretti's plan. I don't want to leave you here unguarded. And I'm not convinced you would be safe with your aunt." He tugged her toward him. "From my perspective, the safest place for you to be is with me. And Moretti. Unfortunately, in order to investigate this clue and hopefully find more, we need to go into areas that proper, young ladies have no business being. Were you to go the way you are dressed now, you would stand out like a beacon in the dark. And that wouldn't help us at all. As a matter of fact, it would make it even more dangerous."

So he was worried about her. He wasn't just trying to tell her what to do. Obviously, he had far more experience in this area than she so perhaps he was right to be worried. Despite her irritation at being largely ignored while decisions were made about her welfare, she didn't want to do anything to change their minds about taking her with them so she bit back the scathing set down she longed to give them both. Instead she regally inclined her head. "I understand."

His eyes narrowed with suspicion. "You do?"

"I have no problem disguising myself if that is what it would take to keep all of us safe."

"Even if that disguise includes trousers?"

She shrugged. "I've never understood why women couldn't wear them anyway. After all, split skirts are becoming more popular. And they're basically wide legged trousers."

He considered her. "I must admit that I'm surprised."

"Why?"

"My mother and sisters would have fainted dead away at the thought of wearing pants."

She shrugged. "Mother thinks I have spent far too much time on the back of horse. And being a practical sort of person, it only makes sense to wear what makes your life easier and more comfortable."

"And safer."

She bobbed her head. "Agreed."

"Good." He took her hand. "Well, while we wait for Moretti, let's see about finding you the other things you'll need."

 25

WITHOUT thinking, Vernon led Phoebe to his room. He didn't realized she had stopped until she asked, "Whose room is this?"

Vernon peered around the door of the armoire he had opened. "Mine. Why?"

"I've never been inside a gentleman's bedroom before." Her eyes darted around the room.

"Never? Not even one of your brothers'?" He couldn't help himself from teasing her.

She all but rolled her eyes. "If we're counting either of them as gentlemen, then I suppose I gave you a false statement."

He grinned. "Are you saying neither of your brothers are gentlemen?"

"Were you always a gentleman to your sisters?"

"Of course I was." He dug through the pile of clothes he had stashed there. "Nothing less would have been acceptable to Father."

"Hmmm." She peered into the armoire.

Holding up the shirt he thought might work he asked, "What do you think of this one?"

She held it against her chest and looked down the front. "It's a little long."

"It should be a little long. The rule of thumb is that it should hit…" He pressed his lips together and shifted uncomfortably.

Her brow arched in question. "Yes?"

Embarrassment had rarely been a problem yet it washed over him like a wave. "Never mind." He couldn't believe he almost told her about the relationship between a man's shirt length and where his genitals hung. His mother would have been mortified.

"Why?"

He waved his hand dismissively. "Just forget it."

For a moment he feared she would argue, but she let it drop.

To change the subject he handed her a pair of trousers. "Let's see what else we can find."

"Those are probably too big."

"Maybe so. But it can't hurt to have options in case Moretti comes up empty handed."

"I suppose that's true."

He handed her a couple more things. "Why don't you try those and see if any will work?"

"All right." She glanced over her shoulder at the bed. "Um..."

He pointed to the open door. "You can use the washroom if that makes your more comfortable."

Her cheeks turned pink. "I don't suppose it matters much. You have already seen me in a state of undress."

"I have." He moved closer and put his hand on her hip. "And I wouldn't mind seeing it again."

Her gaze drifted to his lips. "You wouldn't?"

"Not at all." He lowered his head until their lips were only a heartbeat away." As matter of fact, I would very much like to see all of you. In my bed. With nothing between us."

In a husky whisper she asked, "Nothing?"

The kiss he gave her was light as a feather but it lit a flame within him that if he wasn't careful might burn them both up. "Not a thing."

"I would wager that feels divine."

He fisted his hand in the fabric of her skirt and groaned, "God, how you tempt me."

"I do?" Her body brushed against his, heightening his awareness.

"Indeed." He couldn't resist tasting her lips. Almost immediately, his head swam as if he had been drinking aged whiskey.

He was only vaguely aware of the clothes she had been

holding cascading to the floor. Then her arms circled his waist and she melted against him.

This was what he needed.

Ever since he saw she had been shot. He needed to hold her, to feel her heart beating against his chest. To know that she was indeed well.

He had long-ignored the close calls he's experienced. In his mind, the risk was nothing more than a part of his assignment. But it wasn't for Phoebe. The thought that she came so close to receiving a serious wound, or worse, being killed, did not sit well with him.

Not at all.

"You should push me away," he whispered.

"I know I should." She slid her arms up and wrapped them around his neck. "But I don't want to."

He groaned and drank in her eagerness. Her kisses, while untutored, inflamed him to the point of madness. He knew he shouldn't press his advantage, but damned if he could help it.

She tugged and pulled at his jacket, until he relented and ripped the annoying fabric of and tossed it aside.

Phoebe went to work on the buttons of his vest and shirt while he loosened the ties to her corset.

A moment of clarity crept through his passion-drenched mind. He broke free of her kiss. "Are you sure this is what you really want?"

She blinked up at him. "What?"

"I need you to be certain. We cannot undo this if we take this step." He gestured to her arm. "Not to mention, your injury."

She blinked away the dazed expression she wore. "I want this. And I want it with you." The shy grin she gave him eroded what was left of his doubts. "And to be honest, whenever you kiss me, I don't notice my arm."

Nothing in her tone or expression even hinted at uncertainty. "Then I should probably lock the door."

She nodded.

It only took a few strides to reach the latch. When he turned around the raw beauty of the woman standing in the middle of his room struck him. With her flushed cheeks, mussed hair, and clothing in disarray she was simply breathtaking.

He held her gaze while he crossed the span between them. As he stood before her, he ran his finger across her cheek. "Do you know how beautiful you are?"

She bit her lip and shook her head.

"Very."

He kissed her again and reveled in the way she immediately sank against him. As if she too wanted to touch him everywhere. The way he wanted to with her.

She deserved to be worshped. From the soles of her feet to the top of her head. And everything in between. He wished like hell that he had the time to do so. But that didn't mean that he couldn't make the best use of what time they did have.

Piece by piece, he undressed her. Every time he exposed a patch of skin, he dropped a kiss there. By the time he was finished there was only one place that remained unexplored. And he very much looked forward to kissing her there.

"Lay back on the bed." Her movements were slow and somewhat uncoordinated as she crawled up on the mattress. He loved knowing he was responsible for the dazed look in her eye.

After stripping out of his clothes he joined her on the bed. A strange sense of rightness passed through him when his body made contact with hers. Skin to skin.

Taking care with her injury, Vernon lay on his side and rolled her to face him. She slowly looped her arm around his neck as she stretched forward to meet his lips.

She was soft in all the right places. Her skin felt like satin and held faint traces of some kind of flower.

He slid a hand between them and reached down to touch that place between her legs. She tensed for a second but then relaxed and opened to his explorations. Her hips bucked every time his finger flicked across her sensitive bud.

Anxious to taste every part of her, he dragged his lips across her cheek then down her neck. He nipped her collarbone, then kissed his way down her chest to her bared nipple. The rosy pebble beckoned to him, begging for attention. Attention he was more than happy to supply.

She gasped when his lips closed around it. Her shock quickly turned to murmurs of pleasure as he suckled and teased the tip with his tongue.

As her excitement grew, so too did his. Seeing her experience ecstasy for the first time had been one of the most beautifully erotic things he'd ever witnessed. He longed to see her come apart again.

He inched his way down her belly. Kissing and licking as he went.

When she realized his intent she tried to scoot away. "What are you…"

He halted her movement by gently pressing his hand against her belly. "Shhhh. Let me do this for you."

"But you shouldn't…"

"Yes, I should. I want to taste you everywhere." He grinned as he held her gaze and slowly lowered his mouth to the V between her thighs.

She blinked owlishly at him. "Oh, my."

When his tongue made contact with her sensitive folds she gasped and her head fell back against the mattress. He proceeded to indulge his fantasy of pleasing her beyond her imagination. Her uneven breathing and throaty moans were music to his ears.

He slowly pushed one finger into her channel to prepare her for what was to come. By the time she found her pleasure he was more than ready to bury himself inside of her. The last thing however, that he wanted to do was hurt or overwhelm her.

After kissing his way back up her belly and chest he cradled her against his body until her breathing returned to something close to normal.

"That's such a wondrous thing." She smiled up at him with a dreamy expression on her face. "It's no wonder people do crazy things to be with their lovers."

"Oh, sweetheart." He chuckled. "There's so much more for you learn."

She blinked. "More?"

He rolled onto his back and pulled her astride him.

"What...?" Phoebe's confused expression quickly turned into one of interest. She bit her lip as she found her balance atop his hips. In a whisper she asked, "Would you consider it very naughty of me if I confessed that I had read about women being able to take their lovers from on top?"

"Not at all." He gripped her waist and edged her into a more comfortable position for both of them. "And what did you think when you read that?"

Her cheeks were already slightly pink from her previous exertion but his question spread a darker pink flush across her face and neck. "I couldn't quite figure out the mechanics of it." She wiggled her hips as if testing her abilities in this new position. "But it did intrigue me."

"Good." Prior to her confession he wouldn't have thought his erection could get any harder. He was wrong. "Perhaps you would like to give it a try."

"You will help me, won't you?"

She was the perfect blend of innocent virgin and temptress and it was driving him mad. "You can count on it."

He didn't think it possible but she glowed with anticipation. "What do I do?"

"Lift up on your knees a bit."

When she did he aimed his erection at her opening. The slick remnants of her previous release coated him, letting him slid inside of her with relative ease. Her eyes widened with wonder and discovery. As soon as he felt the barrier of her innocence, he halted her movement.

A tiny V formed in the center of her brow and she tensed as if sensing something amiss.

Through gritted teeth he asked, "I assume you know this might hurt? I've been told it is only a brief pain though."

She nodded.

Sweat beaded on his forehead from fighting the urge to

drive into her willing body and reach his pleasure. "Lean forward and kiss me."

She did as he asked. As soon as their lips touched, he devoured them. He was riddled with need for her and since he couldn't yet slake it he found a way to distract them both. When he felt the tension drain from her he surged his hips upward, breaking through the thin membrane that had been her virginity.

She winced and sucked in a breath.

"I'm sorry," He whispered against her lips. "It's done. It will only be pleasure again from here out. I promise."

He may have said a few nonsensical things about how beautiful she was and how much the moment meant to him, but his brain couldn't think of anything except the fact that he was now embedded inside of her. And how he needed to release some much-pent up tension.

With a quick flip he reversed their positions.

He bent so he was able to take one of her nipples into his mouth. He suckled and teased the pink tip while he slipped one hand between them. He found the tiny nub that would once again bring her to pleasure and worked it back and forth until he re-built her desire. When he felt certain she was nearing the peek he told her, "Wrap your legs around my hips."

The new angle allowed him to sink deeper into her heat then set a rocking pace that worked for both of them. Blood pounded in his ears as he drew closer and closer to the pinnacle.

When she tensed beneath him, he quickened his pace and let himself go.

It wasn't until his brain began working again that he realized that he was still holding on to her. But somehow, it felt right. Unlike any of his previous lovers, he didn't have the urge to spring out of bed.

Unfortunately, they would have no choice about that before long. Moretti and the men would arrive and plans needed to be made.

But for now, he was content to hold her for as long as he

could.

 26

PHOEBE couldn't believe one person could make her feel so much. Every poem or story she had read that described le petite mort fell short in their descriptions. She would have sworn that she had burst apart into a million pieces of bliss only to be remade whole again.

But was she still the same? She couldn't answer that with certainty.

All she knew for sure was that it felt positively divine to lay in the circle of Vernon's arms and listen to the sound of his heart beating inside his chest. No matter what else happened she wanted to remember this. The warmth of his skin. The way he smelled. And how safe she felt.

For the first time since her sister disappeared, she felt a measure of peace. He had done that for her. But as much as she wanted to stay in the cocoon of his arms, she knew she couldn't.

She let out a long sigh.

"Your mind is awfully busy."

She lifted her head. "Was I thinking out loud again?"

He chuckled. "Not literally. But I can tell from the change in your breathing that you've regained use of your faculties."

"Ah." She lay her head back on his chest. "You know I still need to try those clothes on, don't you?"

This time he sighed. "Yes, I know."

"You could help me, you know," she said suggestively. Lord. Did the fact that she wanted him to keep touching her mean that she had she turned wanton?

"I could?"

The small patch of hair in the center of his chest tickled her nose when she nodded. "Mm-hmm. And I wouldn't have to worry about explaining why my corset was uneven if you helped me with it."

He lay still for a moment before responding. "I don't think I've helped a lady into a corset before."

"Then it will be good for you to practice." She grinned at him. "And I'd like to be dressed before your friends arrive."

He nodded. "That would probably be best."

When she sat up she realized she had a few aches in new places. "I should probably clean up a little before getting dressed."

His head rolled to the side and he looked directly at her. "Do you want me to run a bath for you?"

"No, I can manage." She stroked his chest. "Thank you though."

He took her hand from his chest and kissed her palm. That simple gesture did funny things to her heart. She swallowed the lump that suddenly formed in her throat. "I will be back in a moment." She slid from the bed and hurried to the safety of the bathing room. She pulled a towel from the shelf and wrapped it around her middle. After turning on the water in the sink, she sank on the edge of the tub and dropped her head into her hands.

What was she doing?

She might have no regrets about being intimate with Vernon but what should she do now? How was she expected to behave? She needed to be careful and not place too much importance on what they had done. It was extremely likely that he did not feel the same about their encounter. After, he was a man. Men were expected to have sex many times over before marriage. Sowing their wild oats, as her father often said of her brother.

She was likely just one out of a dozen or more women he fell into bed with.

A tiny voice whispered that she might be wrong. She gently pushed that voice to the back of her mind. Even if by some chance he did feel some level of feeling for her the likelihood of them having a chance to be together was small.

He was busy traveling the world, protecting the Queen's interests.

And she…

Well she would be expected to marry a sensible titled gentleman and raise babies. Why set herself up for disappointment in thinking that perhaps someday he might be that sensible titled gentleman?

Besides, all of her confusion and angst over a man didn't help get her sister back. That was what was important. That was what she should focus on.

She washed her hands in the warm water and splashed some on her face. Since her bandage had become twisted during their lovemaking, she untied it and cleaned the wound with a fresh linen. Then used another to clean the rest of herself.

When she looked in the mirror she reminded herself, "You can do this. Find Sophia. Get her home safely."

There would be time to sort her feelings about Vernon later.

With the towel still wrapped around her middle she returned to the bedroom. Vernon had donned a pair of trousers and was sorting through the clothing they had left scattered on the floor.

"We did make a bit of a mess, didn't we?" She bent to retrieve her discarded shift.

His face brightened when he faced her. "We did." He put his hand in the small of her back and pulled her close. "And I would do it again." He dropped a gentle kiss on her lips.

Phoebe's insides warmed and her knees went weak.

He really was an excellent kisser. Not that she had a lot of experience in that area.

"Not that I have any complaints about you wearing that towel, but you should probably find something that covers all of you." He kissed her again. "If you don't I'll be tempted to keep you're here all night."

"All night?"

"Indeed."

He kissed her one more time. Just enough to make her

thoughts scatter.

His gaze dropped to her injury when he pulled away. "How is your arm?"

"It still hurts but I think it will be fine."

"I'll get you a fresh bandage just to be sure." When he returned from the washroom, he spread salve on the open wound then wrapped it with a new strip of linen. Without the hindrance of her dress sleeve he was better able to cover it.

After tending to her injury, he helped her sort through the rest of the clothes. She wasn't certain, but she strongly suspected that he helped her in and out of the clothes far more than was truly necessary. Not that she minded. By the time they finished she was ready to fling herself into his bed and demand that he make the needy feeling that had built inside of her go away.

But she remained strong. She had to. For Sophia.

After trying all of the clothes, including the items Moretti returned with, they settled for a serviceable dress Moretti had procured. Phoebe refrained from asking where he had obtained it. As long as it was clean and the disguise worked, she was satisfied. Coupled with the shawl Vernon had purchased for her the day before covering her head, Vernon and Moretti agreed she could pass for a seamstress or maid.

While they waited for the last man to arrive, the men armed themselves and readied their weapons. Vernon let her know he had sent a note to Signor Bianchi informing him she was safe despite the attacks and how she would not return for dinner.

Phoebe made a concerted effort to slip back into the mindset of their previous relationship status. Remembering what it was like to simply be friends was harder than she expected. She knew what his hands felt like on her bare skin. She also knew how he kissed. And she wanted more of both.

Oh, lord. She was becoming a hussy.

After the last man arrived, they gathered around the dining room table to brief all of the men on their objective and to work out their plan.

Since the places they wanted to investigate were spread

along the coast, Moretti and Vernon divided them between the men so that everyone only needed to check three apiece. They all agreed to meet at the final location even if the ship in question was found. It would be foolish—and very likely suicide—to attempt a rescue operation without assistance.

Under the cover of darkness, and taking care to spread out their departures, they all headed to their assigned destinations.

Vernon insisted Phoebe remain with him. It both thrilled and worried her. She could keep up her charade of being nothing more than friends as long as she kept her head. Focusing on her sister helped temper her wayward feelings about Vernon.

When they had finished inspecting their locations, Vernon hailed a hackney. He had a driver drop them near their destination so as to not draw attention to their entry. Like the other locations, they walked the remaining distance.

"I don't see Moretti or the others anywhere," Phoebe whispered as they drew closer.

"Nor I."

"What should we do?"

"It's late. The watch should be making rounds before long. I think we can at least check the exterior of the building while we wait."

As with the previous locations, they pretended to be a romantically involved couple out for a stroll. Phoebe was thrilled to be included in the search. And it was enlightening to see Vernon at work. Truth being told, she also enjoyed having an excuse to be in Vernon's arms. He swung her around, as if the two of them were dancing to their own music when in reality, he searched the area for clues. Every time he needed to take a longer look at something he whispered into her ear, sending goosebumps down all of her limbs.

It wasn't hard to play her part of the receptive love interest. So easy, in fact, that she felt certain her cheeks were flushed and her eyes glazed, with absolutely no effort on her part. Despite her repeated reminders that so long as he worked for the RIO, he was unlikely to become involved with anyone.

"Perhaps we should return to the villa," he told Phoebe. "I don't see anything unusual here."

"But we haven't looked inside any of these buildings or below them. How can you be sure?"

"I'm not. But my gut says we should leave."

She wrapped her uninjured arm around his back, snuggling closer to his side. "Why?"

"I can't really say."

From the corner of her eye Phoebe caught movement near a stack of crates. She tensed, which drew Vernon's attention.

He shifted, putting her behind him, then his stance relaxed. "It's Moretti."

"Did you find anything?" Vernon asked as they drew close to where Moretti hid.

"No," Moretti grumbled.

"What took so long then?'"

"A couple of Romano's men managed to corner me. Took longer to deal with them than I care to admit." Moretti touched a fresh cut he had received above his eye.

"Are you all right?" Phoebe asked.

"Uh...Yes," Moretti seemed surprised by her show of concern. "I'm fine." Almost as an afterthought he mumbled, "Thank you."

"Good," she said. "Now what?"

"I checked the piers and didn't see anything unusual," Moretti reported. "Dante was going to walk a little farther around the cove. Fabio is keeping watch near the main gate."

Vernon said, "As far as I can tell they have three primary entrances to this main building. The smaller, most obvious one at the front, a large bay door on the back, and a slightly smaller bay door next to the big one."

"Would the big one admit a carriage?" Moretti asked.

"I would say so, yes."

"Let's go see what kind of locks they use and if any are open," Moretti suggested.

The three of them headed to the back. The men flanked her on each side. While she was flattered they both wanted to protect her, she worried they would be the next one to get shot. Wasn't it strange how your perspective changed when you cared deeply about someone else's wellbeing?

Vernon checked the area near the bay doors before drawing close to it. "That's a fairly simple lock."

"What about the smaller one?" Moretti asked.

Before Vernon could protest, Phoebe checked the other lock. "Same. As a matter of fact, it's may be identical. But it's not locked."

"Does that make anyone else uncomfortable?" Moretti mumbled.

"A little," Vernon admitted. "But we still need to know what's inside."

She waited with Vernon while Moretti peeked through the door before entering. Once inside, Moretti let them precede him. Vernon, took the lead. Moretti brought up the rear.

The further they went the more Phoebe's heart beat against her chest. It wouldn't have surprised her if Vernon could hear it "If the building was left unlocked, shouldn't there be guards?"

"You would think," Vernon said.

"I don't like it," Moretti grumbled said from his place in the shadows.

They split up, and slowly made their way around the perimeter of the building. With every step, Phoebe expected someone to intercept them. When they met Moretti on the other side of the room, they all had similar expressions of confusion.

"Are we in the wrong place?" Phoebe asked.

"No. This was definitely on the list," Vernon reassured her.

"But there's no one here," she pointed out. "Not even a guard like we found at the other places we checked."

"I know." Vernon frowned. "Something feels off here."

"I agree," Moretti said. "Perhaps we should—"

A clang of metal echoed around the room then a section of wall began sliding to the left.

"Hide." Vernon grabbed Phoebe's hand and pulled her

behind a crate, while Moretti scrambled for cover near another stack.

Footsteps echoed through the room as a group of well-armed men filed out of what had previously been an unnoticed door.

Phoebe barely contained her gasp when she spotted Romano in the center of the group.

He barked out orders to the men to bring his carriage around. To the man hovering closest to him, "I want to know as soon as the last one is found. We're overdue as it is. I don't want to hold up the departure any longer than necessary."

"Of course not, sir."

"And make sure you tell the captain I expect a full accounting when he returns. There had better not be any mishaps this time."

"Yes, sir."

All of the men filed out of the warehouse. The door slammed closed behind them with a clang.

After the room fell silent Vernon peeked from behind their hiding place. He gestured to Moretti something about the secret door.

Moretti nodded enthusiastically.

It seemed they both wanted to go through the door. Just as they neared it, the door clanged again. Vernon and Moretti leapt in different directions. Vernon pulled her with him and pressed against the wall next to the door.

Two more men marched out. Vernon signaled to Moretti which two he would take. The two of them knocked the guards out, stripped their weapons, and dragged them into a dark corner. They used the men's clothes to bind and gag them. She was amazed by how well they worked together. She would have never guessed they had only been working together for a few months.

At the secret door, Vernon peered around the edge. The only thing she could see was a steep metal ramp. Cold air billowed up from below along with the tangy smell of saltwater.

Hope flared.

"Anyone want to make bets about whether we find a boat at the bottom of this ramp?" Moretti asked.

Vernon mumbled, "I'd say that's a fairly safe bet."

 27

THE passage wasn't bright. The small faintly glowing lanterns on the walls only put off enough light to allow them to see where they were going. Vernon pulled a pair of green-tinted spectacles from one of his pockets and put them over his eyes. He adjusted the dial on the side and brought more of the space into focus. Moretti followed suit, wearing his own pair of after-dark spectacles.

Vernon gestured for Moretti to go ahead of them then took Phoebe's hand and whispered, "Stick close but remember, if I tell you to run, you run. Preferably whichever way is out."

She nodded.

Ever cautious, they followed the path downward. When they reached the bottom their path changed from metal ramp to moss covered rock. The moss had been trampled enough that there was little doubt they were headed in the right direction. Before the rock path split.

"Should we each take a path?" Moretti asked.

"No. I think that's one of the worst things we could do right now." Vernon flicked his head at the passages. "Pick one," he told Moretti.

Moretti pointed.

"Okay," Vernon gestured for him to go ahead. "We'll check this one first then the other." They followed the passage to a darkened room that had been stacked shoulder high with crates.

"I'm dying to know what is in these," Moretti mumbled.

"Maybe there will be time after we finish looking for the ship."

They back tracked their steps and followed the other

passage. The further they went, the brighter the tunnel became until they no longer needed their glasses. At the end, a weatherworn wood pier came into view. A metal, cylinder-shaped ship floated next to the pier. The three of them hovered in the shadows, pressed up against the wall of the cavern while they assessed the situation.

"Do you see any guards?" Vernon whispered.

"No. And I don't like it," Moretti whispered back.

"Me either. That's a long span of open space to reach the boat. Suggestions?"

Moretti leaned forward and checked the space overhead. "As far as I can see we only have one choice. There's nothing above us except rock. I doubt we could get under the walkway for at least ten meters and that would mean getting into the water." Moretti's gaze swung back to Vernon. "I don't know about you, but I'd rather not take an ice bath."

"Agreed. Any trip wires or alarms of any kind?" Vernon asked.

"Not that I've noticed."

Both men frowned.

"I guess we just have to risk it," Moretti said.

"I guess so." Neither man sounded enthusiastic about the idea.

"What do you want me to do?" Phoebe asked.

"I'd like to tell you to go back upstairs but that's really not an option," Vernon grumbled.

"You said she's an ace shot?" Moretti asked.

"She is." While her skill with a revolver impressed him, he hoped she wouldn't be forced to use it.

"Perhaps if we stationed her somewhere out of immediate sight, she could cover our backs and warn us if anyone comes in while we're boarding?"

"But who will protect her back?" Worry for her safety made Vernon's gut clench.

"I'll be fine." Phoebe patted Vernon's arm but it did little to reassure him.

"I don't like it," Vernon frowned even more.

"I want to help. My sister might be on that ship."

"I know. Which is why you need to stay well away from it." Vernon gestured to the ship in frustration.

"But—"

Vernon cut her off with a harsh whisper. "I don't like putting you in danger."

"But you're fine with putting yourself in danger?" Her question echoed in the alcove where they hid.

He leaned closer. "I don't think you understand. This is what I am here to do."

"Hey." Moretti interrupted them. "Can the two of you save your argument until after the honeymoon? We need a plan for getting onboard."

Honeymoon? Images of Phoebe in a white dress with a bouquet of flowers popped into his head. It was followed quickly by one of her sitting on the edge of his bed wearing only her shift, brushing out her hair. "Yes." Vernon cleared his throat and forced the images to the back of his mind. "Of course."

"Phoebe, why don't you follow us up the boarding ramp?" Moretti suggested. "Once we're on board, go around to the other side." He pointed to the area he meant. "Find an out of the way spot where you can see us but are unlikely to be seen by any guards they might have."

"Okay." She nodded. "I can do that."

Vernon didn't care for the plan but since he had no other argument he didn't say more.

With weapons drawn, the three of them quietly made their way aboard the ship. When they reached the top of the ramp Moretti gestured for Phoebe to move around the center part of the ship. She glanced back at Vernon before rounding the turn. "Be careful," she mouthed to him.

If he thought for a moment that the worry he saw in her eyes had been for herself he would have demanded she stay with them. Knowing Phoebe all of her fear was for him and her sister, not herself. "You too."

He waited until she disappeared around the bend to join

Moretti at the door.

"You ready?" Moretti whispered.

Vernon gave him a nod.

The door groaned as they swung it open heightening Vernon's tension. The narrow passage they found themselves in only went left or right.

"Are you back so soon?" A man said from one of the rooms to their left.

Vernon and Moretti hurried to that door. Moretti jerked the man through the open doorway into the passage while Vernon kept an eye out for more guards. Moretti incapacitated the guard who had been napping on the bunk in that room. For good measure, they bound and gagged both guards and left them where they wouldn't immediately be spotted. Vernon closed the door as they left and he and Moretti moved farther down the passage. They crossed paths with another man. This one was far easier to overtake, making Vernon wonder if he might have been a scientist or navigator rather than security.

They moved quickly and quietly, using hand signals to communicate. Lower and lower they descended through the ship, checking every door and every room they passed. By the time they reached the third level, Vernon wondered if they weren't on a fool's errand.

"Over here." Moretti's ominous tone immediately caught Vernon's attention.

He swiveled on his heel to see what Moretti had found. His partner had crouched next to a metal gate that covered an opening in the floor. Vernon's heart leapt in excitement and fear of what they might find inside.

"I have never seen anything like this." Moretti tapped the lock that secured the gate. "There's no place to put a key." He looked up at Vernon. Do you think they mean to cut the lock when they reach their destination?"

Vernon squatted next to Moretti. When he did, he would have sworn the shadows moved in the darkness below the gate. He peered at the lock then smiled. "Actually, no. I have seen this kind of lock before." He moved closer so he could flip the mechanism around the way he needed. "It's a keyless lock. They probably chose it so that anyone on the ship could open it without keeping track of a key. It works around this bolt here." He pointed to the knob situated below the lock's arch. "Let me see if I can remember how to open it." It took several tries but he finally managed it.

Once the lock was out of the way they raised the grate and peered down into the dark. Vernon cursed under his breath when he saw how many women and children were detained in there.

Those closest to the opening cautiously moved away as Vernon used the metal rungs to descend into the dark. Fear stained every face he saw.

He prayed that whoever was responsible for this would pay dearly.

"Ladies, we're here to rescue you," Vernon assured them. "But I need for you to remain calm and quiet as we get you out of there."

His statement only generated a few whispers and muffled sobs. An older woman, likely someone's mother or grandmother, boldly asked, "How do we know you do not lie?"

"I have no way to prove that to you other than to walk away and leave this door unlocked."

Many of the women and girls looked to the same woman for guidance.

"Oh, but one thing," Vernon switched from Italian to English. "I'm looking for Sophia Ashdown. Sophia, if you're in here, Phoebe sent me to find you."

There was a gasp, followed by a broken sob. The crowd in one corner moved as Sophia pushed her way to the front. "Mr. Bennett. Is…" She stammered. "Is it really you?"

"Yes." Vernon motioned her forward. "Come. We don't have much time."

"Oh, thank God." Tears streamed down Sophia's dirt stained cheeks. She turned to face the women. In Italian, she told the others, "I know him. He is a friend to my sister. I believe he really is here to free us."

There was a gasp of relief from the group. Finally, the women began to get up. Those with children grabbed pulled them into their arms and began moving toward the hatch.

"The man at the top is my partner, Mr. Moretti. Do as he says, okay, Sophia?"

She nodded then Vernon helped Sophia up the metal rungs. Moretti assisted her when she reached the top.

When all of the women and children were out, Vernon climbed up. The room at the top was very near to bursting. "We need to go up two levels to get off this ship. Moretti will lead the way. Stay together and make as little noise as possible since we don't know who else might be aboard."

There were murmurings of agreement from many but others simply stood mutely, waiting for one of the other ladies to show them what to do.

Their filthy clothes and hollow faces fueled Vernon's temper. Someone needed to pay for this.

Sophia waited as the other women trailed after Moretti. She tugged at Vernon's sleeve then whispered, "Did Phoebe really send you? Is she all right? What about Aunt Gladys? Were they taken too?"

Vernon motioned her ahead of him. "Phoebe is fine. She is waiting for us on deck."

"Why did you bring her here?" Sophia's voice squeaked as it rose, forcing Vernon to shush her.

"I'll let her explain that when we get out of here." Seeking to offer her some sort of reassurance, he added, "You should know that we would not have found you without her help."

Sophia pressed her fist to her mouth and stifled her sob. "This really is happening, isn't it? We really are going home?"

"I sure hope so," Vernon muttered. "We have a few obstacles to get past first."

"Hey! What are you—"

Vernon turned to confront the man had who snuck up behind them. He threw a small knife and hit the man in the chest.

Sophia gasped. Vernon grabbed her hand and turned her

away. "Don't look."

Her slight form shuddered but she complied. At least it stifled her flow of questions. Somehow their group managed to make it all the way to the top without another incident. When they reached the top level Moretti held everyone at the door. Vernon pushed his way to the front of the line of people. "What's wrong?"

Moretti jerked it head toward the door. "We have company."

"Damn."

The women around them gasped and a few began to sob. The woman who had spoken before joined them. "What is it? Why do we wait?"

Vernon and Moretti exchanged looks. Vernon shrugged.

Moretti told her, "There is a group of men blocking the pier. They didn't come with us so they must be part of the group that took you all."

The woman let out an expletive that made both men's brows rise. "What weapons do we have?"

"Only the few we carried. Even if we had more, who amongst you knows how to use them?"

"I can shoot," She told them with a lift of her chin. "I also know how to wield a knife."

Moretti gestured to the first room they had entered. "There are two men tied up in the corner in there. We didn't take the time to strip them of any weapons. You're welcome to any that you find."

She pushed her way back thought he crowd and disappeared into the room.

"So what do you think?" Vernon asked.

"Since neither of us can operate this ship, we only have one exit. It's simply a matter of how you want to play it."

"Guns blazing versus polite diplomacy?"

"Exactly." Moretti smirked. "You know which way I'd vote."

Vernon snorted. "Perhaps we could come up with a compromise?"

"I knew you'd say that," Moretti grumbled.

"How about if I go out first?" Vernon suggested.

"You just want to see where your lady friend is."

"Of course, I do." He shrugged. "She may once again be the ace up our sleeve."

"We'll see," Moretti said hopefully.

28

ANTICIPATION surged through Vernon's veins. But the thrill of an upcoming fight was tempered by fear. Strangely enough, his fear was for Phoebe instead of himself. He regretted ever letting her leave his sight. It was killing him to not know if she was safe.

"Did you find anything you could use?" Moretti asked the woman leading the victims when she returned.

She held up a pistol and a knife. "I found a few things."

"You do know how to use that, don't you?" he asked.

"Yes, of course. My husband taught me well." She shrugged. "Much to his embarrassment."

Moretti snickered.

"I'm going out to assess the situation." Vernon told her. "Moretti will stay with you until I signal. Ideally we would like to take out all of those men. But based on sheer numbers, they have the advantage over the three of us. And I highly doubt they will hesitate to kill any of us."

"Understood." She nodded. "I am no weak-kneed female and I will not hesitate to shoot any of them for what they have done."

"Then we understand each other," Vernon told her. He looked at Moretti. "You know my signals."

Moretti nodded once.

Vernon stepped cautiously through the door. His eyes darted around the cavern, searching the shadows for any hidden threats as well as for Phoebe.

As before, Romano lingered in the midst of his men. The coward. "Signor Bennett." Romano's shout echoed around the cavern. "What ever are you doing aboard my ship?"

Vernon made an exaggerated inspection of both sides of the ship where he stood. "My apologies. Is this yours?"

"It is." Romano still hadn't moved from his group of men. "Perhaps you could tell me how you came to be here?"

"Well…" Vernon stepped toward the railing to get a better view of the length of the ship. He very much needed to know if anyone waited above or along the sides. "A friend of mine contacted me a couple of days ago. She was distraught because her sister had disappeared."

"Why would this friend reach out to you, Signor Bennett?"

"Because I was one of the few people she knew in Genoa."

Romano wagged his finger at Vernon. "I think that is perhaps not the only reason."

Vernon shrugged and chuckled. "I'd like to think it's because I'm a charming gentleman." He smiled his best smile. "But that could just be me making assumptions."

A couple of Romano's men scoffed.

Vernon paced back to the door and signaled to Moretti behind his back that there were two men hidden on the dock, just below the ship's ramp. He still had not spotted Phoebe however and his worry only grew.

"I admit that I wondered about you when we met at the party. You don't strike me as a typical tradesman."

"I don't know whether to be flattered or insulted, Signor Romano."

"It is no matter." He gestured Vernon forward. "Why don't you come down from there and we will discuss this as gentlemen?"

"Or you could come up?" Vernon suggested. "Without your men, of course. After all, gentlemen have no need for armed guard."

"That's not really an option."

"Then I believe we are at a stalemate, Signor Romano."

"Are we?" Romano held his hands out. "The way I see it, you have no way out except through us. And, unless I am mistaken, you are sadly out numbered."

"That's partly true. We do however have control of your

ship. We could simply put it out to sea."

Romano's cocky grin faltered a bit.

"And are you certain that I am outnumbered?" Vernon raised his hand as he asked the question. "And how do you know we do not have men en route as we speak? I could be stalling simply to allow them time to arrive."

As intended, his questions caused several of Romano's men to cast worried glances behind them.

"Perhaps if you and your men were to stand aside and allow us to leave without incident, we could all go back to whatever we were doing before this," Vernon suggested.

"I'm afraid that I cannot allow that, Signor Bennett."

"Well..." Vernon leaned against the wall. "I'm prepared to wait. Are you?"

"Enough of this nonsense." Romano gestured to someone to his left. "Rocco, bring the girl."

Vernon tensed. There was a scuffle off to his right then his deepest fear was realized. A man holding Phoebe by the arm steered her into view. At least she was still aboard the ship.

"Unhand me you oaf." Phoebe winced as she tried to jerk her arm free, but the man refused to relent.

"Phoebe!" Sophia tried to launch herself out of the doorway, but Moretti jerked her back inside to safety. "Let me go!" Sophia sobbed and struggled against Moretti's hold.

"Sophia just stay there," Phoebe called out then she pointed at Romano. "It was you that took her, you bastard!"

Romano chuckled.

"Let her go," Phoebe demanded.

"I see no reason why I should." Romano stepped forward. "Unless you want her killed, I suggest that you and your friends do as I say and come down from my submersive before I lose what is left of my patience."

"No." Vernon was jostled to one side when the woman in charge of the captives barreled through the door with her gun raised. She fired at the men below. They scattered like rats.

Vernon looked up in time to see Phoebe pull her knife out and stab the man who held her in the thigh and make a run for it. The man grabbed his leg but before he could level his gun at her, Vernon let his own knife fly. The blade caught the man in the chest making him drop his weapon. Bullets flew as Moretti joined the woman at the railing. The two of them fired shots while Vernon sprinted toward Phoebe. He provided cover as best he could until Phoebe reached him. "I've got to help Moretti," Vernon told her. "Stay here."

Vernon pushed her into an open doorway and slammed the door shut on her protest. He pulled his extra gun from his pocket, took cover behind a post, and fired at the men below the ship's ramp.

After what seemed like an eternity the gunfire stopped. Vernon looked toward Moretti to check how they fared. Moretti squatted next to the woman and inspected her shoulder. When Moretti met Vernon's questioning gaze he nodded once. Vernon prayed that meant she was fine. Or, in this case, perhaps just a minor injury.

The door he had shoved Phoebe through opened part way. Vernon held up a finger to caution her to wait a moment longer before coming out.

She angled her head and looked toward Moretti and the woman.

Vernon eased his way around the column to get a better look at the dock and the men below.

Unless he was very much mistaken, most of Romano's men had deserted him. Romano had collapsed against a barrel on the dock. Blood oozed through his fingers where he grasped a wound to his neck.

Based on how much red had stained Romano's shirt, Vernon's suspected the man didn't have long to live. There were a few other injured men lying about the dock, but they were obviously in no hurry to help Romano.

"I'm going to go down," Vernon mouthed to Moretti. Moretti nodded once as he finished reloading his gun.

Vernon added a few bullets to his own gun, then headed to the gangplank. He kept his eye on Romano as he made his way down the ramp in case it was a ruse. When he drew close,

Vernon kicked Romano's gun out of reach. He hovered over Romano as he assessed the wounds. Every time Romano drew breath, a larger spurt of blood oozed between his fingers.

"Tell me, Romano. Was it worth it?"

Romano's glazed expression cleared for a moment when he looked up at Vernon. "Was what worth it?"

"All of it. The money, the killing. Ripping families apart. All of those deals that eroded a little more of your soul."

"You would…" Romano wheezed and gasped for breath but it gained him little. "You would think so." Finally, Romano's wheezing stopped and his head lolled to the side.

It was hard to feel sorry to someone who spent most of his adult life destroying other people's lives. Yet still. Vernon couldn't help but think about the fate that awaited Romano on the other side. It couldn't be pleasant. If there was any justice, it wouldn't be.

A shot rang out startling Vernon. He crouched in a defensive position as he scanned the area for the threat.

"I recommend that you do not do that." Phoebe stood at the top of the ramp with her gun pointed at one of Romano's men.

The would-be attacker must have crawled out of his hiding place while Vernon wasn't looking. The man dropped the weapon that had likely been pointed at Vernon and ducked his head. Once again, if it hadn't been for Phoebe watching his back, he might have been shot.

Phoebe gestured for the man to move away from the crates toward Vernon.

"Get down on your knees. Lock your fingers together behind your head," Vernon ordered.

The man grumbled under his breath.

"Those had better be nice things that you're saying or I'll have her shoot you. Just enough to make it hurt but not actually kill you." Vernon leaned closer and whispered. "She doesn't like to kill people but now that she has seen what was done to her sister, she will probably make an exception."

The man finally complied.

Vernon took the man's weapon then gave Phoebe a thumbs-up to let her know he was all right. She pointed off to the right. "I think there's another one over there."

He nodded and hurried to see what she had noticed. He found another guard. This one however had been shot in the shoulder. The injury wasn't life threatening, but probably did make him re-think his participation in Romano's scheme.

Once he was certain there were no other immediate threats, he signaled Moretti to come down. Together they checked the area to confirm it was safe.

"We have three dead and four wounded." Moretti shrugged. "It looks like the others ran off."

"I saw several make for the exit when the shooting started."

"They weren't terribly reliable bodyguards," Moretti mumbled. "Guess Romano didn't buy their loyalty after all."

Vernon snorted. "Guess not." He gestured for Phoebe to come down. "It's clear."

Phoebe motioned for the women hiding behind the closed door to come out. Sophia burst through the door and launched herself at Phoebe.

Seeing the sisters reunited even made Moretti's countenance soften.

Two of the women stopped to help their leader as she slowly made her way to the ramp.

Vernon and Moretti went to lend their assistance. He couldn't stop himself from dropping a kiss on Phoebe's hand as he helped her from the ramp. Once all of the victims made it to the dock, Vernon asked the leader, "Is that everyone?"

Her gaze bounced on each of the faces around them. "It appears so."

One of the women helping her added, "There's not a single one of us that wants to stay here, Signor."

"I wouldn't think so but that many gunshots can make even trained soldiers freeze."

"Once we get everyone to safety I'll bring a group of men back and make a sweep of the area," Moretti told him.

"I hope you'll also consider sinking that horrible

contraption there." The leader pointed to the ship. "I don't want it carrying anyone else away."

Moretti grinned. "I made a few modifications while we were searching the ship. If anyone tries to move the ship they'll find the boiler and the rudder uncooperative."

The woman dipped her head. "Thank you, Signor."

Moretti jerked his head to the path they used to find their way in. "Now, let's get everyone out of here."

As before, Moretti took the lead. The women fell in line behind him. Vernon brought up the rear, just behind Sophia and Phoebe. As much as he longed to pull Phoebe into his arms to assure himself she was well, he knew Sophia needed her more.

At the top of the ramp, Moretti stopped everyone before they crossed through the last door leading to the warehouse. "There hasn't been anyone to intercept us so far, but I don't want to get lax now and assume the rest of the way is perfectly safe. Wait here while I take a look."

Vernon took the opportunity to check the leader's wound. He repacked it with another linen strip one of the ladies had ready. "I wanted to thank you for being so brave. I'm not certain which of us actually killed Romano, but you deserve credit for stopping him."

"I hope I was the one to kill that bastard." She didn't even flinch when he tightened the bandage holding the rolled linen against her wound.

"What is your name, by the way?" Vernon asked.

"Belladonna Mariogalia."

Vernon took her hand. "Belladonna, I am happy to know you. I'm just sorry it has been under such horrible conditions."

"You as well, Signor." She squeezed his hand. "You and Signor Moretti will be in my prayers every day for what you have done for me and the others."

"Thank you."

Moretti returned. He made no effort to quiet his voice or to hide. "It's the damnedest thing." He shook his head and shrugged. "There is no one out there."

"You mean we can just walk out of here and no one will say anything?" Phoebe asked.

"That's what it looks like," Moretti told her.

The ladies whispered to each other. A few made the sign of the cross on their chest and murmured prayers of thanks.

"I guess Romano really was the keystone. Without him the whole organization fell apart," Vernon speculated.

"I guess so," Moretti said with a shrug.

"Well, then let's get everyone out of here."

"Agreed."

They led the women and children out the warehouse doors and to the street. Moretti whistled for the other men and sent them in search of carriages. As they waited, Vernon and Moretti debated the best place to take the women.

"Take them to the Bianchi villa," Phoebe suggested. "I feel certain that they would agree to take them in until arrangements could be made for them."

Sophia, still clinging to her sister's side, nodded her agreement.

"Signor, if it isn't too much trouble, if we pass near the cathedral could I walk home from there?" One of the younger ladies asked. "It wouldn't be far." Her voice trembled as she spoke.

"Absolutely not," Vernon told her. Her face crumpled until he added, "I won't be happy with doing anything less than taking you directly to your doorstep."

Tears flowed down her cheeks. "Thank you, Signor. Thank you."

"Anyone else live within the city?" Moretti asked.

The other women shook their heads.

Moretti's men returned with what Vernon guessed to be Romano's horseless carriage. Behind it, the men had connected an open wagon that was likely used to carry supplies.

"Signora Mariogalia will you be all right to ride?" Vernon asked.

"I can manage," she told him.

"We will help her Signor," the woman next to her assured

him.

Vernon nodded. "Very well. Let's get everyone aboard and set off."

 29

PHOEBE joined the teary reunion between Sophia and Aunt Gladys in the middle of the entryway at the Bianchi villa. As expected, Signor Bianchi and Lady Charlotte generously offered to shelter the women and children that had been rescued until transportation could be arranged to take them home. Phoebe helped settle them in guestrooms while Vernon and Moretti related the day's events to Signor Bianchi and Lady Charlotte.

Signor Bianchi promptly sent word to the Polizia di Stato so that an investigation could be conducted. Their hope was that with all the Romanos out of the way and so many victims to testify, the Polizia would be willing to take action. Of course, there would be little they needed to do other than collecting evidence and testimonies. Arresting any men who had been hired by Romano seemed like a distant hope.

Vernon and Moretti agreed to stay long enough to speak to the Polizia. Phoebe returned to the sitting room just as they finished. She had, in truth, hoped to see Vernon before he left.

"How is Sophia?" Vernon asked after pulling her aside.

"She is well. It may take her a little time for her to trust again, but she will recover. She's stronger, I think, than even she realizes."

"Good." His voice dropped to a near whisper. "Signor Bianchi told the Polizia that while Sophia had been treated roughly, they had left her...untouched. But some of the other ladies were not so fortunate."

"Yes. Belladonna said she believed Sophia's virginity would have brought them a handsome price." Phoebe shuddered. "I just can't believe some men would—"

"Stop. Don't dwell on it." He took her hand. "Will you be returning to England soon, you think?"

"Most likely." She took a deep breath. "I feel certain Sophia will want to go home as soon as possible. Especially with Christmas coming up."

"Your parents will be relieved to hear that Sophia has been returned safely."

"Actually, my aunt never told them. Thankfully." Phoebe tugged her shawl back up to her shoulder. "She said she tried to write the letter a dozen times and could never find the right words."

"That would be a hard thing to do."

Phoebe's expression brightened. "But now she doesn't have to. We will wait and explain everything once we are home safely." Phoebe cringed. "Of course that also means Mother will likely never let any of us out of her sight again." She gave him a sad smile. "So my dreams of seeing Greece and the Alps may be thwarted.

His brow arched. "Until she deems you old enough to travel on your own?"

"Hard to say with Mother."

"Well, don't give up on that dream just yet. Perhaps your trips will simply be delayed."

She nodded. "I hope you're right." Perhaps if she had a worldly gentleman to accompany her it might happen.

"I, uh..." He glanced toward the front entrance where Moretti was still saying goodbye to Belladonna. "Might I beg a favor of you?"

"Of course. Anything."

He gave her a wicked grin and dropped his voice, "Don't promise to give me anything I want unless you really mean it."

Her cheeks turned pink. "And if I do?"

"I may just hold you to it."

The heated look in his eyes set the butterflies loose in her belly. "And your favor?"

"Since I'm unsure if I will be home in time for Christmas, would you mind terribly delivering a gift for my mother?"

A flash of disappointment rolled through her. She scolded herself for being selfish. Vernon was the reason Sophia had been found. She owed him far more than that simple favor. "I would be more than happy to deliver a gift for your mother." She tilted her head. "But won't you be leaving soon also? Surely you would rather deliver it yourself."

"My return is indefinite. I should know more in the next few days. Even though this case is technically resolved, my departure from Genoa does not necessarily mean I'll be given a direct path home."

"Ah, I see." She forced a smile. "But I shall see you again then before we leave?" she asked hopefully.

"I do hope so." He brought her hand to his lips and placed a kiss on the top, lingering perhaps a little longer than proper. "Until then."

His lips against her skin made her breath catch. "Yes."

With what might have been regret, he released her and went to joint Moretti at the door. He said his farewells to Belladonna before casting one last glance at Phoebe.

Exhaustion hit Phoebe as soon as the door closed behind the men. She barely remembered making her way to Sophia's room.

She found Aunt Gladys sitting next to the bed reading to Sophia. Hardly surprising, Sophia had not yet fallen asleep. Her coloring however looked much better after having a bath and donning a clean night robe.

Sophia lifted her head. "There you are."

Phoebe went to her own side of the bed. She sat down then reached for Sophia's hand. "How are you feeling?"

"Tired." Sophia crinkled her nose. "But I cannot sleep."

"We've been reading," Aunt Gladys told her as she stifled a yawn.

"If you wish to retire, Aunt Gladys, go ahead. I believe tonight's excitement is done."

"Will you be all right, dear?" Aunt Gladys asked Sophia.

Sophia gave her a weak smile. "Yes. Phoebe is here."

"All right." Aunt Gladys closed her book and got up from

her chair. She leaned over and placed a kiss on the top of Sophia's head. "Good night, dears. Wake me if you need me."

"Good night, Aunt Gladys," Phoebe said. After her aunt left, she curled up next to her sister. "How are you faring? Really."

Sophia shrugged. "I still can't believe that it happened. It doesn't seem real." She met Phoebe's gaze. "And yet I can still smell that ship. It won't to go away." A shudder racked her thin frame.

"I would think it would fade soon." Phoebe wanted to reassure her but didn't know what else to say.

"I hope so."

"In the morning we should talk about our return home."

Sophia nodded.

"Will you be able to sleep?" Phoebe asked.

"I don't know. I will try though."

"Well I'm not going anywhere. You can always wake me if you need to." She patted her sister's hand where it gripped her own. "But I do need to put my night robe on."

"All right."

Phoebe hurried to her room, stripped out of her borrowed dress and wiggled into her sleeping gown on. Her injured arm had throbbed ever since the man in the cavern grabbed her. But there had been far more important things to worry about so she said nothing. Now, however, she almost wished she had asked Lady Charlotte for a tonic to ease the ache.

She draped the borrowed gown over the back of a chair and reminded herself it would need be returned to Moretti so he could give it back to its rightful owner. The simple dress had been surprisingly comfortable though.

As she made her way back to Sophia's room the last of her strength faded. She sat on the edge of the bed and pulled the remaining pins from her hair using her uninjured arm. Almost absently she ran her brush through her somewhat tangled tresses and tried to still her mind from the day's events.

"Phoebe?"

Phoebe looked over her shoulder at her sister. Every time

she saw the bruise on Sophia's cheek she became both angry and sad. It took effort to not let her emotions show. "Yes?"

"Thank you."

She could have pretended she didn't know what Sophia meant, but there was no point. "You're welcome. You would have done it for me."

"I might have wanted to save you but I don't know that I was as capable as you."

Phoebe took a breath. "Sometimes we surprise even ourselves."

Sophia's reply was just above a whisper. "Maybe."

She set the brush aside then turned down the mechanical flame on the lamp next to the bed. When she crawled under the covers she reached for Sophia's hand. Phoebe gave it a squeeze as she gave silent thanks that they had found all of the women and managed to get them to safety.

The next thing Phoebe knew the pink light of dawn was peeking through the drapes. She woke to find Sophia watching her.

"Good morning." Phoebe rubbed the sleep from her eyes. "Were you able to sleep?"

Sophia shrugged. "A little."

"Have you eaten yet?"

Sophia shook her head and looked down. "You will likely think me a coward, but I didn't want to leave without you."

Phoebe stroked Sophia's cheek. "You're not a coward. I wouldn't blame you if you stayed in bed all morning."

"You wouldn't?"

"Not at all." Phoebe sat up then winced as all of her aches and pains reminded her of the previous day's activities. "I wouldn't mind it myself. However, Mother Nature is insisting that I get up and take care of a personal issue." She retrieved her robe from her trunk and eased her arms into the sleeves. "Would you like to go to the dining room with me? Or would you rather I bring you a tray?"

"I am a little hungry." Sophia chewed her lip in indecision. "I suppose I could dress and go with you."

Phoebe smiled encouragingly. "I think that would be a good way for you to prove to yourself that you made it through an ordeal and are stronger for it."

Sophia blinked as she considered what Phoebe said. "I am, aren't I?" She slowly sat up in bed as if testing her stability.

Phoebe prayed that Sophia's stubbornness would push her onward. While Sophia had never been a shrinking violet, an ordeal like she experienced would forever mar her outlook. Pride warmed her when Sophia's feet finally hit the floor.

"Okay." Sophia nodded. "I'm ready."

"Good." Phoebe beamed at her sister. However as soon as her hand touched the doorknob, for the briefest of moments, Sophia looked wary.

"It's just a normal morning," Phoebe reminded her as she opened the door. "We'll dress and have breakfast and visit with Lady Charlotte."

As they made their way to the bathing room a few doors away, Sophia said, "I would like to visit with Milia to see how she is doing."

"Milia?"

"She was one of the girls from last night. I—" Sophia swallowed. "She and I talked while we were on the ship. I feel guilty because I abandoned her as soon as I saw you."

Phoebe stopped Sophia. "Do not feel guilty about anything that happened while you were there. But yes, we can go and check on all of them. I had planned to anyway."

Sophia nodded and brushed a tear away.

They cleaned up and dressed then headed to the dining room. Phoebe was surprised to find Aunt Gladys already at the table.

"There you are." Aunt Gladys beamed at them. "Cook has been busy this morning. She has a much larger group to feed so it is a lighter fare than usual. Not that I need much."

"That's fine," Phoebe assured her. "We always had plenty."

"I just want tea and toast anyway," Sophia told her.

Lady Charlotte bustled in, updated them on the day's events and drank a cup of tea, then hurried out. The local physician was due some time that morning. They wanted everyone checked for injuries so they could be treated properly.

It seemed that Signor Bianchi had wasted no time in making inquiries into suitable transportation. It was the general belief that the sooner everyone was returned to their homes, the sooner they would recover.

After breakfast Phoebe and Sophia went to see how they could help. Phoebe immediately went to work organizing linens and extra clothing to determine what else they were in need of. Sophia and one of the younger women tasked themselves with tending to the children.

By luncheon, Phoebe felt they had the situation well in hand. Everyone had bathed and now wore clean clothes. Food had been laid out to anyone who wanted to eat. Lady Charlotte had eschewed all propriety and created a picnic-like environment in that wing of the house. She even insisted that the physician who had been tending the women should take time to eat as well.

As Phoebe delivered a basket of rolls from the kitchen she turned a corner and ran into someone. "I'm so sorry!"

Two strong hands caught her by the waist and steadied her "There you are."

"Vern-um, I mean, Mr. Bennett." Phoebe's smile grew. "When did you arrive?"

"Not long ago." He gestured toward the front of the house. "Moretti and I met with Signore Bianchi. He told me I would likely find you here." He reached for the basket. "Here. Let me help you."

"Thank you." She gladly handed over her bundle. "Did you take lunch yet?"

"No, I didn't."

"I was going to deliver these then rest for a bit while I ate. Did Signore Bianchi invite you to join us? I'm sure there is plenty for you and Mr. Moretti."

"He did, actually." He tipped his head. "Would you mind terribly if I joined you?"

"Not at all." She showed him where to leave the basket. "I

should be glad for your company."

He set the basket down then both of them helped themselves to soup and bread. Vernon pulled two chairs together in a quiet corner where they could visit.

"How is your sister faring?"

"She seems better this afternoon." She glanced around the room for Sophia but didn't spot her right away. "I was not so sure this morning."

"Oh?"

"I believe helping the others took her mind off her own misfortune. And perhaps made her realize how much worse her fate could have been."

Vernon nodded. "Well I am glad she's able to help them."

"Physical wounds will heal soon enough. It's the internal ones that worry me."

"Not everyone is willing to open themselves up and share their pain though." He tipped his head toward the left. "It seems however, your sister had made a few friends."

Phoebe followed his gaze to where Sophia was sitting on the floor with two young girls, one on each side. Sophia demonstrated how to fold pieces of paper into different shapes. A boy, slightly older than the girls watched over Sophia's shoulder. It did Phoebe's heart a world of good to see the hollow look that had been in Sophia's eye that morning replaced by a far lighter emotion.

"I'm glad she's recovering well."

Phoebe nodded. It took a moment to swallow the lump that had formed in her throat. "I am too."

"And what about you?" Vernon dipped the chunk of bread he had torn off into his soup. "Have you recovered from your own brushes with danger?"

"I suppose." She shrugged. "The doctor agreed with your assessment that it did not need stitches. He said as long as I keep it clean it should have only a little scaring."

He nodded. "Good."

"It will likely sound odd..." She paused as she carefully considered her words. "But after yesterday's excitement, today's activities seem rather…well…somewhat dull." Almost instantly she regretted saying anything. She probably sounded like a crazy person. "I don't mean to imply that I want to repeat our run in with Romano, but…well…"

He chuckled. "I know what you're saying." He wiped his mouth with a linen. "I often experience similar feelings when I complete assignments. It's as if I don't quite know what to do with myself when my target has been acquired." He shrugged. "But it soon passes."

"When you receive another assignment?"

His grin grew. "Most likely."

"Yes well, I don't expect to receive an assignment any time soon so I guess I'll just have to manage."

"Oh, I don't know." He glanced around them. "I imagine you often create assignments for yourself." He gestured to the table of food across the room. "Helping serve food to those in need. Or touring foreign cities."

She blinked as she considered his words. Then her smile widened. "I suppose you are right."

His expression became pensive. "I remember you saying you wanted to travel. Where would you like to go?"

"That list is quite long. Are you sure you have time to hear it all?"

"I will make the time."

"Greece for certain. If I make it there then I could go just a little farther and cross into Egypt. It would be oh-so-interesting to see the Pyramids, don't you think?"

"The idea of hot desert sands doesn't bother you?"

"Not at all. A parasol goes a long way to providing relief from the sun." She grinned. "Besides, I understand it's cool and dark inside the pyramids."

He gestured to her with his spoon. "I do believe you are correct." After taking another sip from his soup he asked, "Where else might you want to go?"

"Oh, my list is quite long. Aunt Gladys has talked so fondly of her time in Paris that I think I would like to go. India holds some interest for me." She tried to think of the more interesting places on her list. "The States, too. But I'm not sure about spending so long aboard a ship. I think it would be interesting to travel into Prussia even."

"Most people are content to see cities within a day's ride of their home." His gaze turned contemplative. "You truly do wish to travel, don't you?"

"Oh, yes, I really do." She wished she could express how giddy the idea of seeing all of those far off places made her. "There are places in England I'd like to see too but those feel far more accessible. Someplace I could jump in a carriage or hop a train and visit in a day or two. Or maybe even an airship." Her grin probably reached ear to ear. "I'd dearly love to fly on one of those someday. I think it would be grand."

"Would you?" She wondered which surprised him more, the fact that she wanted to fly or her enthusiasm for it.

"For certain. I imagine the views from that high up are breathtaking." Just thinking about soaring above the trees like a bird made her heart race.

"Well, I think you should do it."

"So do I." She nodded once. "As soon as the opportunity presents itself." And she meant it. After the events of this week, she knew how short life really was. And how things often got in the way. She wanted to have dozens—no, hundreds—of memories of exotic places and interesting people to recall in her old age. Stories of adventures and chances taken. Not a parade of ball gowns at the same functions where the stories never changed.

Phoebe considered the man next to her. After the past few days, her heart insisted that she knew him and yet he still remained a bit of a mystery. Was it because he lived two lives? How similar were the Earl's son and the Royal Intelligence spy, really? "What about you? What do you dream of doing?"

He shrugged. "In some ways I am doing it. My assignments let me travel. More often than not, I live under the guise of someone else. And I get to experience the thrill of the chase."

"So you have it all then?"

The intensity of his gaze made her heart skip a beat. "I

wouldn't say that."

She had to swallow the lump in her throat before asking, "What would you say is missing?"

"There you are." Aunt Gladys' ill-timed appearance cut off anything Vernon was going to say.

Vernon got to his feet as Aunt Gladys approached.

"Do pardon my interruption, my dears. But Mr. Moretti has offered the use of his carriage to take two of the girls who live to the north home. Would you be able to assist him in picking it up, Mr. Bennett?"

"Of course. Did he happen to say when?"

"Now, if you don't mind. Signor Bianchi believes if you all leave immediately, they can return before dark."

"Ah." Vernon looked down at Phoebe. "Miss Ashdown, I appreciate you letting me join you for luncheon."

"The pleasure was mine, Mr. Bennett. I do hope you and Mr. Moretti are able to deliver our guests with little inconvenience to yourselves."

"The weather is quite fine today. I'm sure it will be no trouble."

"Mr. Moretti was just finishing with Signor Bianchi in the study," Aunt Gladys told him. "I'm certain you can still find them there."

"Thank you." Mr. Bennett dipped his head to Aunt Gladys. Then paused, before turning away. "I wondered, Miss Ashdown, if I might call on you tomorrow. If you're not too busy, that is. I would very much like your opinion on the gifts for my mother that I mentioned."

Phoebe glanced at her aunt. "I should be happy to help you select something for her."

Her aunt's smile brightened further. Obviously she approved of her answer.

"Excellent. I shall call on you in the morning, if that is convenient?"

"Yes. That would be agreeable."

He smiled. "Until tomorrow then."

She watched him wind his way through the crowded room.

"He is a handsome man, is he not?" Aunt Gladys asked with a knowing twinkle in her eye.

"Indeed."

"If I were you, I would be loath to return to England without some understanding between you two."

"I believe his business dealings give him plenty to think about. I doubt there is room for anything beyond that."

"We make room for the things we think are important."

Phoebe sighed. What Aunt Gladys didn't know was that Vernon had made time for the important things. His duty to his country. She couldn't possibly hope to compete with that.

But wouldn't it be nice if she could?

 30

PHOEBE added the last of her things to her trunk and closed the lid. Vernon's gift for his mother had been carefully rolled in one of her gowns to pad it. She didn't want to be responsible for breaking the delicate teapot he had purchased. Hopefully the storekeeper's wrappings and her clothes would be enough for it to make it all the way to England in one piece.

She smiled. It had been kind of him to take her shopping with him. He even taken her suggestions for the gifts he purchased for his sisters. Those were tucked into her trunks as well.

It had been lovely to see him when people weren't chasing them or trying to kill them. But that time with him also made her sad knowing that it might be a long while before she crossed paths with him again. If at all.

She sighed as she took one last look around the room looking for any personal items she may have missed. It had been a lovely room for their stay but she was glad to finally be going home.

A knock at her door startled her from her thoughts.

"*Mi scusi.*" Rosa pushed the door open further. "Angelo wanted to know if you were ready for him to take your trunks."

"Yes, I am." Phoebe gestured to the heavy box on the floor beside her bed.

"Just the one?"

"Yes. Just the trunk. I'll keep this bag with me."

"I'll let him know he can put it with the others to be taken to the station."

"Thank you so much, Rosa."

Phoebe gathered her pelisse and bag and headed to the

front entrance. She had expected to find Sophia there given how antsy she had been the last couple of days to leave. Not that Phoebe blamed her. At least, Sophia had given into Aunt Gladys' suggestion and took a tonic each evening before bed in order to rest.

Which allowed Vernon a chance to sneak into Phoebe's room during the night. Those glorious hours spent in his arms would be forever etched into her memory. But how she would ever be able to face him in a ballroom again? Most especially if he were to escort someone else.

She shook off that depressing thought.

"There you are, my dear girl." Aunt Gladys said as she breezed into the room with Signora Bianchi. "Did you break your fast yet?"

"Yes, I had tea and toast earlier."

Aunt Gladys waved off her comment. "Of course you did. You are always up with sun, aren't you?"

Phoebe smiled without comment. Better to say nothing than to lie. Thanks to Vernon's midnight visit, she barely slept at all. But there would be plenty of time to make up her missing sleep on the train.

Sophia was the next to join them. While her naturally buoyant personality had lost some of its original shine she did seem, if not happy, at least content.

"And you, my dear. Are you quite ready to depart?" Aunt Gladys asked Sophia.

"Yes. They came and took my trunk earlier. I have the things I will need for the train here." She held up her tapestry bag.

"Excellent. I believe that Signor Bianchi has the carriage waiting for us out front."

They said their farewells to Signor Bianchi and Lady Charlotte then headed to the waiting carriages. No sooner had Aunt Gladys settled into the seat when a horseless carriage came racing up, spooking their horses.

Vernon jumped out of the automated carriage and hurried toward them. "I took a chance that you had not left yet."

"We are just about to." Phoebe gestured to where Aunt Gladys and Sophia watched them out the window. "Why? What's wrong?" Alarm skittered up Phoebe's spine. By her aunt's expression, she was equally as concerned by his sudden appearance.

He shook his head. "Nothing is wrong per se. I had some news that I wanted to share with you and something to ask before you left."

"What is it?" She reached for his hand. "Is everything all right?"

He led her a little distance from the carriage. Why he even bothered was beyond her. It seemed her aunt and sister had forgotten about their need to depart and were watching him as if expecting him to sprout wings.

"My employer, for a lack of a better word, arrived this morning."

Phoebe gasped in surprise and whispered, "The Queen came here?"

He shook his head. "The man who relays my orders and provides information back to the Queen."

Some of her tension dissipated. "Ah."

"How he knows what is happening with his agents still baffles me, but that is a story for another time. He arrived this morning to say that my assignment here in Genoa was complete and that another agent would be taking over the clean-up work."

She frowned. "Are you in trouble for helping us rescue my sister?"

"No, as a matter of fact, quite the opposite. They had expected us to observe and report but since I was directly involved in the rescue of multiple victims, the Prince Regent has recommended that I receive a medal for my efforts. The ceremony is to be held in two days' time in London."

"That's wonderful." She beamed up at him. Then she frowned. "But how ever will you get back in time? It's at least a four-day trip by train."

He grinned. "They sent a ship for me."

She frowned. "But traveling by ship will take even longer." She gestured to their carriage. "That's why we opted for the train."

"Not if it's an airship."

An airship? "Oh, how exciting!" She beamed up at him. "So you will likely arrive before us then."

"Not if you go with me."

She blinked up at him. "You want me to go on the airship? With you?"

"Yes."

Her heart skipped a beat and her mind raced. "I... "She glanced at Aunt Gladys and Sophia. "What about your employer? What would he think?"

"I'm far more worried about your opinion."

"Mine?"

"I know this is quite sudden, but as soon as Glas—I mean, my employer—told me about the medal, the first person I thought of when I imaged who would be there with me, is you."

"Me?"

"Yes, you." He smiled. "I have spent the last couple of days dreading your return to England. Knowing that I wouldn't be with you. Every worst-case scenario I could think of popped into my head. Everything from your train wrecking to you meeting the man of your dreams at a ball while I was away."

"That's not—"

"The bottom line is this. I can't picture the rest of my life without you in it. And I would be most honored if you would consider coming with me, marrying me, and spending the rest of your life with me."

Her mouth fell open in what was likely a most un-ladylike manner.

"I would love to be the one who took you to all those places you wanted to go," he continued. "To see all of the things you've dreamed of seeing through your eyes."

Her vision blurred as tears clung to her lashes.

"All I ask is that you stay by my side, through thick and thin.

In return, I swear that I'll love you until the day I die."

She sniffed. "If a lifetime of love really is what you are offering then, yes. I would be very much willing to join you on your airship. And I suspect that marrying you would be an adventure of its own."

He grinned from ear to ear then swooped her up into his arms and swung her around. Before letting her feet touch the ground he kissed her soundly on the lips.

They were both grinning like fools when her aunt and sister clamored from the carriage. In a breathless rush, Phoebe explained what Vernon had told her.

"Oh, my dears, I am so happy for you," Aunt Gladys gushed. "Your mother will be beside herself with joy."

Phoebe's grin faltered. "But if I go with Vernon, that means I'll be leaving the two of you to ride the train alone."

Aunt Gladys waved her concern away. "We will be just fine my dear. Poor Sophia likely need the time to herself and you know I'm perfectly content as long as I have a book and my needlework."

"You don't think I'm being to rash?"

"Pish posh. I wouldn't let that man get away from me for all of the gold in the world. You grab this moment and make the most of it. We'll handle any naysayers the ton might have later. For all they know you two were married while in Genoa. Who am I to tell them otherwise?" Aunt Gladys winked at Phoebe. "Now off with the two of you. I have a train to catch."

"Oh! Yes, you do." Phoebe hugged her aunt one more time. "Wait. What about my trunk?"

"We'll see to it. I doubt you'll be needing it any time soon anyway." Her aunt climbed back into the carriage. "Just meet us at the train station so that I know that all is well."

With that her aunt waved the driver onward.

"Shall we depart then?" Vernon asked her.

"I believe we should."

He escorted her to the carriage he had absconded with and tossed her bag into the cabin. "I'll have to ride up front since I didn't wait for anyone to navigate this beast."

"Then so too will I."

Her offer must have surprised him for it took a moment for him to help her up. When he climbed up beside her, his expression radiated love. "What did I ever do to deserve you?"

"Just lucky I guess."

He kissed her once again. "I do love you, you know."

She gasped and once again tears pooled in her eyes. "I love you, too."

He rubbed noses with her then handed her a pair of goggles. "Let's get this thing back to Moretti so we can make it to London before dark."

"Oh, yes. I want to see what it looks like from the tree tops."

"And so you shall."

# EPILOGUE

Christmas Morning

"MERRY Christmas, Mrs. Wright."

Phoebe grinned from ear to ear. "Merry Christmas, Mr. Wright."

Vernon kissed Phoebe gently as he wrapped his arms around his beautiful wife.

His wife.

He still wasn't used to that word.

"Did you sleep well?" He asked as he rested his forehead against hers.

"I did. And you?"

"It seems that I sleep better when I'm with you than I have in decades."

She pressed up against him. "I'm glad."

He kissed her one more time then took a step back. Reluctantly. But he knew if he didn't he would be tempted to carry her back to their bed. "Do you have everything you need for this morning's visits?"

"I believe so." She bit her lip.

He pressed gently on her chin with his thumb. "What's wrong?"

"I'm just a little nervous about going to your parent's for lunch."

"Why?"

She shrugged. "It's the first time I'm meeting them as your wife. I'm well…I am a little nervous."

He grinned. "Just be yourself. You have nothing to worry about. It's me who will be lectured for not waiting or including them in the wedding. Not to mention the long list of reasons our family has never eloped that I expect my father to carry on about."

Her eyes widened.

"In private, of course." He tapped her gently on the nose. "To you he will be perfectly charming, so you have nothing to worry about."

He took Phoebe's pelisse from the maid and held it so Phoebe could slip her arms into the sleeves.

"Thank you." His pretty bride still blushed whenever he touched her especially when others were nearby.

"As for my sisters and brothers," Vernon continued. "They'll be thrilled to have a new addition to the family."

"You really think so?"

"I know so."

Vernon offered his arm to her. "You do realize I'll be facing the same scenario from your family later this evening."

"Oh, pish posh. My family is terribly informal. You have nothing to worry about there. Especially since I'm certain that Sophia and Aunt Gladys have already divulged most of the story."

"That's true."

As Vernon helped Phoebe into the carriage out front, a messenger boy came running up. "Excuse me sir, but I'm looking for Mr. Wright? Are you he?"

"I might be," Vernon said cautiously. "What's the trouble?" Surely his superiors wouldn't be contacting him this soon.

"No trouble sir, just a delivery." The boy pulled a letter from his pocket and handed it over. Vernon exchanged the envelope for a couple of coins.

"Thank ye, sir and Merry Christmas!" The boy touched his cap and hurried off.

"Merry Christmas," Vernon said absently as he inspected the seal on the letter.

"Who is it from?" Phoebe said from inside the coach.

"No one I wish to hear from today." He settled into the seat next to her.

She pressed her shoulder against his and looked meaningfully at the letter. "Are you going to open it?"

"I've found more bad news comes from letters such as these than good, so I'm tempted to leave it until later this evening."

"How can you wait that long without knowing what it says?" She jostled his arm. "I would never be able to stand the suspense."

"You haven't been on the receiving end of these missives," he muttered.

"Is it work related, do you think?"

"Most likely."

"Ah." She nodded but didn't press him further.

The morning after they had been married at Gretna Green, he confessed what his employment truly entailed and who he worked for. If she were going to be a part of his life, he saw no point in hiding such a significant part. He omitted names where ever possible, and didn't give her specifics about past missions, but enough information that she could understand the importance of his role.

As the carriage began rolling down the lane he caught her making frequent glances at the letter he still held in his hand. "Would it make you feel better if you read it?"

"I don't have to read it, I just want to know that you have and that there's nothing in there that we need to worry about." She crinkled her nose. "But nor do I want our Christmas ruined either."

His wife had a curious nature. "Very well. I'll read it."

Her smile brightened. "Good."

It never failed to make him happy whenever he saw her happy. It was the oddest thing.

He broke the seal on the letter and unfolded the sheet. As he scanned the words, he summarized for her.

"He sends his congratulations on our nuptials and wishes us a Merry Christmas."

She nodded.

"And he says that they have new reports on the Mastermind

making a move to Germany."

He read a little further. Then folded the letter.

"That's it?" She asked.

His brow furrowed. "No. I'm just not certain how I feel about the last part."

"Why? What did it say? Is it something you can tell me?"

He squeezed her hand. "I made you a promise that I would tell you everything I could as long as it didn't directly disobey orders or place you in immediate danger."

She nodded again. "Does this missive infringe one of those?"

He paused. "Not immediately, no."

"But it could?"

"Perhaps."

She let him think through the information in peace, which he was grateful for. Phoebe was proving to be remarkably perceptive. Before they made it to the outskirts of town, he reached his decision. "The letter says that an assignment has come up that they believe would be perfect for a young married couple."

She turned to him in surprise. "An assignment?"

He dipped his head. "Yes. He said he had reports of how well we worked together and how much of an asset you were to the case in Genoa. He wants to speak with us further on the possibility of incorporating you into a new persona for my case work."

"And what do you think?" She asked.

"My instinctive reply is absolutely not."

Her form deflated, ever so slightly.

"But then I remembered how capable you are and how well you handled yourself under pressure despite the danger that not only you were in, but also your sister. You kept a level head and, as he pointed out, without you we wouldn't have been able to intercept that journal and find those women in time."

Her breath caught. "What are you saying?"

"I guess I'm saying that if you are interested in working cases with me, then I would be willing to give it a shot."

The smile she gave him radiated from her face. She threw her arms around him and kissed him soundly.

"I guess that you like that idea?"

"I am excited by the possibility." She took his hand and intertwined her fingers through his. "I admit that what you do frightens me a bit. But I love the idea of contributing to a worthy cause, such as the one you just finished."

He started to say something, but she held up a finger. "I know that was just one strand in a much larger spider's web that would have to be untangled, but it made a huge difference to those women. And I'm proud to have played a part in their rescue. I guess what I'm saying is that I'm thrilled that you are open to the idea of my working with you. But I don't expect to go on every assignment that you're given. You're good at what you do for a reason and I would never want to hold you back from that. As long as you come home to me at the end of every case hale and healthy, I'll be fine. But I would be happy to help anywhere they believe I can be an asset."

He kissed the back of her hand. "And here I didn't think I could be more proud of you. Once again you surprised me." He turned in the seat. "I love you, Mrs. Wright."

"No more than I love you, Mr. Wright."

He kissed her until both of them regretted their decision to leave their house instead of spending all day in bed together.

But, oh, did they have something to look forward to when they returned that evening.

THE END

If you enjoyed this book, please consider leaving a review!

 # EXCERPT

During her search for her missing brother, Trixie is reunited with Nathaniel, the man she never stopped loving. Sensing that Trixie might be in danger, Nathaniel lends his skills as an investigator to her efforts. Their love is rekindled as they race across the country looking for clues to more than one mystery.

Turn the page to read an excerpt from *Her Clockwork Heart*.

1

NATHANIEL Dennison rubbed the spot between his eyes where his head throbbed. He'd been reading files for the last three—he glanced at his pocket watch—correction, four and a half hours. After all that time, he had more questions than answers.

There was a connection between the disappearances he'd been asked to investigate. He just couldn't put his finger on it.

He took a deep breath. He had to be missing something. The blank lines of his notebook mocked him. When had he ever come up with so few clues on a case?

Only with the Mastermind.

He scowled at the stack of files he'd reviewed. The Mastermind had all members of the Royal Intelligence Office on edge, investigators and officers alike. They had been searching for the men behind the political unrest and outright attacks on the royal family for almost three years. No one could pin down who was behind the espionage and hints of treason. His Royal Highness had become increasingly insistent on answers.

Not that Nathaniel blamed him at all. No one in the RIO did. They wanted answers almost as much as he did. Smoke would be easier to catch.

With a sigh, he straightened his mess and tucked his notebook away in the breast pocket of his coat. He reached for the lamp to douse the light but paused when something banged against the wall of the records room.

Most of the RIO staff had left for the evening. By now he should have the offices to himself, with the exception of the security officer who patrolled through the night. But he would have sworn he recently heard the officer's footsteps echoing down the hallway.

As silently as possible he exited the file room. At the door to the records room, he paused and listened. There were shuffling sounds, like boxes being moved about, as well as odd clicks and whirls. Almost like a clock with a gear out of alignment.

"No, not that one," someone whispered on the other side of the door.

Was that a woman's voice?

"Hurry. We don't have much time."

Again, no response to the whisper, but the clicking sounds multiplied.

Nathaniel checked the lock on the door. It had been opened. The intruder either had a key or a considerable talent with locks. The locks used at the RIO were unusual and gave even the most experienced lock picks trouble.

He pulled his derringer from his pocket then as quietly as possible turned the door handle. The last click of the latch set off a flurry of activity inside the room.

So much for a stealthy entry.

He positioned himself against the wall, yanked the door open, and leveled his gun on whatever he found inside the room.

Some kind of insect jumped off one of the file cabinets onto Nathaniel's outstretched hand and pinched him.

"Ouch!" He shook his hand and tried to dislodge the bug, but it moved too fast. "What the bloody hell?" He bellowed when the bug ran across his arm then down his chest and leg to the floor.

"Don't hurt her. She won't hurt you," a woman called out from the other side of the cabinet. "Nid, get over here." Papers were shuffled and more clicks came from that side of the room.

Her voice was familiar. Nathaniel lowered his gun but kept

it at the ready as he made his way to the other side. As he crept forward he looked left and right for more bugs. "Who is that and what are you doing in here?"

More shuffling of papers. A drawer slammed shut. The woman whispered, "Squeaks. Hopper. Get in."

Nathaniel stepped around the end of the cabinets and leveled his gun at the person crouched next to the cabinet. He blinked in surprise at the woman who looked up at him. "Trixie?"

Beatrix Wadeworth froze with her hand extended to two small creatures that resembled a toy mouse and small rabbit. "Nathaniel?" She started to stand, then paused and scooped up the toys and slipped them into her pocket. "I uh..." She glanced behind him toward the door.

He took two steps forward and grabbed her by the arm. "Don't even think about it."

"Wh... what are you doing here?" she asked breathlessly.

"I work for the Royal Intelligence Office so I'm allowed to be here but you're not." He tightened his grip on her arm. "What are you doing here?"

Two of the bugs ran up his arm. He tried to brush them off, but only managed to hit one of them.

"Nid, it's okay." She nabbed the one shaped like a spider. "Come here."

"What are those?" They looked like bugs, but the whirling noise and clicks gave away the fact that they weren't.

"They're my, well..." She shrugged and dropped the one she'd taken off his arm into the pouch at her waist. "They're my friends."

"Friends?" One of her other toys scratched at his pant leg as it tried to climb it.

"Oh, sorry." She reached for the creature but stopped when her face drew too close to an area of his anatomy that no proper young woman should be near.

"I'll get it." He released her arm, slid his pistol back into its holster, then plucked the tiny mechanical insect from his thigh. He examined it for a moment then dropped it into her open palm. The strange assortment of metal gears and parts were shaped to resemble a scorpion.

"Thank you," she murmured.

"How many more of those do you have?"

"I only brought five of them with me."

He opened his mouth to say something then shook his head. "You can't be here."

"What the deuce is going on in here?"

Trixie's eyes widened with alarm. Nathaniel groaned. Great, the security officer had found them. "I was just finishing up for the night, Adam," Nathaniel told him.

"No one other than RIO personnel is allowed in the records room," Adam said sternly.

"I'm sorry. That's my fault," Trixie said.

Nathaniel tried to grab her but she swatted his hand away.

"You see, we were supposed to have dinner tonight, but someone..." She gestured at Nathaniel. "Forgot." Then she looked back at the guard. "He gets so forgetful when he's working. I insisted that if he had work to finish, then I should at least sit with him."

"That doesn't explain why you're in the records room," Adam said stiffly.

Nathaniel opened his mouth to say something but Trixie cut him off.

"Oh, pish posh." She waved one of her dainty hands at the guard. "I wasn't about to be left alone in that boring old office. I need to make sure he finishes whatever he needs to do so that he has plenty of time to take me to dinner." Her eyes grew wide. "Oh wait." She faced Nathaniel. "Is that why you said I needed to stay in your office? Because I'm not allowed to be in here?" She looked back and forth between the guard and Nathaniel in mock surprise.

"Something like that," Nathaniel said through gritted teeth as he slipped his pistol into his pocket.

"That's right, miss. No one other than authorized personnel is allowed in the records room."

"Oh, no. I thought you were just trying to avoid me." Her

eyes grew round and filled with tears.

Despite his annoyance, Nathaniel couldn't help but be impressed with Trixie's display. If he didn't know better, he would have sworn she'd had some kind of training for the stage.

"I'm so sorry. I didn't mean to break any of the rules."

His breath lodged in his chest when she closed in on him, practically grasping the lapels of his coat.

"I didn't mean to get you into trouble. We haven't seen much of each other lately and I just wanted to stay with you. Please don't be cross with me." She suddenly released him and turned to the guard. "Please don't turn him in. He didn't do anything wrong. Not really. It's my fault. I followed him in here. He really did try to make me stay in his office. You're not going to tell his superiors, are you?"

She turned her attention back to Nathaniel. "I'll explain to them what happened. Surely they'll understand." She drew one finger across her lashes, as if to wipe away a tear.

"I'm not sure—" Nathaniel said, momentarily distracted by the delicate floral scent that teased his senses when she had pressed against him.

"Please don't get him into trouble." She took a few steps toward the officer. "I'll go back to his office right now. I promise. I won't move a muscle from the seat. Just please don't tell on him."

"Now, Miss. Just calm down." Adam told her in a placating manner.

"I'll go right now."

She tried to brush past Adam but Nathaniel rushed forward and grabbed her by the arm. "How about if we leave so Adam can get on with his patrol?"

"No harm done, Miss." Adam said. "I'm sure you didn't mean to break the rules."

She turned large, pleading eyes on him. "No, I didn't. Truly."

"My apologies, Adam," Nathaniel said. "I should probably take her to dinner. I've made her wait longer than I should have."

"Yes, sir." He tipped his hat to Trixie. "Good night, Miss. And just remember, if you visit again the Inspector there knows where you are allowed and where you're not."

"I will remember that."

Nathaniel tugged her toward his office.

"And thank you," Trixie called back to the guard.

When they reached his office she said, "Oh, my, that was close."

He glared at her. "You have no idea."

~ Look for *Her Clockwork Heart* at any major ebook retailer ~

ABOUT THE AUTHOR

Dena Garson is an award-winning author of contemporary, paranormal, fantasy, and sci-fi romance. She holds a BBA and a MBA in Business and works in the wacky world of quality and process improvement. Making up her own reality on paper is what keeps her sane.

She is the mother of two rowdy boys and two rambunctious cats (AKA the fuzzy jerks). When she isn't writing you can find her at the sewing machine or stringing beads. She is also a devoted Whovian and Dallas Cowboys fan.

Find Dena on the web at:

Website - http://www.denagarson.com/
Facebook - https://www.facebook.com/AuthorDenaGarson
Twitter - https://twitter.com/DenaGarson
Email – Dena@DenaGarson.com

OTHER BOOKS BY DENA GARSON

Steampunk
Her Clockwork Heart
To London, With Love

Paranormal/Fantasy/Sci-Fi Romance
Ghostly Persuasion
Mystic's Touch
Rege's Rescue
Vordol's Vow
When Ash Remains
Who Wants Forever
Your Wild Heart

Contemporary Romance
Down to Business
Loss of Control
Risky Business
Snow Effect

Find detailed information on all of Dena's books at:
http://www.denagarson.com/books.html